The Case of the Missing Servant

from the files of
Vish Puri, India's "Most Private Investigator"

TARQUIN HALL

SIMON & SCHUSTER
New York   London   Toronto   Sydney

Simon & Schuster
1230 Avenue of the Americas
New York, NY 10020

First Simon & Schuster hardcover edition June 2009

SIMON & SCHUSTER and colophon are registered trademarks of Simon & Schuster, Inc.

For information about special discounts for bulk purchases,
please contact Simon & Schuster Special Sales at 1-866-506-1949
or business@simonandschuster.com.

The Simon & Schuster Speakers Bureau can bring authors to your live event. For more information or to book an event contact the Simon & Schuster Speakers Bureau at 1-866-248-3049 or visit our website at www.simonspeakers.com.

Manufactured in the United States of America

10 9 8 7 6 5 4 3 2 1

Library of Congress Cataloging-in-Publicatin Data
Hall, Tarquin.
   The case of the missing servant : a Vish Puri mystery / Tarquin Hall.
      p.   cm.
   1. Private investigators—India—Fiction.   2. India—Fiction.   I. Title.
   PR6108.A495C37   2009
   823'.92—dc22   2008032438

ISBN 978-1-4165-8368-4
ISBN 978-1-4165-8402-5 (ebook)

This book is dedicated to the memory of
Grandpa Briggs

One

Vish Puri, founder and managing director of Most Private Investigators Ltd., sat alone in a room in a guesthouse in Defence Colony, south Delhi, devouring a dozen green chili pakoras* from a greasy takeout box.

Puri was supposed to be keeping off the fried foods and Indian desserts he so loved. Dr. Mohan had "intimated" to him at his last checkup that he could no longer afford to indulge himself with the usual Punjabi staples.

"Blood pressure is up, so chance of heart attack and diabetes is there. Don't do obesity," he'd advised.

Puri considered the doctor's stern warning as he sank his teeth into another hot, crispy pakora and his taste buds thrilled to the tang of salty batter, fiery chili and the tangy red chutney in which he had drowned the illicit snack. He derived a perverse sense of satisfaction from defying Dr. Mohan's orders.

Still, the fifty-one-year-old detective shuddered to think what his wife would say if she found out he was eating between meals—especially "outside" food that had not been

* See glossary on page 297.

prepared by her own hands (or at least by one of the servants).

Keeping this in mind, he was careful not to get any incriminating grease spots on his clothes. And once he had finished his snack and disposed of the takeout box, he washed the chutney off his hands and checked beneath his manicured nails and between his teeth for any telltale residue. Finally he popped some sonf into his mouth to freshen his breath.

All the while, Puri kept an eye on the house across the way and the street below.

By Delhi standards, it was a quiet and exceptionally clean residential street. Defence Colony's elitist, upper middle-class residents—army officers, doctors, engineers, babus and the occasional press-wallah—had ensured that their gated community remained free of industry, commerce and the usual human detritus. Residents could take a walk through the well-swept streets or idle in the communal gardens without fear of being hassled by disfigured beggars . . . or having to negotiate their way around arc welders soldering lengths of metal on the sidewalks . . . or halal butchers slaughtering chickens.

Most of the families in Defence Colony were Punjabi and had arrived in New Delhi as refugees following the catastrophic partition of the Indian subcontinent in 1947. As their affluence and numbers had grown over the decades, they had built cubist cement villas surrounded by high perimeter walls and imposing wrought-iron gates.

Each of these minifiefdoms employed an entire company of servants. The residents of number 76, D Block, the house that Puri was watching, retained the services of no fewer than seven full-time people—two drivers, a cook, a cleaner-cum-laundry-maid, a butler and two security guards. Three of these employees were "live-in" and shared the barsaati on the roof. The overnight security guard slept in the sentry box positioned outside the front gate, though strictly speaking, he really wasn't meant to.

The family also relied on a part-time dishwasher, a sweeper, a gardener and the local press-wallah who had a stand under the neem tree down the street where he applied a heavy iron filled with hot charcoal to a dizzying assortment of garments, including silk saris, cotton salwars and denim jeans.

From the vantage point in the room Puri had rented, he could see the dark-skinned cleaner-cum-laundry-maid on the roof of number 76, hanging underwear on the clothesline. The mali was on the first-floor balcony watering the potted plants. The sweeper was using up gallons of precious water hosing down the marble forecourt. And, out in the street, the cook was inspecting the green chilis being sold by a local produce vendor who pushed a wooden cart through the neighborhood, periodically calling out, "Subzi-wallah!"

Puri had positioned two of his best undercover operatives, Tubelight and Flush, down in the street.

These were not their real names, of course. Being Punjabi, the detective had nicknames for most of his employees (and this being India, his company was as labor intensive as they came), relatives and close friends. For example, he called his wife Rumpi; his new driver, Handbrake; and the office boy, who was extraordinarily lazy, Door Stop.

Tubelight was so named because he was a heavy sleeper and took a while to flicker into life in the morning. The forty-three-year-old hailed from a clan of hereditary thieves, and therefore had been highly adept at cracking locks, safes and ignitions since childhood.

As for Flush, he had a flush toilet in his home, a first for anyone in his remote village in the state of Haryana. An electronics and computer whiz, during his career with Indian intelligence he had once managed to place a microscopic bug inside the Pakistani ambassador's dentures.

The other member of the team, Facecream, was waiting a few miles away and would play a crucial part in the operation later that evening. A beautiful and feisty Nepali woman who had run away from home as a teenager to join the Maoists but became disillusioned with the cause and escaped to India, she often worked undercover—one day posing as a street sweeper; the next as irresistible bait in a honeytrap.

Puri himself was known by various names.

His father had always addressed him by his full name, Vishwas, which the detective had later shortened to Vish because it rhymes with "wish" (and "Vish Puri" could be taken to mean "granter of wishes"). But the rest of his family and friends knew him as Chubby, an affectionate rather than derisive sobriquet—although, as Dr. Mohan had pointed out so indelicately, he did need to lose about thirty pounds.

Puri insisted on being called Boss by his employees, which helped remind them who was in charge. In India, it was important to keep a strong chain of command; people were used to hierarchy and they responded to authority. As he was fond of saying, "You can't have every Johnny thinking he's a Nelson, no?"

The detective reached for his walkie-talkie and spoke into it.

"What's that Charlie up to? Over," he said.

"Still doing timepass, Boss," replied Flush. There was a pause before he remembered to add the requisite "Over."

Flush, who was thirty-two, skinny and wore thick, milk-bottle-bottom glasses, was sitting in the back of Puri's Hindustan Ambassador monitoring the bugs the team had planted inside the target's home earlier, as well as all incoming and outgoing phone calls. Meanwhile, Tubelight, who was middle aged with henna-dyed hair and blind in one eye, was disguised as an autorickshaw-wallah in oily clothes and rubber chappals. Crouched on his haunches on the side of the street among a group of bidi-smoking local drivers, he was gambling at cards.

Puri, a self-confessed master of disguise, had not changed into anything unusual for today's operation, though seeing him for the first time, you might have been forgiven for thinking this was not the case. His military moustache, first grown when he was a recruit in the army, was waxed and curled at the ends. He was wearing one of his trademark tweed Sandown caps, imported from Bates of Jermyn Street in Piccadilly, and a pair of prescription aviator sunglasses.

Now that it was November and the intense heat of summer had subsided, he had also opted for his new grey safari suit. It had been made for him, as all his shirts and suits were, by Mr. M. A. Pathan of Connaught Place, whose grandfather had often dressed Muhammad Ali Jinnah, founder of Pakistan.

"A pukka Savile Row finish if ever I saw one," said the detective to himself, admiring the cut in a mirror in the empty room. "Really tip-top."

The suit was indeed perfectly tailored for his short, tubby frame. The silver buttons with the stag emblems were especially fetching.

Puri sat down in his canvas chair and waited. It was only a matter of time before Ramesh Goel made his move. Everything the detective had learned about the young man suggested that he would not be able to resist temptation.

The two had come face-to-face on Day One of the operation, when Puri had entered number 76, the Goel family residence, disguised as a telephone repairman. That encounter, however brief, had told the detective all he needed to know. Ramesh Goel, who had spiky hair and walked with a swagger, lacked moral fiber. It was the same with so many young middle-class people these days. Infidelity was rife, divorce rates were on the up, elderly parents were being abused and abandoned in old people's homes, sons no longer understood their responsibilities to their parents or society as a whole.

"Many thousands of males and females are working in call centers and IT sector side by side and they are becoming attached and going in for one-night stands," Puri had written in his latest letter to the *Times of India*, which the honorable editor had seen fit to publish. "In this environment, in which males and females are thrust together without proper family supervision or moral code, peer group pressure is at the highest level. Even young females are going in for premarital affairs, extramarital affairs—even extra extramarital affairs. So much infidelity is there that many marriages are getting over."

American influence was to blame with its emphasis on materialism, individuality and lack of family values.

"A fellow is no longer happy serving society. Dharma, duty, has been ejected out the window. Now the average male wants five-star living: Omega watch, Italian hotel food, Dubai holiday, luxury apartment, a fancy girl on the side," Puri had written. "All of a sudden, young Indians are adopting the habits of goras, white people."

Sixty years after Gandhi-ji sent them packing, Mother India was, being conquered by outsiders again.

"Boss, Flush this side, over." The voice broke into the detective's private lament.

"Boss this side, over," replied the detective.

"Mouse made contact, Boss. Leaving shortly, over." "Mouse" was code for Goel.

The detective made his way as quickly as he could down into the street and, a little short of breath after his exertion on the stairs, joined Flush in the back of the waiting Ambassador.

Tubelight folded his hand of cards, made a hasty apology to the other drivers, collected up his winnings (nearly sixty rupees; not bad for an hour's work) and revved up the three-wheeler he had rented for the day from his cousin Bhagat.

A few minutes later, the gates to the Goel residence swung open and a red Indica hatchback pulled out. The vehicle turned right. Tubelight waited five seconds and then followed. Puri's Ambassador, with Handbrake at the wheel, was not far behind.

The team kept a safe distance as Goel sped along the old Ring Road. There was little doubt in the detective's mind where his mark was heading.

"This Charlie might be having Angrezi education, but he is like a moth to Vish Puri's flame," he said with a grin.

Flush, who held his employer in high regard and had learned to tolerate his boastfulness, replied, "Yes, Boss."

The Ambassador and the auto took turns tailing the Indica through the streets of south Delhi, the rush hour traffic helping the team remain inconspicuous. Cars, motorcycles, scooters, cyclists, bicycle rickshaws, trucks, hand-pushed carts, bullock carts, sacred cows and the occasional unroadworthy hybrid vehicle that defied description vied for space on the road. Like bumper cars at a fairground, vehicles cut across one another, drivers inching into any space that presented itself, making four and a half lanes out of three.

Horns blared constantly, a clamor as jarring as a primary school brass brand. Loudest of all were the Blueline buses. Driven by charas-smoking maniacs who were given financial incentives for picking up the most passengers, even if they ended up killing or maiming some of them. "Bloody goondas," Puri called them. But he knew that the harshest penalty these men would ever face was a few hours in a police station drinking chai. Politicians and babus owned all the buses and had the police in their pockets. The going rate for expunging the record of a "manslaughter" charge was about three thousand rupees.

The detective watched one of these battered Blueline buses lumbering through the traffic like an old wounded war elephant, its sides scarred by previous battles. Faces peered down from the scratched windows—some with curiosity, others with envy and perhaps contempt—into the plush interiors of the many thousands of new luxury sedans on Delhi's roads. For the have-nots, here was a glimpse of the lifestyle that hundreds of thousands of the nouveaux riches had adopted. For Puri, the scene was a reminder of the widening economic disparity in Indian society.

"Mouse is turning right, Boss," said Handbrake.

Puri nodded. "Tubelight, keep ahead of him," he said into his walkie-talkie. "We'll keep back, over."

Goel's Indica passed over the new spaghetti junction of "overbridges" in front of the All India Institute of Medical Sciences and continued in the direction of Sarojini Nagar. Had it not been for the occasional ancient tomb or monument—echoes of Delhi's previous incarnations, now jammed between all the concrete and reflective glass—Puri would not have recognized the place.

In his childhood, Delhi had been slow moving and

provincial. But in the past ten years, Puri had watched the city race off in all directions, spreading east and south, with more roads, cars, malls and apartment blocks springing up each day. The dizzying prosperity attracted millions of un-educated and unskilled villagers into the capital from im-poverished states across north India. With the population explosion—now 16 million and rising—came a dramatic in-crease in crime. The vast conglomeration of Old Delhi, New Delhi and its many suburbs had been officially renamed the National Capital Region—or the "National Crime Region," as most newspapers wrote mockingly.

For Puri, this meant more work. Most Private Inves-tigators Ltd. had never been busier. But the business was not all welcome. There were days when the detective found his natural optimism waning. Sometimes he would battle home through the honking gridlock wondering if perhaps he should turn his hand to social work.

His dear wife, Rumpi, always reminded Puri that India was making great progress and talked him out of throwing in the towel. She would point out that he was already doing the public a service. His current investigation was but one example. He was on the brink of saving a young woman from a terrible fate and bringing an unscrupulous individual to account.

Yes, it would not be long now before Ramesh Goel was brought to book. Puri would have him in another ten minutes or so.

The detective made sure Handbrake remained three cars behind the Indica on the last leg of his journey down Africa Avenue to Safdarjung Enclave. Predictably, the young man turned into A Block.

Unbeknownst to Goel, as he pulled up outside A 2/12—

"Boss, he's at A-two-oblique-twelve, over"—he was being filmed with a long lens from a nearby vantage point. It made no difference that he was wearing a baseball cap, sunglasses and a dark raincoat in an effort to disguise himself. Nor that he was using the alias Romey Butter.

Vish Puri had got his man.

Two

The detective was not looking forward to the conclusion of the Ramesh Goel case. It rarely gave him any satisfaction to convey bad news to a client, especially such a successful and powerful man as Sanjay Singla.

"But what to do?" Puri said to Elizabeth Rani, his loyal secretary, who had worked for him since Most Private Investigators had opened above Bahri Sons bookshop in Khan Market in south Delhi, in 1988.

"I tell you, Madam Rani, it's a good thing Sanjay Singla came to me," he added. "Just think of the bother I've saved him. That bloody Ramesh Goel would have made off with a fortune! A most slippery fellow if ever I met one. Undoubtedly!"

Elizabeth Rani, a stolid widow whose husband had been killed in a traffic accident in 1987, leaving her with three children to provide for, did not have a head for mysteries, intrigue or conspiracies, and often found herself lost in all the ins and outs of his many investigations—especially given that Puri was usually working on two or three at a time. Her job required her to keep Boss's diary, answer the phones, manage the files and make sure Door Stop, the office boy, didn't steal the milk and sugar.

11

But unofficially, it was also Elizabeth Rani's remit to listen patiently to Puri's expositions and, from time to time, give his ego a gentle massage.

"Such a good job you have done, sir," she said, placing the Ramesh Goel file on Puri's desk. "My sincerest compliments."

The detective grinned from his executive swivel chair.

"You are too kind, Madam Rani!" he answered. "But as usual, you are correct. I don't mind admitting this operation was first class. Conceived and carried out with the utmost professionalism and secrecy. Another successful outcome for Most Private Investigators!"

Elizabeth Rani waited patiently until he had finished congratulating himself before giving Puri his messages.

"Sir, a certain Ajay Kasliwal called saying he wishes to consult on a most urgent matter. He proposes to meet at the Gym tonight at seven o'clock. Shall I confirm?"

"He give any reference?"

"He's knowing Bunty Bannerjee."

A smile came over the detective's face at the mention of his old friend and batchmate at the military academy.

"Most certainly I'll see him," he said. "Tell Kasliwal I'll reach at seven come rain or shine."

Elizabeth Rani withdrew from the office and sat down behind her desk in reception.

Her tea mug was halfway to her lips when there was a knock at the door. Apart from the various clients coming into Most Private Investigators Ltd., there was a small army of wallahs, or people charged with specific tasks vital to the rhythm of everyday Indian life. Ms. Rani found the lime and chili woman at the door and remembered it was Monday. For three rupees per week, the woman would come and hang a fresh string of three green chilies and a lime above the door of each business in the market to ward off evil spirits. Ms. Rani was also in charge of paying the local hijras during the festival season, when they approached all the businesses in the market and demanded bakshish, and ensured that the local brass-plaque polisher kept the sign on the wall next to the doorbell shiny. Engraved with a flashlight, the company's symbol, it read:

MOST PRIVATE INVESTIGATORS LTD.
VISH PURI, MANAGING DIRECTOR,
CHIEF OFFICER AND WINNER OF ONE
INTERNATIONAL AND SIX NATIONAL AWARDS
"CONFIDENTIALITY IS OUR WATCHWORD"

Meanwhile, Puri turned his attention to the evidence he had compiled against Ramesh Goel and, having satisfied himself that everything was in order, prepared for the imminent arrival of his client, Sanjay Singla.

Reaching into his drawer for his face mirror, he inspected his moustache, curling the ends between his fingers. His Sandown cap, which he only ever took off in the privacy of his bedroom, also required adjustment. Next, he glanced around the room to check that everything was exactly as it should be.

There was nothing fancy about the small office. Unlike the new breed of young detectives with their leather couches, pine veneer desks and glass partitions, Puri remained faithful to the furniture and décor dating back to his agency's opening in the late 1980s (he liked to think that it spoke of experience, old-fashioned reliability and a certain rare character).

He kept a number of artifacts pertaining to some of his most celebrated cases on display. Among them was a truncheon presented to him by the Gendarmerie Nationale in recognition of his invaluable help in locating the French ambassador's wife (and for being so discreet about her dalliance with the embassy cook). But pride of place on the wall behind his antique desk belonged to the Super Sleuth plaque presented to him in 1999 by the World Federation of Detectives for solving the Case of the Missing Polo Elephant.

The room's focal point, however, was the shrine in the far corner. Two portraits hung above it, both of them draped in strings of fresh marigolds. The first was a likeness of Puri's guru, the philosopher-statesman, Chanakya, who lived three hundred years before Christ and founded the arts of espionage and investigation. The second was a photograph of the detective's late father, Om Chander Puri, posing in his police uniform on the day in 1963 when he was made a detective.

Puri was staring up at the portrait of his Papa-ji and musing over some of the invaluable lessons his father had taught him when Elizabeth Rani's voice came over the intercom.

"Sir, Singla-ji has come."

Without replying, the detective pressed a buzzer under his desk; this activated the security lock on his door and it swung open. A moment later, his client strode into his office—tall, confident, reeking of Aramis.

Puri met his visitor halfway, shaking him by the hand. "Namashkar, sir," he said. "So kind of you to come. Please take a seat."

Puri sounded obsequious, but he was not in the least bit intimidated at having such a distinguished man in his office. The deference he showed his client was purely out of respect for hierarchy. Singla was at least five years his senior and one of the richest industrialists in the country.

Private detectives on the other hand were not held in

great esteem in Indian society, ranking little higher than security guards. This was partly because many were con men and blackmail artists who were prepared to sell their aunties for a few thousand rupees. Mostly it was because the private investigation business was not a traditional career like medicine or engineering and people did not have an appreciation—or respect—for the tremendous skills the job required. So Singla talked to Puri as he might to a middle manager.

"Tell me," he said in a booming voice, adjusting his French cuffs.

The detective chose not to begin immediately. "Some chai, sir?"

Singla made a gesture with his hands as if he were brushing away a fly.

"Some water?"

"Nothing," he said impatiently. "Let us come to the point. No delay. What you have found? Nothing bad, I hope. I like this young man, Puri, and I pride myself on being an excellent judge of character. Ramesh reminds me of myself when I was a young man. A real go-getter."

Singla had made it clear to Puri during their first meeting a fortnight earlier that he had reservations about commissioning an investigation. "This spying business is a dirty game," he'd said.

But in the interest of his daughter, he'd agreed to make use of the detective's services. After all, Singla did not really know Ramesh Goel. Nor Goel's family.

How could he?

Up until two months ago, they—the Singlas and the Goels—had never met. And in India, marriage was always about much more than the union between a boy and a girl. It was also about two families coming together.

In the old days, there would have been no need for Puri's services. Families got to know one another within the social framework of their own communities. When necessary, they did their own detective work. Mothers and aunties would ask neighbors and friends about prospective brides and grooms and their families' standing and reputations. Priests would also make introductions and match horoscopes.

Today, well-off Indians living in cities could no longer rely on those time-honored systems. Many no longer knew their neighbors. Their homes were the walled villas of Jor Bagh and Golf Links, or posh apartment blocks in Greater Kailash and NOIDA. Their social lives revolved around the office, business functions and society weddings.

And yet the arranged marriage remained sacrosanct. Even among the wealthiest Delhi families, few parents gave their blessing to a "love marriage," even when the couples belonged to the same religion and caste. It was still considered utterly disrespectful for a child to find his or her own mate. After all, only a parent had the wisdom and foresight necessary for such a vital and delicate task. Increasingly, Indians living in major towns and cities relied on newspaper ads and Internet websites to find spouses for their children.

The Singlas' advertisement in the *Indian Express* had read as follows:

SOUTH DELHI HIGH STATUS AGRAWAL BUSINESS FAMILY SEEKS ALLIANCE FOR THEIR HOMELY, SLIM, SWEET-NATURED, VEGETARIAN AND CULTURED DAUGHTER. 5'1". 50 KG. WHEATISH COMPLEXION. MBA FROM USA. NON-MANGLIK. DOB: JULY '76 (LOOKS MUCH YOUNGER). ENGAGED IN BUSINESS BUT NOT INCLINED TO PROFESSIONAL CAREER. BOY MAIN CONSIDERATION. LOOKING FOR PROFESSIONALLY QUALIFIED DOCTOR/INDUSTRIALIST BOY FROM DELHI OR

OVERSEAS. PLS SEND BIODATA, PHOTO, HOROSCOPE.
CALL IN CONFIDENCE.

Ramesh Goel's parents had seen the advertisement and applied, providing a detailed personal history and a headshot of their son.

At twenty-nine, he ticked all the boxes. He was an Agrawal and was Cambridge educated. His family was not fabulously wealthy (Goel's father was a doctor), but for the Singlas, caste and social status were the main concern.

From the start, their daughter, Vimi, liked the look of Ramesh Goel. When she was shown his head shot, she cooed, "So handsome, no?" Soon after, the two families had tea at the Singlas' mansion in Sundar Nagar. The rendezvous was a success. The parents got along and provided their consent for Vimi and Ramesh to spend time together unchaperoned. The two went out on a couple of dates, once to a restaurant, a few days later to a bowling alley. The following week, they agreed to marry. Subsequently, astrologers were consulted and a date and time was set for the wedding.

But with less than a month before the big day, Sanjay Singla, acting on the advice of a sensible friend, decided to have Goel screened. That was where Puri had come into the picture.

During their initial meeting at Singla's office three weeks ago, the detective had done his best to assure the industrialist that he was doing the right thing.

"You would not invite a stranger into your house. Why invite any Tom, Dick or Harry into your family?" he'd said.

The detective had told Singla about some of the cases he had handled in the past. Only recently, he'd run a standard background check on a Non-Resident Indian (NRI) living in London who was betrothed to a Chandigarh businessman's daughter and discovered that he was a charlatan. Neelesh Anand of Woodford was not, as he claimed, the owner of the Empress of India on the Romford Road, but a second-order balti cook!

As Puri had put it to Singla: "Had I not unmasked this bloody goonda, then he would have made off with the dowry and never been heard of again, leaving the female in disgrace."

By disgrace he'd meant married, childless and living back at home with her parents—or worse: on her own.

Of course, the Anand case had been a straightforward investigation, a simple matter of calling up his old friend, retired Scotland Yard inspector Ian Masters, and asking him to head down to Upton Park in east London for a curry. Most prematrimonial cases that came Puri's way—there were so many now, he was having to turn them away—were simple.

The Goel investigation, however, had been far more involved. Singla had been persuaded to commission the Pre-Matrimonial Five Star Comprehensive Service, the most expensive package Most Private Investigators provided. Even Ramesh Goel's parents' financial dealings and records had been scrutinized by forensic accountants.

The file now lying on Puri's desk was testimony to the long hours that had gone into the case. It was thick with bank statements, phone records and credit card bills, all acquired through less than legitimate channels.

There was nothing in the family's financial dealings to raise suspicion. It was the photographic evidence that proved so damning.

Puri laid a series of pictures on the desk for his client to see. Together they told a story. Two nights ago, Goel had gone to a five-star hotel nightclub with a couple of male friends. On the dance floor, he had bumped into Facecream, who'd been dressed in a short leather skirt, a skimpy top and high heels. The two had danced together, and afterward, Goel had offered to buy her a drink, introducing himself as Romey Butter. At first she'd refused, but Goel had insisted.

"Come on, baby, I'll get your engine running," he'd told her.

The two had downed a couple of tequila slammers and danced again, this time intimately. At the end of the evening, Facecream, going under the name Candy, had given Goel her phone number.

"On the coming night, he set out for the female's apartment at two-oblique-twelve, A Block, Safdarjung Enclave," Puri told Singla. "Inside, he consumed two pegs of whisky and got frisky with the female. He said—and I quote— "Wanna see my big thing, baby?" Then he got down his trousers. Unfortunately for him, the female, Candy, had dissolved one knockout drug in his drink and, forthwith, he succumbed, passing out."

An hour later, Goel awoke naked and in bed, convinced that he had made love to Candy, who assured him that he was "the best she'd ever had."

Lying next to her, Goel confessed that he was getting married at the end of the month. He called his fiancée, Vimi Singla, a "stupid bitch" and a "dumb brat" and proposed that Candy become his mistress.

"He said, 'I'll soon be rich, baby. I'll get you whatever you want.'"

The detective handed the last photograph to his client. It showed Goel leaving Candy's apartment with a big grin on his face.

"Sir, there is more," said Puri. "We have done background checking into Goel's qualifications. It is true he attended Cambridge. Three years he spent there. But he never so much as saw one university lecture. Actually, he attended Cambridge Polytechnic and concerned himself with drink and chasing females."

The detective paused for breath.

"Sir," he continued, "as I intimated to you previously, my job is gathering facts and presenting evidence. That is all. I'm a most private investigator in every sense. 'Confidentiality' is my watchword. Rest assured our dealings will remain in the strictest confidence."

Puri sat back in his chair and waited for Singla's reaction. It came a moment later, not in English, but Punjabi.

"Saala, maaderchod!"

With that, the industrialist gathered up the photographs and roughly shoved them back into their file. "Send me your bill, Puri," he said over his shoulder as he headed for the door.

"Certainly, sir. And if I can ever be . . ."

But the industrialist was gone.

No doubt he was heading home to call off the wedding.

From everything Puri had read in the society pages, his client would be out of pocket by crores and crores. No doubt the Umaid Bhavan Palace in Jodhpur was already paid for. So, too, Céline Dion and the Swarovski crystal fountains.

The detective heaved a sigh. Next time he hoped the Singla family would consult with Most Private Investigators before they sent out four thousand gold-leaf-embossed invitations.

Three

The rubber soles of Puri's new shoes squeaked on the marble floors of the Gymkhana Club reception. The noise caused Sunil, the incharge, to look up from behind the front desk. He was holding a phone to his ear and murmuring mechanically into it, "Ji, madam, o-kay madam, no problem madam." He gave the detective a weary nod, placing the palm of one hand over the receiver.

"Sir. One gentleman is awaiting your kind attention," he said in a hushed voice.

It was not unusual for a prospective client to ask to meet Puri at the club. The prominent members of society who came to him often guarded their privacy and preferred not to be seen coming and going from the detective's offices.

"Mr. Ajay Kasliwal is it?" asked Puri.

"Yes, sir. Thirty minutes back only he reached."

The detective acknowledged this information with a nod and turned to look at the notice board. The club secretary, Col. P. V. S. Gill (Ret.), had posted a new announcement. It was typed on the club's letterhead and, in no fewer than five places, blemished with whitener.

21

NOTICE
THE DIFFERENCE BETWEEN A SHIRT
AND A BUSH SHIRT IS CLARIFIED AS UNDER:
UNLIKE A SHIRT, THE DESIGN OF THE
UPPER PORTION OF THE BUSH SHIRT
IS LIKE THAT OF A SAFARI.

This made instant sense to Puri (as he believed it should to anyone coming to the club wearing bush shirts or indeed safaris) and his eyes turned to the next notice, a reminder from the undersecretary that ayahs were not permitted on the tennis courts. The chief librarian had also posted a note appealing for funds to replace the club's copy of the collected works of Rabindranath Tagore, which had "most unfortunately and due to unforeseen and regrettable circumstance" been "totally destroyed" by rats.

Next, the detective cast a quick eye over the dinner menu. It was Monday, which meant mulligatawny soup or Russian salad for starters; a choice of egg curry, cabbage bake with French fries or shepherd's pie for mains; and the usual tutti-frutti ice-cream or mango trifle for dessert.

The thought of shepherd's pie followed by tutti-frutti ice cream stirred the detective's appetite and he regretted not having come over to the club for lunch. As per Dr. Mohan's instructions, Rumpi was packing his tiffin with only weak daal, rice and chopped salad these days.

Finally, Puri turned to the list of new applicants for club membership. He read each name in turn. Most he recognized: the sons and daughters of existing members. The others he jotted down in his notebook.

As a favor to Col. P. V. S. Gill (Ret.), Puri ran background checks on anyone applying for membership who was not already known in the right Delhi circles. Usually this meant making a couple of discreet phone calls, a service Puri gladly provided the Gym for free. Standards had to be kept up, after all. Recently, a number of Johnny-come-lately types had made applications. Just last month, a liquor crorepati, a multimillionaire, had asked to join. Puri had been right to flag him. Only yesterday, the man had been featured in the social pages of the *Hindustan Times* for buying the country's first Ferrari.

The detective slipped his notebook back into the inner pocket of his safari suit and made his way out of reception.

Usually he reached the bar by cutting through the ballroom. This route avoided the main office, which was the domain of Mrs. Col. P. V. S. Gill (Ret.). A bossy, impossible woman who ran the club while her husband played cards in the Rummy Room, she regarded Puri as an upstart. He was, after all, the son of a lowly policeman from west Delhi who had only gained entry to the hallowed establishment through Rumpi, whose father, a retired colonel, had made him a member.

Unfortunately, the ballroom was being decorated—a dozen paint-splattered decorators working on bamboo scaffolds bound with rope, were applying lashings of the only color used on every exterior and interior wall of the Gym: brilliant white—and so Puri was left with no choice but to take the corridor that led past Mrs. Gill's door.

He proceeded slowly, painfully aware of his new squeaking shoes, specially made for him to account for the shortness of his left leg. He passed the Bridge Room and the ladies' cloakroom and a row of prints of English country scenes depicting tall, upright gentlemen in top hats and tails.

As he passed Mrs. Gill's office, he went on tiptoe, but the door immediately swung open as if she had been lying in wait.

"What is all this squeaking, Mr. Puri?" she screeched, her flabby midriff bulging from the folds of her garish sari. "Making quite a racket."

"My new shoes, I'm afraid, madam," he said.

Mrs. Gill looked down at the offending footwear disapprovingly.

"Mr. Puri, there are strict rules governing footwear," she said. "Rule number twenty-nine, paragraph D, is most specific! Hard shoes are to be worn at all times."

"They are orthopedic shoes, madam," he explained.

"What nonsense!" Mrs. Gill said. "Hard shoes only!"

She pulled back into her office, closing the door behind her.

Puri continued down the corridor, resolved not to wear his new shoes in the club again. Such Punjabi women were not to be tangled with; in his experience they could be more fearsome adversaries than Mumbai's crime bosses.

"Imagine spending sixty years with such a woman," he mumbled to himself. "One can only imagine what the colonel did in his past life to deserve such a fate."

The detective pushed open the door to the bar and stepped into the relative quiet he so cherished. This was the only truly civilized spot left in Delhi, a place where a gentleman could enjoy a quiet peg or two among distinguished company—even if some of his fellow members barely acknowledged him.

Judge Suri was sitting in the far corner in his favorite chair, smoking his pipe and reading the *Indian Journal of International Law*. Puri recognized Shonal Ganguly, professor of history at Delhi University, sitting with his wife.

Next to the fireplace slouched L. K. George, the former in-
dustrialist who had given away his family fortune to the
League for the Protection of Cows and their Progeny and
now lived in a crumbling Lutyens bungalow on Racecourse
Road. Propping up the bar stood Major-General Duleep
Singh along with his eldest son, a surgeon and resident of
Maryland visiting from the USA.

Apart from the waiters, the only other person in the room
was a distinguished-looking gentleman sitting on his own at
one of the little round tables near the French windows with
an empty glass in front of him. Puri guessed this must be his
guest because his brow was deeply furrowed with worry, a
feature prospective clients often shared.

"Sir, your good name, please?" asked the detective, ap-
proaching the stranger.

"Ajay Kasliwal," he answered, standing up and offering his
hand.

Despite the bar's cool temperature, his palm was moist.
"Vish Puri, is it? Well, I'm certainly glad to meet you. Bunty
Bannerjee put me on to you. Said you were to be found here
most evenings. He sends his best wishes, by the way."

"Most kind of you," replied the detective. "How is the old
devil? It's been such a very long time!"

"Very good, very good. No complaints. In and out of
trouble," replied Kasliwal with a jovial chuckle.

"Everyone is well?"

"World class! Flourishing, in fact!"

"And Bunty's factory? Thriving, is it?"

"Thriving, absolutely thriving."

Puri gestured for Kasliwal to take his seat. He sank back
into the armchair and his weight caused it to wheeze air like
an old bellows.

"You'll join me?" asked the detective.

25

"Please," sighed Kasliwal.

The detective snapped his fingers and an elderly waiter who had been working at the club for some forty years approached the table. He was hard of hearing so the detective had to shout his order.

"Bring two Royal Challenge and soda! Two portion chili cheese toast!"

The waiter nodded, picked up Kasliwal's empty glass and methodically wiped the surface of the table. This provided Puri with an opportunity to study his guest up close.

Kasliwal, who was in his late forties, had an air of privilege about him. His manicured fingernails, contact lenses, and well-groomed salt-and-pepper hair, swept back from his forehead, indicated that he spent a good deal of time tending to his appearance. His gold watch, two thick gold rings and the gold pen glinting from his shirt pocket left others in no doubt of his wealth and status. There was an intellectual gravitas about the man too. In his thoughtful eyes, Puri perceived a certain striving.

"Accha," said Kasliwal, once the waiter had finally withdrawn. He leaned forward in his armchair. The furrows on his brow deepened. "Firstly, Puri-ji please understand one thing. I'm not a man to panic easily. Not at all."

He spoke English with a strong accent and "not at all" was rolled into one word as "naataataall."

"Believe me, I've faced many obstacles and challenges in my life. This I can say with utmost confidence. Also, I'm one man who prides himself on honesty. That much is well known. Ask anyone. They will tell you that Ajay Kasliwal is one hundred and fifty percent honest!"

He went on: "Puri-ji, I understand you are a man of integrity and discretion, also. That is why I've come. Frankly,

I'm facing a serious situation. A crisis. It can be my ruin, actually. That's why I've *air-dashed* here to see you."

"You are a lawyer residing in Jaipur, is it?" interrupted Puri.

Kasliwal looked taken aback. "That's correct," he said. "But, how . . . Ah, Bunty told you, I suppose."

Puri enjoyed impressing prospective clients with his deductions, despite the simplicity of his observations.

"I've not spoken with Bunty, actually," he said, plainly. "But from your Law Society of India monogrammed tie and type of briefcase, I deducted you are a man of the Bar. As to your hometown, traces of red Rajasthani sand are on your shoes. Also, you mentioned air-dashing to Delhi. You arrived here thirty minutes back. So should be you came by the five o'clock flight from Jaipur."

"Amazing!" exclaimed Kasliwal, with a clap of his hands. "Bunty said you were a gifted fellow, but never would I have believed!"

The lawyer edged even closer, looking from side to side to make sure no one could overhear their conversation. The waiters were at a safe distance behind the bar. None of the other members appeared to be paying Puri and his guest any attention.

"Yesterday I was paid a visit by the cops," he said. "Someone has lodged an FIR against me."

Kasliwal handed Puri a copy of the "First Information Report." The detective read it carefully.

"You're ordered to produce one female named Mary within seven days, is it?" he noted once he'd finished, passing back the document. "Who is she exactly?"

Before Kasliwal could answer, the waiter returned with their drinks and snacks. Slowly, he placed them on the table one by one and then presented Puri with the bill. The club did not accept cash, so all purchases made at the bar or in the restaurant had to be signed for. This system produced piles of paperwork, which kept at least four clerks employed in the club's accounts department. Puri had to sign one bill for the drinks he'd ordered, another for the double Scotch Kasliwal had downed earlier, and another for the food. Naturally, the guest book required a signature as well.

It was several minutes before Kasliwal was able to answer Puri's last question.

"Mary was a maidservant in the house—did cleaning, laundry and all," he said.

"And where is she now?"

"I'm not having the foggiest! She left two, maybe three months back. Just disappeared one night. I wasn't home at the time. I had work to attend to."

Puri tucked into a slice of chili cheese toast as he listened.

"My wife says Mary stole some household items and ran away. But a rumor has circulated that, well . . ." Kasliwal took a swig of his whisky to fortify his nerves. "There's no truth in it. You know how people talk, Puri-ji."

"Most certainly I do. India is one giant rumor mill, actually. Tell me what all they're saying?"

There was a pause.

"That I got Mary pregnant and did away with her," admitted Kasliwal.

"By God," intoned the detective.

"This has been the complaint made against me and, as you know, in case of FIRs, the police are obliged to investigate."

There was a silence while Puri retrieved his notebook from his inside pocket and then pulled out one of the four pens he kept tucked into the breast pocket of his safari suit.

After jotting down a few details, he asked: "Any body has been discovered?

"No, thank heavens!" exclaimed Kasliwal. "The police searched my house and grounds and some media persons have been on the doorstep asking questions."

"Sounds like someone's trying to ruin your good name, is it?" asked the detective.

"That's it! You've hit the nail on the head, Puri-ji! That's exactly what they're trying to do!"

The lawyer went on to explain that in the past few years he had launched a number of public litigation cases in the Rajasthan High Court. This was something many honest lawyers and individuals were doing across India: working through the legal system to bring inept local and national authorities to account.

"I've had some success tackling the water mafia. I've managed to stop a lot of the illegal water drilling in the driest parts of the state," he explained. "But with so much corruption in the judiciary itself, it's been a tough innings. So earlier this year, I decided to take on the judges themselves. I've launched a public litigation case calling for them to declare their assets."

Puri sipped his whisky. Out of the corner of one eye he registered Major-General Duleep Singh and his eldest son leaving the bar.

"Must have made a few enemies along the way," he said.

"At first they tried to buy me, but I'm not a bowler to do ball tampering. I turned them down flat. To hell with them. So now they're gunning for me. They've seized on this missing servant to muddy my name."

"It seems there's no hard evidence against you, so surely you've got nothing to worry—" said the detective.

"Come on, Puri-ji, this is India!" interrupted Kasliwal. "They can tie me up in knots for years to come."

Puri nodded knowingly; he knew what a long, drawn-out court case did to a family. The similarities between the Indian legal system and the Court of Chancery as described in Dickens's *Bleak House* were startling.

"The circumstances are certainly unusual," he said, eventually. "What is it you want from me?"

"Puri-ji, I'm begging you, for God's sake, find this bloody Mary!"

"You have her full name?" he asked, biting into a piece of chili cheese toast.

Kasliwal shrugged. "She was there for two months. I believe she was a tribal."

"You have a photograph, personal possessions, copy of ID?"

"Nothing."

Puri's tone became measured. "She was a verified domestic, registered with the cops at least?"

Kasliwal shook his head.

"Sir, allow me to understand," said Puri. "It is your suggestion I locate one tribal-type girl called Mary with no second name, no idea where she is coming from, no idea where she is alighting?"

"That is correct."

"Sir, with respect, I think you must be some kind of joker."

"I can assure you that while I'm enjoying a good joke, I am no joker," objected Kasliwal. "Such an accomplished private investigator as yourself should have no difficulty in such a matter. It's a straightforward thing, after all."

Puri's eyes bulged with incredulity.

"It is certainly not straightforward locating one missing female in a population of one billion plus personages," he said. "It will take time and resources and *all* of my considerable skills. Looking in Yellow Pages will not suffice."

Puri explained that he worked on a day rate and would require two weeks in advance, plus expenses. The total amount caused Kasliwal to gag on his Scotch.

"So much? Surely you can do better than that, Puri-ji! We can reach some accommodation. Funds are a bit tight these days, you know."

"I don't work for farthings and I don't do negotiation," said the detective, munching on the last piece of chili cheese toast. "My fee is final."

Kasliwal thought for a moment and, with a grave sigh, drew a checkbook from the inside pocket of his jacket.

"Sir, rest assured I will find this female by hook or crook," said Puri. "If I fail, then I will return my fee minus expenses."

The detective drained his glass.

"There is one other thing," he added.

The lawyer, who was bent over the table writing a check, looked up.

"Cash, banker's draft or electronic transfer only," insisted Puri with a smile.

Four

Puri woke the next morning to the sound of water dribbling into an empty bucket in the bathroom. This was his anomalous alarm, a signal that it was 6:30, the hour when Sector Four received its daily supply of water and each household filled up buckets, tanks and all manner of receptacles to carry them through the day.

Puri sat up and glanced over at the single bed next to his. It came as no surprise to find it empty. Hardly a day had gone by during the past twenty-six years when Rumpi had not risen at five. Even during the months when she was heavily pregnant with each of their three daughters, Puri's devoted wife had insisted on getting up at the crack of dawn to oversee the running of the house. No doubt she was downstairs now churning fresh butter for his double-roti. Or she was in the second bedroom rubbing mustard oil into her long, auburn hair.

The detective reached for the light switch, which, like the radio alarm and world clock, was fitted into the astonishingly shiny imitation-mahogany headboard. The side lamp did not come on, which prompted him to glance over at the electric mosquito repellent plugged into the far wall to see if its red light was glowing. It was off. Sector Four was experiencing more load shedding.

Muttering a curse, Puri reached for his flashlight, switched it on and slipped out of bed. His monogrammed slippers—"VP"—were lying next to each other on the floor where he had carefully positioned them the night before. He wriggled his feet inside their furry lining and reached for his silk dressing gown. His collection of fourteen Sandown caps were arranged on a shelf inside one of the fitted cupboards. He chose the tartan one, pulling it snug over his head. Then he surveyed himself in the mirror, gave the silk handkerchief protruding from the breast pocket of his dressing gown a tug and, pleased with what he saw, walked out into the hallway.

The beam of his flashlight fell on the marble floor, partially illuminating the large silver-plated Ganesh idol and the gilded legs of the hallway table, which supported a vase of plastic sunflowers. Puri walked to the top of the stairs, where the sound of giggling from the kitchen caused him to pause.

Listening intently, the detective was able to make out the voice of his new houseboy, Sweetu, who was in the kitchen joking around with Monica and Malika rather than attending to his morning duties. The detective couldn't quite make out what Sweetu was saying, so he crept over to the door of his private study. This was the one room of the house which no one, save Rumpi (who cleaned it every Friday), was allowed to enter. There were only two keys in existence: one hung on his key chain; the other was hidden in a secret compartment built into the shrine in the puja room.

Like his office, Puri's study was simply furnished. In one corner stood a fireproof safe containing his private papers, various important files, a selection of fake passports and IDs and his Last Will and Testament. The bottom half of the safe also contained 100,000 rupees in cash, some of his wife's gold and diamond jewelry (the rest she kept in a bank vault), and a loaded .32 IOF pistol—a copy of the .32 Colt Pistol made by the Indian Ordnance Factory.

Puri sat at his desk and pulled open one of the drawers. Inside lay a battery-operated receiver set to the frequency of the bug he had concealed in the kitchen. He switched it on, pushed the mono earpiece into his left ear, adjusted the volume and sat back in his chair to listen.

Rumpi frowned upon his practice of listening in on the servants, but Puri made it a policy to monitor all new recruits at home and at the office. He himself relied on servants as primary sources of intelligence and often planted his own operatives inside other people's households. As a man who fiercely guarded his privacy and had a number of dangerous enemies and unscrupulous competitors, he needed to be sure that his own staff were not spying on him or unwittingly passing on details about his private affairs to interested parties.

Furthermore, Puri was well aware of just how lazy servants could be. Village types like Sweetu were often under the illusion that city people did not work for a living, and saw no reason why they should behave any differently. Living in a modern house in comparative luxury could give them delusions of grandeur. The boy before Sweetu had had the audacity to seduce a part-time cleaner on Puri's bed. The detective had come home unannounced one afternoon when Rumpi was away visiting her sister and found them at it.

Puri spent ten minutes listening in on the conversation in the kitchen. The talk was mostly about the latest Shahrukh Khan film, a double-role. It all sounded harmless enough, as gossip went. But it was obvious that Sweetu was keeping the girls from their duties and shirking his own. The detective decided to put a stop to it and reprimand the boy. Switching off the receiver and locking the study door behind him, he walked to the top of the stairs.

"Sweetu!" he bellowed.

The sound of Sahib's voice brought the boy scuttling from the kitchen into the hallway below.

"Good morning, sir," he stammered, awkwardly,

"Why are you being idle?" demanded Puri in Hindi. "You are not employed to discuss Shah Rukh's double-roles!"

"Sir, I—"

"No argument. Where is my bed tea?"

"Sir, power cut—"

"Tell Malika to bring it to the roof. And," he added in English, "don't do chitter chatter!"

Puri headed upstairs, satisfied with the manner in which he had handled Sweetu. The boy was young, only fifteen, and an orphan. What he needed was discipline. But Puri was never one to abuse, exploit or treat his servants badly, as he had known so many other people to do. He believed in looking after the interests of all his employees, providing they were hardworking and loyal. In Sweetu's case, Puri had arranged for the boy to attend school two afternoons a week so that he would learn to read and write and acquire a skill. And in a few years' time, the detective would also help him find a suitable wife.

Had not Chanakya taught that it was the duty of the privileged to help the underprivileged?

Puri climbed the stairs and stepped out onto the flat roof of the house. The sun was climbing into what should have been a clear, azure sky. But as was so often the case these days, a brown pall of dust and pollution blanketed Delhi, smothering the city like some Vedic plague.

The family had hoped to escape the smog when they had moved to Gurgaon nine years earlier.

When Puri had bought his plot of land, it had lain many miles from the southern outskirts of the capital. It had taken more than two years to build his and Rumpi's dream house—a white, four-bedroom Spanish-style villa with orange-tiled awnings, which they'd furnished from top to bottom in Punjabi baroque.

On the roof, Puri had established a garden of potted plants, tending to them every morning at dawn.

In those days, the vistas in all directions had been breathtaking, the sun shimmering off mustard fields and casting long shadows over clutches of mud huts. Goatherds and their flocks wove along time-worn tracks that dissected the complex patchwork of land. Farmers drove oxen and wooden plows, kicking up dust in their wake. Barefoot women in bright reds and oranges walked from the hand pump to their homes, brimming brass pots balanced on their heads.

Away from the drone of Delhi traffic and the roar of jets making their approach into Indira Gandhi International Airport, Puri had been greeted by peacock calls and the laughter of boys washing at the nearby village pump. When the wind was right, he had also been treated to the smell of chapatis cooking over dung fires and the scent of jasmine, wafting over the exterior wall.

Little had Puri known that in building a new home in Gurgaon, he had become a trendsetter. His move from Punjabi Bagh coincided with the explosion of India's service industries in the wake of the liberalization of the economy. In the late 1990s, Gurgaon became Delhi's southern extension, and was made available for major "development." First, a few reflective glass buildings appeared along the main road to Rajasthan. Then, one by one, the local farmers sold up, and their little fields disappeared under the tracks of bulldozers and dump trucks.

In their place came Florida-style gated communities with names like Fantasy Island Estates. They boasted their own schools, medical facilities, shops, fitness centers and mega-malls.

Concrete superstructures shot up like great splinters of bone forced from the body of the earth. Built by armies of sinewy laborers who crawled like ants along frames of bamboo scaffolding, these were the apartment blocks for the 24/7 call center and software development workforce.

LUXURY IS A PLACE CALLED PARADISE and DISCOVER A VE-NETIAN PALACE LIFESTYLE read the plethora of billboards that invited India's newly affluent to share in the dream.

All this was built on the backs of India's "underprivileged classes," who were working for slave wages. They had arrived in Gurgaon in their tens of thousands from across the country. But neither the local authorities nor the private contractors provided them with housing, so most had built shacks on the building sites alongside the machinery and brick factories. Before long, shantytowns of corrugated iron and open sewers spread across an undeveloped no-man's-land.

The Puris now found themselves living between five hundred homes built on a grid of streets with names like A3; and a slum with a population of laborers and carrion that was growing exponentially. To the north, the view was marred by towering pylons and, beyond them, a row of biosphere-like office blocks bristling with satellite dishes.

The smog, too, had caught up with them. The new four-

lane highway to Delhi had encouraged more traffic, poison-
ing the air with diesel fumes. Legions of trucks stirred dust
into the atmosphere.

These days, the detective found himself struggling to keep
his beloved plants clean. Each morning, he came up onto the
roof armed with a spray gun and gave each of them a bath,
and each morning he found them coated in a new deposit of
grime.

Puri had just got around to tending to his favorite ficus
tree when Malika arrived with his bed tea and biscuits. She
laid the tray on the garden table.

"Namaste, sir," she said shyly.

"Good morning."

He was always happy to see Malika, who had been with
the family for six years. She was a bright, cheerful, hardworking girl, despite having an alcoholic husband, a tyrant
of a mother-in-law and two children to care for.

"How are you doing?" asked Malika, who was keen to
try out her English, which she picked up from watching
American soap operas on Star TV.

"I am very well, thank you," said Puri. "How are you?"

"Fine," she answered, but started giggling, blushed and
then fled downstairs.

The detective smiled to himself and drank some of his tea
before returning to the job at hand. He finished bathing his
ficus and then made his way over to the roof's east side,
where, on the ledge, he was growing six prized chili plants.
He had nurtured each of them from seed (they had been sent
to him by a friend in Assam and came from one of the hottest
chilis Puri had ever tasted) and was pleased to see that after
many weeks of tender care and watering, they were bearing
fruit.

He sprayed the leaves of the first plant and was lovingly

wiping them clean when, suddenly, the flowerpot shattered into pieces. A split second later, a bullet whizzed by Puri's ear and punctured the water tank on the platform behind him.

With some difficulty, given his bulk, he managed to prostrate himself on the roof. A third bullet smashed into another of his chili plants, showering him with broken pottery and earth. The detective heard a fourth and fifth round hit the side of the house as he remained flat on his front, conscious of the pounding in his chest and the shortness of his breath.

A sixth bullet whizzed overhead, puncturing the tank for a second time. Water began to stream out, soaking Puri's silk dressing gown.

He decided to crawl over to the stairwell. If he could get down to his study and retrieve his pistol from the safe, then he could go after the shooter. It crossed his mind that he would need to put on some shoes as well; his monogrammed slippers would get ruined if he had to give chase through the slums.

But as he reached the door, it suddenly flew open, knocking him squarely on the head. Puri's vision doubled for a moment, and then went solidly black.

Five

Puri came around to find Rumpi kneeling by his side, holding some smelling salts under his nose. Nearby, Malika and Monica stood looking down at him with concerned expressions. In the doorway of the stairwell hovered an anxious Sweetu, wringing his hands.

"Sir, sir, sir, so sorry, sir. I didn't mean to, sir! I heard shots, sir, so I came running and then . . . I didn't know you were there, sir! Sir, please don't die . . ."

Puri's head was spinning and he felt nauseous. It took what seemed like several minutes until he could focus his thoughts and then he whispered to Rumpi, "For God's sake, tell the boy to shut up and go away."

Rumpi complied, assuring Sweetu that "sir" was going to be fine and that he should get back to work.

After seeking further reassurance that his life was still worth living, the houseboy did as he was told and returned downstairs.

The girls soon followed him to the kitchen, leaving Rumpi to apply an ice pack to the bump on Puri's forehead.

"Thank heavens you're all right, Chubby," she said tenderly." "I thought you'd been shot."

"Had I not reacted with lightning reflexes and thrown

myself on the ground, most certainly I'd be lying here permanently," he said. "Just I was crawling over to the door when that . . . that fool burst in. Otherwise I would have caught the shooter. Undoubtedly!"

"Oh please, Chubby, it wasn't the boy's fault," chided Rumpi gently. "He was only trying to help. Now tell me how you're feeling."

"Much better, thank you, my dear. A nice cup of chai and I'll be right as rain."

Slowly, the detective pushed himself up into a sitting position, taking the ice pack from Rumpi and holding it on his forehead.

"Tell me, anyone see the shooter?" he asked.

"I don't believe so," answered Rumpi. "I was in the toilet and the others were downstairs. I heard the shots and the next thing I knew Sweetu was shouting you'd been shot and we all came running."

"You called the police, is it?"

"I've tried several times, Chubby. But I keep getting a message: 'This number does not exist.' You want I should try again?"

"Yes please, my dear. An official report should be made. Most probably the cops have been negligible in paying the phone bill. Last I heard, they were some years behind, so the lines were cut off. If you can't get through, send that Sweetu to the station. Tell him to say that some goonda tried putting Vish Puri in the cremation ground, but very much failed in his duty."

The police—an officer and four constables—arrived an hour later. After stomping around on the roof, they concluded that the would-be killer had positioned himself in the vacant plot behind the house.

Their search of the area yielded nothing of value and, predictably, they turned their full attention on the servants.

"Nine times out of ten, it's the help," the officer told Puri.

The questions put to Monica, Malika and Sweetu were accusatory and misleading, and after all three had answered them in turn and professed their innocence, the policeman told Puri he strongly suspected an "inside job." Sweetu was his "chief suspect."

"You think he's dangerous, is it?" asked Puri, playing along.

"I'd like to take him down to the station and get the truth out of him," replied the officer.

The detective pretended to give this suggestion some thought and then said, "Actually, I'd prefer to keep him here. That way I can keep an eye on him and he'll lead me to the hit man."

Puri showed the cops to the door and, after watching them drive away and pausing for a moment to contemplate their crass stupidity, headed up onto the roof.

A careful inspection of the holes in the water tank and the pits made by the two bullets that had impacted on the exterior wall indicated that the hit man had positioned himself on top of the half-constructed building that stood a few feet to the east of the Puris' home.

Five minutes later, the detective was standing on the spot, behind a half-built wall, from where his assailant had shot at him.

There, on the ground, amid some broken bits of brick and lumps of dried concrete, he found six empty slugs and a few cigarette butts. These he scooped up one by one, wrapping them carefully in his handkerchief, and then returned to ground level.

From a number of boot impressions left in the earth, which matched those visible in the dust on the top of the building, he determined that the hit man had entered the site through an open back gate and could easily have come and gone without anyone seeing him.

Puri spent a fruitless hour asking the neighbors and their servants if they had seen anything unusual that morning and then returned home.

Once seated on the big blue leather couch in the sitting room, he wrote down everything he knew so far.

1. Hit man waiting 15 mins. at least.
2. Hit man expecting subject.
3. Hit man uses country-made weapon.
4. Hit man is man—size nine boots.

Next, Puri turned to his Most Usual Suspects file, which he'd retrieved from the safe in his study.

It contained up-to-date information on all the individuals with a strong motive for having him murdered and whom he judged to be a grave threat. In the event of his untimely death, Rumpi was under instruction to take the file to his rival, Hari Kumar. Despite their differences, he and Hari had an understanding that they would not allow each other's murder to go unsolved.

The Most Usual Suspects file contained details of four individuals. A fifth name, that of a serial killer known as Lucky, had recently been removed after he had been awarded the death sentence.

"Not so lucky after all." Puri chuckled to himself as he looked over the other names. In no particular order, they were:

Jacques "Hannibal" Boyé, the French serial killer, serving a life sentence in Tihar jail for murdering and eating seven Canadian backpackers.

Krishna Rai, the opposition MLA from Bihar, whose son Puri had helped convict for murdering a bar girl.

Ratan Patel, the head of India Info Inc., serving six years for insider trading.

Swami Nag, the swindler, confidence man and murderer.

Without doubt, this last individual posed the greatest threat. There was a note on his page that read "absconding, whereabouts unknown." Before going into hiding, the Swami had sworn to kill Puri himself "by any and all means."

The detective decided to call his usual sources within the criminal underworld to find out about Swami Nag's whereabouts and whether any of the other three had put out a contract on his life recently. He would also ask Tubelight to make some inquiries; no one else had better informants.

Beyond that, there was not much more Puri could do.

There were hundreds of hit men for hire in Delhi; nearly all of them were ordinary, everyday people desperate to do anything to provide their families with their next meal. Their fingerprints were not on record; their weapons of choice were often "country-made" pistols and rifles, which were impossible to trace. Puri closed the Most Usual Suspects file, put it on the couch next to him and opened another dossier containing details of the attempts that had been made on his life.

Today's incident brought the tally to twelve.

On six occasions, his enemies had tried shooting him; twice, they'd attempted poison (once using a samosa laced with arsenic); and during the Case of the Pundit with Twelve Toes, a hired thug had tried to force Puri's car over the edge of a hairpin bend on the road to Gulmarg.

The most ingenious attempt had been orchestrated by a cunning murderer (a naturalist by profession) working in Assam's Kaziranga Park, who had secretly sprayed Puri's clothes with a pheromone that attracted one-horned rhinos.

The closest anyone had come (not including the three rhinos, who could move surprisingly quickly) had been a criminal hijra who had pushed a pile of bricks off the top of a building into an alley in Varanasi where Puri had been walking.

Hardly a day went by when Puri didn't relate one of these stories to someone. Prospective clients, journalists, visiting children doing school projects and Scotland Yard detectives had all heard one or more.

"Danger is my ally," he would tell eager listeners.

Fostering an image of fearlessness was vital to his reputation as a detective. But Puri was not lax about his own security. His Ambassador was a customized model fitted with bulletproof glass and a reinforced steel undercarriage. He kept two Labradors in the garden and employed an alert chowkidar armed with a shotgun. And he varied the route he took home.

Puri was also careful to appease the gods, visiting the temple at least once a week and observing all the major festivals.

If all that failed to protect him . . . well, the detective had not stared death in the face without being somewhat fatalistic. As he was fond of saying, "We're all one breath from this life to the next, only."

A couple of hours after the shooting, with the bump on his forehead no longer throbbing, Puri decided he was well enough to drive to Jaipur.

Rumpi had other ideas.

"Chubby, you must rest," she insisted in Punjabi, the language the two usually spoke with each other, returning from the kitchen with some tea for him.

"I'm making you some khichri and later I'll rub mustard oil on your head."

Obediently, the detective sat on the couch again. He knew when it was prudent to do as he was told. Besides, spending the day at home would not be all bad. He could repot his chili plants, watch some cricket and, in the evening, visit the temple.

Rumpi returned to the kitchen and Puri switched on the TV, surfing through the inordinate number of satellite channels until he found one showing the India vs. West Indies match in Hyderabad. It was the second test—the Indian batsmen having collapsed in the first—and the tourists were nearly eighty-two for one, with Lara two runs short of a half-century.

Half an hour later, as Puri was enjoying Rumpi's khichri with homemade curd and tart mango pickle, and reflecting on the perks of being shot at, a car honked its horn outside the front gate and the dogs began barking.

The detective listened as the gate was opened and a vehicle's tires ground against the gravel. Two doors banged shut and footsteps approached the house. A few seconds later, Puri heard the sound of his mother's voice in the corridor.

"Namaste," she said to Rumpi. "I came directly, na. But traffic delay was there. So many cars you can't imagine. At Ring Road junction, the light was blinking, causing backup. Police were being negligent in their duty. Drivers were just honking and shouting and such. But what a terrible thing has happened! Everyone is all right, though, na?

Thank God. Where is Chubby? He is OK? That is the main thing."

Puri heaved a drawn-out sigh and looked affectionately at the TV like a lover bidding his sweetheart a reluctant adieu. He switched it off and pushed himself off the couch. As his mother entered the room, he bent down and touched her feet.

"Thank God you are all right, my son," she said, tears welling in her eyes as she raised him up by the shoulder. "As soon as I came to hear, then directly I called your number. But the line was totally blocked. Must be there is commotion here and such. So I rushed right away. Of course, I felt certain everything would be all right. But Ritu Auntie was in agreement I should come. This shooting person must be found and I've little else to do."

The fact that Ritu Auntie, an insatiable gossip, had encouraged Mummy to drive over came as no surprise to him. Nor did the fact that his mother had learned about the shooting so quickly. Although recently retired and living with the detective's eldest brother twelve miles away, Mummy-ji had a staggering number of mostly female friends and acquaintances who acted as her own intelligence network across the city (and often well beyond).

Puri was in little doubt that the leak had emanated from his servants. One of them had told the subzi-wallah about the shooting and he in turn had passed on the news to one of his other customers, more than likely one of the drivers working for a household a few doors down. This driver had told his mistress, who in turn had informed her cousin-sister, who in turn had called up the auntie living next door. In all likelihood, this auntie was a bridge player who had paired up with Mummy at a recent kitty party and they had swapped telephone numbers.

Puri had learned from hard experience that it was impossible to hide dramatic developments in his life from his mother. But he would not tolerate her nosing about in his investigations.

True, Mummy had a sixth sense and, from time to time, one of her premonitions proved prescient. But she was no detective. Detectives were not mummies. And detectives were certainly not women.

"Mummy-ji, there is no need to come all this way," said Puri, who always sounded like a little boy when he addressed his mother. "I am fine. Nothing to worry about. No tension."

She made a disapproving tut. "Tension is there most definitely," she replied firmly. "Quite a bad bump you've got, na."

Mummy found the armchair nearest the door and perched on the edge of the seat, her back perfectly straight. Despite the abruptness of her departure from home and the race through Delhi's pollution and traffic, she was calm and composed. The former headmistress of Modern School, she wore her silver hair, which had only been cut once in her life, pulled back from her face into a sedate bun. Her cotton sari was a conservative green and matched her emerald earrings.

"For tension, bed rest is required. Two days minimum," she continued.

"Mummy-ji, please. I don't need bed rest," protested Puri, who was sitting back on the blue leather couch. "Really, I am fine."

A silence fell over the room. Puri noticed the Most Usual Suspects file still lying next to him and hoped that his mother wouldn't notice it.

"There are clues?" asked Mummy, suddenly.

Puri hesitated before answering. "No clues," he lied.

"Empty cartridges?"

"No, Mummy-ji."

"You've made a thorough investigation of the scene?"

"Of course, Mummy-ji," he said, sounding as stern as he could when addressing his mother. "Please don't get involved. I have told you about this before, no?"

Mummy replied impatiently, "Peace of mind will only be there once this goonda is behind bars. He may be absconding, but he will revert. Meantime, there is one other matter I wish to discuss." She hesitated before continuing. "Please listen, na. Chubby, last night, I was having one dream . . ."

The detective let out a loud groan, but his mother ignored him.

"Just I see you walking through one big house," she said. "Lots of rooms there are, and peacocks, also. I believe it is in Rajasthan, this place. You're entering one long passage. It is dark. One flashlight you are carrying, but it is broken. At the end, there is one young girl. Just she's lying on the ground. She is dead. So much blood, I tell you. Then from behind comes one goonda. Most ugly he is. And he's carrying a knife and . . ."

Mummy stopped talking and looked confused.

"And what, Mummy-ji?" interrupted Puri.

"Well, see, at that moment I was waking."

"So you don't know the end?"

"No," she admitted.

"OK, Mummy-ji, thank you for telling me," he said to appease her. "Now, let's have no more talk of knives or goondas or shootings. We'll take tea and then, you are right, I should take bed rest. Tension is most definitely building."

The detective called out to Sweetu, who was in the kitchen. In double time, he appeared in the doorway, looking uncharacteristically alert.

"Bring masala chai and biscuits," instructed the detective.

"Sir, what to do with Auntie's tachee?" he asked.

"Tachee?" repeated Puri.

"My trunk case," explained Mummy. "I'll be staying for some days. It's my duty to remain, to make sure you are all right, na? I'm your mummy after all. When you are safe, then I will revert. Meantime, don't go to Rajasthan, Chubby. I forbid it. There is grave danger and such awaiting you there."

Six

The following morning, Puri left the house at the usual time, saying good-bye to Mummy and Rumpi on the doorstep. He took with him his briefcase, stainless steel tiffin and a cardboard box holding files and papers.

The detective was not heading for the office, but he did not tell anyone his destination, not even Rumpi, for fear of having to listen to another of Mummy's lectures.

Handbrake only found out where they were headed once he had pulled away from the gate.

"We are going out-of-station," said Puri, nursing the bump on his head, which was less sore than the night before but had turned a dark purple.

He addressed the driver in Hindi peppered with the odd English term and phrase.

"Where to, Boss?" asked a surprised Handbrake, regarding Puri curiously in the rearview mirror.

"Jaipur."

"No bags, Boss?"

"I have packed my overnight things in that cardboard box. It was not possible to explain all this to you at home." Puri reverted to English: "Everyone is doing gossip."

Handbrake decided not to pry further; he knew it was not his place to ask questions about his employer's business or to complain about the sudden departure and the fact that he had not been given the opportunity to bring along a change of clothes. Such was the lot of the Indian chauffeur. Still, he could not help wondering why Puri was being so secretive about his plans. Surely it must have something to do with the shooting yesterday?

Working for the detective was certainly proving exciting. Handbrake had started the job almost a month ago, a busy month in which he had found himself tailing errant spouses and working alongside undercover operatives. On one occasion, Boss had asked him to follow a client whom he suspected of keeping two wives. Last week, he had driven his employer to South Block for a meeting with the defense minister. Yesterday, someone had tried killing him. And now, it seemed, they were on the trail of a hit man.

Handbrake still couldn't quite believe his luck. For the past five years, he had worked at the Regal B Hinde Taxi Service behind the Regal Hotel. Home had been a dirty tarpaulin erected by the side of the road, where he'd slept on a charpai shared on a shift basis with two other drivers. The hours had been grueling and the owner, "Randy" Singh, had been a miser who exacted a punishing percentage of all fares.

To add to Handbrake's woes, he had rarely been able to visit his wife and new baby girl, who remained in his father's house in the family's "native place," a village in the hills of Himachal Pradesh, a ten-hour drive north of the capital.

But after visiting the Sai Baba temple on Lodhi Road, Handbrake had seen his fortunes change for the better.

That very afternoon, Puri's former driver had suddenly resigned due to ill health, and Elizabeth Rani had had to call the Regal B Hinde Taxi Service and ask for a car. Handbrake had been first in line for a fare, and after picking up the detective from Khan market, he spent the day driving him all over the city.

That evening, Boss had complimented him on his knowledge and asked him four questions.

Did he have a family? Yes, Handbrake had replied, telling Puri about little Sushma, whom he missed so much it hurt.

Did he drink? Sometimes, he admitted, feeling ashamed because of the many times since he'd come to Delhi that he'd gotten drunk on Tractor Whisky and blacked out.

Next the detective had asked him whether he knew what color socks he was wearing.

"Yes, they are white," Handbrake had replied, mystified by the question.

"And which newspaper have I been reading today?"

"*Indian Express.*"

Without further ado, Puri had offered him a full-time job with a monthly salary double his usual earnings. He had thrown in one thousand rupees to buy some new clothes and go for a haircut and shave, and advanced him a further five hundred to rent a room in Gurgaon.

The job came with certain conditions.

Handbrake was not to discuss Puri's business with anyone, not even his wife. To do so was a sackable offense. So, too, were drinking on duty, turning up for work with a hangover, cheating on petrol, gambling and visiting prostitutes.

The driver was banned from sleeping on the backseat of the car during the day. And he was expected to shave every morning.

Handbrake had accepted all these conditions willingly. However, there was one proviso to which he had taken exception: his employer's insistence that he obey Indian traffic rules. Incredibly, Puri expected him to keep to his lane, indicate before he turned, and give way to women drivers. When he attempted going around roundabouts anticlockwise, cutting off autorickshaw drivers or backing the wrong way down one-way streets, he was severely reprimanded. Furthermore, when he exceeded the speed limit on the main roads, he was told to slow down. This meant that he often had to give way to traffic, which was humiliating.

Handbrake found the drive to Jaipur that morning particularly frustrating. The new tarmac-surfaced toll road, which was part of India's proliferating highway system, had four lanes running in both directions, and although it presented all manner of hazards, including the occasional herd of goats, a few overturned trucks and the odd gaping pothole, it held out an irresistible invitation to speed. Indeed, many of the other cars travelled as fast as 100 miles per hour.

Handbrake knew that he could keep up with the best of them. Ambassadors might look old-fashioned and slow, but the latest models had Japanese engines. But he soon learned to keep it under seventy. Time and again, as his competitors raced up behind him and made their impatience known by the use of their horns and flashing high beams, he grudgingly gave way, pulling into the slow lane among the trucks, tractors and bullock carts.

Soon, the lush mustard and sugarcane fields of Haryana gave way to the scrub and desert of Rajasthan. Four hours later, they reached the rocky hills surrounding the Pink City, passing in the shadow of the Amber Fort with its soaring ramparts and towering gatehouse. The road led past the Jal Mahal palace, beached on a sandy lake bed, into Jaipur's ancient quarter. It was almost noon and the bazaars along the city's crenellated walls were stirring into life. Beneath faded, dusty awnings, cobblers crouched, sewing sequins and gold thread onto leather slippers with curled-up toes. Spice merchants sat surrounded by heaps of lal mirch, haldi and ground jeera, their colours as clean and sharp as new watercolor paints. Sweets sellers lit the gas under blackened woks of oil and prepared sticky jalebis. Lassi vendors chipped away at great blocks of ice delivered by camel cart.

In front of a few of the shops, small boys, who by law should have been at school, swept the pavements, sprinkling them with water to keep down the dust. One dragged a doormat into the road where the wheels of passing vehicles ran over it, doing the job of carpet beaters.

Handbrake honked his way through the light traffic as they neared the Ajmeri Gate, watching the faces that passed by his window: skinny bicycle rickshaw drivers, straining against the weight of fat aunties; wild-eyed Rajasthani men with long handlebar moustaches and sun-baked faces almost as bright as their turbans; sinewy peasant women wearing gold nose rings and red glass bangles on their arms; a couple of pink-faced goras straining under their backpacks; a naked sadhu, his body half covered in ash like a caveman.

Handbrake turned into the old British Civil Lines, where the roads were wide and straight and the houses and gardens were set well apart.

Ajay Kasliwal's residence was number 42 Patel Marg, a sprawling colonial bungalow purchased by his grandfather, the first Indian barrister to be called to the Rajasthani Bar. The house bore his name, Raj Kasliwal Bhavan, and sat back from the road beyond two red sandstone pillars crowned by stone Rajasthani chhatris. A driveway led through a well-tended front garden where a mali stooped over the beds, planting marigolds.

Handbrake pulled up in front of the grand, columned entrance and got out to open Puri's door. The detective was stiff after the long drive and grimaced as his knees creaked under his weight.

"I'll be some time," he told the driver, handing him thirty rupees. "Take lunch and then come back. Also, don't call anyone in Delhi and tell them where you are."

Puri mounted the three steps that led to a veranda with its cane furniture and rush blinds, and yanked the brass bellpull. There was a ringing somewhere deep inside the house, and before long, the door was pulled ajar by a young maidservant.

"Ji?" she said, her eyes darting over the top of her chunni, which obscured half her face.

"I am here to see Ajay Kasliwal," explained Puri in Hindi.

The girl nodded and let him inside, her head bent shyly. She closed the door behind them and, without another word, led the detective down a hallway lit by an antique smoky-brown Manoir lamp. The inside of the bungalow was cool thanks to its thick granite walls and stone floors. The sound of the maidservant's chappals scuffling over them was accompanied by the soft squeaking of the detective's shoes. When she came to the second door on the left, the girl indicated it as if something frightening lurked inside.

"Is Mr. Kasliwal inside?" asked Puri.

She shook her head slowly. "Madam," she whispered with lowered eyes.

Puri opened the door and stepped into a large sitting room of diminished grandeur. It was furnished with dowdy couches and armchairs draped in crocheted throws. On the floor lay a twenty-foot Persian rug that was faded and, in places, threadbare. Overhead hung a sooty crystal chandelier that gave a feeble light.

The décor did not detract from Mrs. Kasliwal's regal bearing. She sat on a thronelike armchair next to the fireplace in a priceless silk sari. Although no great beauty, she benefited from strong bone structure, which suggested strength of character. The gold and black mangal sutra necklace, large red bindi on her forehead and the sindoor in the parting of her hair also indicated a certain piety.

"Namashkar, Mr. Puri," she said, putting aside her knitting. Her tone was inviting but also slightly imperious. "Such an honor, no? Not every day a famous detective visits. The Sherlock Holmes of India, isn't it?"

Puri did not like being compared to Sherlock Holmes, who had rather belatedly borrowed the techniques of deduction established by Chanakya in 300 BC and never paid tribute to them. But he hid his irritation well and sat down on the couch in front of the fireplace to the left of Mrs. Kasliwal.

"Quite a bruise you've got there, Mr. Puri. Some criminal type gave you a bash, is it?"

"Nothing so exciting as that," replied the detective, quickly changing the subject. "But what a fine house. Must be quite old."

"They're not making them like this anymore, that is for sure." Mrs. Kasliwal beamed. "It's been in the family for quite some time. Three generations, in fact. But where are my manners? Something to drink, Mr. Puri? Chai?"

"I wouldn't say no, actually, madam," answered the detective.

Mrs. Kasliwal rang a bell that sat on a side table along with a portrait of a young man in his graduation cap and gown.

"What a handsome fellow," remarked Puri.

"So kind of you to say so," she said proudly. "That's Bobby, taken earlier this year graduating out from St. Stephen's. Such an intelligent boy, I tell you. And most considerate, also."

"He is living with you now?"

"Living with us, of course, but currently studying in UK at School of Economics, London. In two years, he should be returning and joining Chippy's practice."

Chippy was evidently Ajay Kasliwal's nickname.

"So it's the legal profession for him, also, is it?" asked the detective.

"Bobby's always wanted to be a lawyer like his father, Mr. Puri. He's got all kinds of idealistic visions. Wants to put the world to rights. But I keep telling him to get into corporate law. That is where the money is. You know these fellows are making crores and crores."

A knock came at the door and the young maidservant reappeared carrying a glass of water on a tray. As she served the detective, Mrs. Kasliwal watched her every movement with a deep frown.

"Will there be anything else, madam?" the girl asked timidly after Puri had taken the glass.

"Bring tea," came the icy reply.

The maidservant nodded and withdrew in silence, closing the door behind her.

"Mr. Puri, I should have told you that Chippy is running late," Mrs. Kasliwal said while the detective sipped his water. "Some urgent business is there. You'll find him at the District and Sessions Court. But first you'll take lunch."

"He's a busy fellow, is it?"

"Never stops, Mr. Puri! One case after another. So many people seeking his advice. And he can never say no. He is far too accommodating, actually. That is his character. You will not find a more respected man in all of Rajasthan. And from such a well-to-do family. His grandfather was one of a kind and his father was a most distinguished person, also. Only problem is . . ." Here Mrs. Kasliwal faltered. "Frankly speaking, I fear for his safety, Mr. Puri. Such powerful people he is taking on. Even politicians and the like. I ask you, is it worth it? Sometimes it's best not to get involved, no?"

"Certainly one has to be careful," said Puri, staying neutral despite his admiration for his client's strong convictions and courage.

"Exactly," said Mrs. Kasliwal. "A man should put his family first and others after. Also, is it for lawyers to fix the whole country? Mr. Puri, such terrible things they are saying about Chippy. But that is why you are here, is that not correct? You'll clear my husband's good name and the family name, also. People are getting all kinds of ideas, I tell you. Everywhere there is talk."

"You can count on Most Private Investigators, madam," he replied.

"But how will you find this girl, Mr. Puri? She could be alighting anywhere, no? Who knows what has become of her? One day she is here, then absconding. Most probably she has made friendship with the wrong sort and paid the consequences."

Puri nodded. "Often shenanigans are taking place," he agreed.

"I tell you, Mr. Puri, I'm facing constant servant tension. I don't dare take my eyes off these people for one minute. Give them an inch and they take more than a mile. You provide good salary, clean quarters and all, but every time, someone is making mischief. I tell you, drivers are making hanky-panky with maidservants. Cooks are stealing ghee. Malis are getting drunk and sleeping under trees. Then they are making demands, also! 'Madam, give me advance. Madam, give my daughter education. Madam, give me two thousand bucks for Mother's heart operation.' Are we expected to take responsibility for every problem in India, I ask you? Don't we have our own stomachs to feed?"

Puri took out his notebook and asked Mrs. Kasliwal how Mary had come to be in her employ.

"Just, she came knocking one day. I had need of one maid-servant."

"You have records? A photocopy of her ration card, a photograph?"

Mrs. Kasliwal regarded Puri with amused pity.

"Why should I have a photograph of her?" she asked.

"What about her last name? You know it?"

"I never asked, Mr. Puri. Why should I? She was just a maidservant after all."

"Is there *anything* you can tell me about her, madam? She was a satisfactory worker?"

"Not at all! Always things were going missing, Mr. Puri. One day my comb; the next, two hundred rupees. When absconding, she took one silver frame, also."

"How do you know?"

"Because it was gone! How else?"

The detective wrote something in his notebook, ignoring Mrs. Kasliwal's testiness.

"Mary vanished on what date exactly?" he asked.

"August twenty-first night. Twenty-second morning there was no sign of the girl. I found her room empty."

"Was Mary having relations with other staff members?"

"You know these Christian types, Mr. Puri. Always putting it about."

"Anyone in particular?"

"She and Kamat, cook's assistant, were carrying on for sure. Twice or thrice, I saw him coming from her room."

Puri made a note of this.

"You have been most cooperative, madam," he said. "But just a few more questions are there. Tell me, when Mary left, her salary was owing, was it?"

Mrs. Kasliwal seemed surprised by the question and took a moment to answer. "Yes, it was due," she said.

"You're certain, madam?"

"Quite certain."

"Did you report her disappearance to the police?"

"And what should I tell them, Mr. Puri? Some Bihari-type maidservant absconded? Police have better things to do with their time."

"You are quite correct, madam," he said. "The police suffer from case overload these days. That is why substitute batsmen like myself are making good innings."

Puri put away his notebook, but he wasn't quite finished with his questions.

"Madam, just you called Mary a 'Bihari-type,' " he pointed out. "But earlier you didn't say where she was from."

"A slip of the tongue, Mr. Puri," said Mrs. Kasliwal. "So many servants these days are coming from Bihar and other such backward places. Naturally I assumed she was from there, also, being so dark."

"She was very dark, is it?"

"Like kohl, Mr. Puri," she said with disdain. "Like kohl."

After an excellent lunch, Puri inspected the servant quarters.

The redbrick building stood in the back garden beyond a wide lawn and a screen of bushes.

There were five small rooms as well as a shared "bathroom" equipped with a cold tap, an iron pail and a squat toilet.

Mary's room had remained empty since her disappearance. It was dingy and bare save for a cotton mattress that lay on the floor and posters of the Virgin Mary and the Bollywood hunk Hrithik Roshan on the wall. Puri knew that in winter, with no source of heating, it must have been brutally cold, and in summer, unbearably hot.

He spent more than five minutes in the room, scouring the place for clues. There were rat droppings scattered across the floor, and in one corner ash from a burnt mosquito coil. Lined up on the windowsill, Puri also discovered a dozen smooth little colored stones. These he slipped into his pocket when Mrs. Kasliwal wasn't looking.

"Regrettably, I found nothing," said Puri as he emerged from the room, noting that the door was warped and it couldn't be closed or locked properly.

Together they made their way back across the lawn and down the side of the house to the driveway, where Handbrake was waiting in the car.

"Madam, one more question is there, actually," said Puri before he headed off to the court. "What all were your whereabouts on August twenty-first night?"

"I was playing bridge with friends, Mr. Puri."

"I see. And you returned at what time exactly?"

"Quite late, Mr. Puri. Some time after midnight, if I'm remembering correctly. Before you ask, Mary's absence came to my attention the next morning only."

"Must be there were other people around the house— servants and all?"

"Certainly, Mr. Puri. But who knows what goes on when I'm not around. I shudder to think, really I do."

"Can you list all of those who might have been present at the time?"

"But of course, Mr. Puri. Let me write the names down for you."

She wrote:

Jaya, maidservant
Kamat, cook assistant
Munnalal, driver
Dalchan, mali

Seven

Outside Jaipur's District and Sessions Court, rows of male typists sat at small wooden desks bashing away at manual typewriters. The tapping of tiny hammers on paper punctuated by the pings of carriage bells was constant—the very sound of the great, self-perpetuating industry of Indian red tape.

Hovering behind each typist stood his clients: complainants, defendants, petitioners and advocates, all watching to ensure their affidavits, summons, wills, marriage applications, deeds, indentures and countless other types of form were completed accurately. A rate of ten rupees per page was charged for this service, an unavoidable fee given the court's stipulation that all official documents should be typed (and one exploited to the full by the typing mafia, who ensured that there was not a word processor in sight).

In front of the courthouse sat rows of advocates whose "offices" were out in the open. Each had a desk with his name prominently displayed on a plaque, a few chairs and a metal filing cabinet packed with bulging files tied with string.

Schools of hangers-on circled the lawyers, like symbiotic

fish feeding off the parasites on sharks. Chai-wallahs moved between the rows of desks with trays of small glasses of sweet milky tea, calling "Chaieee, Chaieee!" Grubby little urchins carrying wooden boxes with brushes, rags and tins of polish offered to shine shoes for four rupees.

Hawkers sold roasted peanuts in newspaper cones.

Various businesses had also set up under a banyan tree. There was a barber—a mirror attached to the gnarled trunk and a high chair—catering to those requiring a haircut or a shave before making their appearance in court. A table with a phone and a meter hooked up to a car battery also served as a "telecon center."

Like any place in India where people gathered, the courts attracted beggars and a collection of wildlife as well. A man with no legs rolled around on a makeshift skateboard, holding his hand up in hopes of a handout. Rats and crows competed for discarded peanut shells. Pye-dogs lazed in the winter sun.

Puri passed through this throng with disdain written large across his face. His aversion to India's courts had developed long before he became a private detective. In the mid-1970s, his father had been falsely accused of bribery and become embroiled in a court battle to clear his name, which had dragged on for nearly fifteen years and had sullied his reputation forever. As a teenager, the young Puri had spent many a morning or afternoon waiting patiently outside the Rohini courts complex, where he had seen for himself how corrupt and inefficient the system was. Often he would meet his cousin Amit there, trying to settle a property dispute that had started between his grandfather and great-uncle some twenty years earlier and embroiled the next two generations in pointless quarrelling and exorbitant legal fees.

According to one newspaper article Puri had read recently, it would take half a century to clear the backlog of cases pending in India. And there were hundreds more being added every day.

The detective passed some of the system's victims in the corridors of the main building as he searched for the courtroom where Ajay Kasliwal was arguing a case. Many of them were poor and illiterate, unable to afford proper representation or the bribe money necessary to grease the palms of the countless gatekeepers to justice. They crouched on their haunches, resigned and helpless in the face of endless adjournments, incomprehensible legal jargon and unchallenged violations of their fundamental rights.

A jostling crowd of advocates, defendants and their families blocked Puri's entrance to Court 19. He found a space on a bench outside and waited for Kasliwal to emerge. Next to him sat an old man with the dry, cracked heels of a farmer who had spent long years plowing parched fields.

Puri asked him what he was doing there and soon the farmer was telling him about his case. It had begun with a dispute over a water buffalo.

"My neighbor stole the animal at night," he said. "When I complained to the police, they beat me. The court said there was no evidence and I was ordered to pay my neighbor's legal fees. Now I am in dispute with his lawyers because I cannot pay and my own lawyer is also charging to represent me. When I come here to appeal, either the lawyers do not appear or there is no time given to me in the court. Meanwhile the bills grow larger and still I cannot pay. In the end I will be bankrupt, they will take my land and I will have no choice but to take my own life."

Puri asked him how much he owed. The amount was two thousand rupees.

"And how long have you been coming here?"

"Three years."

It saddened him to think that in today's India, sixty years after the nation had won its independence, a man's future and that of his family hung in the balance over an amount equivalent to a restaurant bill. He felt inclined to take out his wallet and give the farmer the amount he required. But he knew cash handouts were not the answer; the money would just get swallowed up. What was needed was reform. Perhaps by defending Ajay Kasliwal, he could help achieve it.

"Case adjourned," said Kasliwal, squeezing through the swell of people clambering to get inside Court 19. "That's the third time this week."

"On what grounds?" asked Puri.

"The key witness was supposed to be deposed before the judge, but it seems His Lordship has been bought by the opposition."

The two men left the building and drove over to the Rajasthan High Court, where Kasliwal had his office.

"The problem with the system is such that it is almost impossible to remain honest," said the lawyer. "So much temptation is there, I tell you. Everyone is involved. All these bastards are looking after one another's interests. If you get one good apple, then they're worried it will spoil the batch. They don't want honest fellows like me around who aren't ready to do match fixing.

"It is a great conspiracy of interests," he continued. "I'm fighting the entire system, Puri-ji. My enemies are surrounding me on all fronts. But we must root out this evil. How can India expect to reach superpower status with all this corruption around? It is like a great hand around our throats. I, for one, am prepared to fight it with every bone in my body."

Kasliwal's office was plainly furnished with just a desk, a few chairs and picture of Gandhi on the wall. In the bottom drawer of his desk, he kept a bottle of Royal Challenge.

"It's good for bad purposes." He chuckled, pouring Puri a small glassful, then adding some soda.

The two men clinked glasses and sat down on either side of Kasliwal's desk, facing each other.

"Puri-ji, you are a good man," said the lawyer. "That is as clear as day. Come what may, we will be friends! That is for sure."

The detective drank to his client's health but looked troubled.

"Too much soda?"

"No, no, badiya!"

"Something is wrong?"

"Yes, there is something," answered Puri. "Before I proceed further, one thing should be understood. A detective must be thorough. He must leave no stone unturned. To reach the truth, he must go about where he's not wanted, asking questions people don't want to answer. He must pry into the darkest shadows. Sometimes he will discover skeletons hiding away in closets. Sometimes in trunks, also."

"You've found something already, Puri-ji?"

"Nothing yet. But this is an old friend." He touched the side of his bulbous Punjabi nose. "It is as good as radar. Better, in fact! And it is telling me something terrible has happened. The circumstances surrounding Mary's disappearance are most peculiar. No way a maidservant leaves without taking her salary. However small an amount, such a female will want it."

The detective stared into his whisky, deep in thought.

"If you want me to find out what happened, I must

examine your affairs and those of your family. From top to bottom, inside and out."

"We have nothing to hide," said Kasliwal.

Puri drained his glass and placed it on his client's desk. His countenance was grave. "Let us suppose for a moment you were making mischief with this Mary," he said.

Kasliwal sat up straight. "What kind of question is that?"

"Sir, I need to know everything or no good will come," answered Puri, staring at him across the desk.

"Nothing happened between us, I swear it."

"But you tried to make friendship with her?"

"Listen, I admit she was good for window shopping, but I never touched her. My father taught me never to do hanky-panky with servants."

"And with others?" probed Puri.

The lawyer stood up, looking agitated. He started to pace up and down.

"Sit. It is no good hiding the truth from Vish Puri," prompted the detective.

"My private life is not open for discussion," said Kasliwal firmly.

"Sir, I'm working on your behalf. What is said will remain between us."

Kasliwal stopped by the window of his office looking out on the inner courtyard of the High Court. There was a long silence and then he turned his back on the window and said, "I admit I'm not a man to always eat home-cooked food. Sometimes, I like something extra spicy."

His words were met with a blank look.

"Come on, Puri-ji, you know how it is. I'm only human. Married to the same woman for twenty-nine years. Arranged marriage and all. After so many innings, a man needs some extracurricular activity."

"But not with servants?"

"Life is complicated enough, Puri-ji."

The detective took out his notebook, referring to his notes from his conversation with Mrs. Kasliwal.

"How about Kamat, cook's assistant? He and Mary got involved?"

Kasliwal shrugged. By now, he was standing with his hands on the back of his chair, leaning over it. "I wouldn't know. With so much workload, I'm not around the house much."

Puri flicked back to the notes taken during his first conversation with his client in the Gymkhana Club.

"The night Mary vanished, you were working, is it?" he asked.

The lawyer looked down and exhaled deeply. "Not exactly," he confessed. "I was . . ."

"Making friendship?"

There was a pause. "Something like that."

"Anyone can verify?"

Kasliwal looked torn by the suggestion. "Puri-ji, that could be awkward," he said hesitantly.

The detective referred to the list compiled by Mrs. Kasliwal of everyone who was supposed to have been in the house at the time of Mary's disappearance.

"What about your driver, Munnalal? He was with you?"

"He dropped me at the address, yes."

"I'd like to talk with him."

"I'm afraid one month back, he got drunk and abusive, so I fired him."

"You know his address?"

"No, but he's round about. I pass him in one of those new Land Cruisers from time to time. Must be working for another family. I doubt it will be difficult to track him down."

The detective checked his watch. It was already four o'clock.

"By God, where does the time go? I'd better get a move on, actually," he said.

Kasliwal saw him to do the door.

As they shook hands, Puri asked, "Sir, is your wife aware?"

"Of what? Munnalal's address? Possibly I can ask her."

"I was referring to your like of spicy food."

Kasliwal raised a knowing eyebrow and replied, "I never bring home takeout."

After he left the High Court, Puri asked Handbrake to take him to a hole-in-the-wall cash dispenser, where he took out a wad of new hundred-rupee notes.

Their next stop was Jaipur's Central Records Office, where the detective wanted to check if any unidentified bodies had been discovered in Jaipur around the time of Mary's disappearance.

The building matched the blueprint for most Indian government structures of the post-1947 socialist era: a big, uninspiring block of crumbling, low-quality concrete with rows of air-conditioning units covered in pigeon excrement jutting from the windows.

At the entrance stood a walk-through metal detector that looked like a high school science project. Made out of chipboard and hooked up to an old car battery, it beeped every ten seconds irrespective of whether anyone passed through it.

The foyer beyond was dark with a half-dead potted plant on either side of the lift and several panels hanging precariously from the false ceiling. Two busybody male receptionists sat at a wooden desk cluttered with rotary-dial telephones and visitors' logbooks. A sign on the wall behind them read:

FOLLOWING VIPS ONLY MAY ENTER
WITHOUT SECURITY CHECK:
PRESIDENT OF REPUBLIC OF INDIA
PRIME MINISTER OF REPUBLIC OF INDIA
CHIEF MINISTERS
MEMBERS OF LOK SABHA
MEMBERS OF RAJYA SABHA
FOREIGN HEAD OF STATE
FORMER FOREIGN HEAD OF STATE
FOREIGN AMBASSADOR (ORDINARY DIPLOMATS
NOT EXEMPT NOR AIDES)
DALAI LAMA (RETINUE NOT EXEMPT)
DISTRICT COMMISSIONER
STRICTLY NO SPITTING

Puri did not have an appointment and, since he could not lay claim to being any of the above, had to part with a few minutes of his time and three of his new hundred-rupee notes.

Thus armed with the requisite entry chit, all properly signed and rubber-stamped, the detective made his way up the stairs (the lift was undergoing construction), passing walls streaked with red paan spit and fire buckets full of sand and cigarette and bidi butts.

On the fourth floor, little men with oiled hair wearing the semiofficial uniform of the Indian bureaucratic peon—grey polyester pant suits with permanent creases, and black shoes—made their way up and down the corridor. Coming face-to-face with the sheer size of the Indian bureaucracy never failed to amaze Puri. The system still employed hundreds of thousands of people and, despite the recent rise of the private sector, it remained the career of choice for the vast majority of the educated population.

Puri doubted this would change any time soon. India's love of red tape could be traced back centuries before the British. The Maurya Empire, India's first centralized power, which was founded around 2300 BC and stretched across most of the north of the subcontinent, had had a thriving bureaucracy. It had been a uniting force, implementing the rule of law and bringing stability. But now, the endemic corruption in India's administration was severely hampering the country's development.

Room 428 was near the far end of the corridor. As he strode purposefully inside, Puri took his fake Delhi police officer badge from his wallet, adopting the role of Special Commissioner Krishan Murti, Delhi Crime Branch. At the counter where all requests for records had to be made, he told the clerk that he wanted to see the file for unclaimed bodies found in Jaipur in August.

"Make it fast," he said.

"Sir, request must be made. Procedure is there. Two days minimum," replied the clerk.

At that moment, Puri's phone rang. He had preprogrammed the alarm to go off thirty seconds after he'd entered the office. He pretended to answer it.

"Murti this side," he said, pausing as if to listen to a voice on the other end of the line. He allowed his eyes to widen. "Bloody bastard!" he bellowed. "What is this delay? Where are my results?"

The clerk behind the counter watched him with growing unease.

"Don't give me damn excuses, maaderchod! I want results and I want them yesterday! Top priority! I'm answering directly to the home minister himself. The man doesn't take no for an answer and neither do I! If I don't see action within one hour, you'll be doing traffic duty in Patna!"

Puri hung up the phone, muttered "Bloody bastard" and turned on the clerk.

"What were you saying? Something about two days minimum, huh?"

"Yes, sir." The clerk quivered.

"What bullshit! Get me the incharge. Right away. No delay!" bawled the detective, thoroughly enjoying himself. Oh, how he loved watching bureaucratic types squirm!

Puri was ushered into a partitioned cubicle, the domain of C. P. Verma, whose seniority was denoted by the fact that he wore a jacket and tie.

"I want the record for unidentified bodies discovered in August," Puri told the bureaucrat, who had stood up. "It's of national importance. Top priority."

C. P. Verma, who had overheard the exchange between the desk clerk and Puri, hadn't risen through the ranks without learning how to respond to authority and recognizing when to jump.

"Of course, sir! Right away, sir!" He called for his secretary, who swiftly presented himself in front of his boss's desk. C. P. Verma ordered the man to bring him the file, his tone no less abrupt than Puri's. "Jaldi karo! Do it fast!" he added for good measure, his face contorted with displeasure.

The secretary scampered off to dispense orders of his own to the subordinates ranked below him. The incharge's expression melted into an unctuous smile.

"Sir, you'll take tea?"

The detective brushed away his offer with a motion of his hand, busying himself with his phone.

"Just get me the file," he said flatly, pretending to make another phone call, this time to his assistant, whom he accused of mismatching a set of fingerprints.

Less than five minutes later, the secretary returned with the file. Puri snatched it out of his hands and began searching through the pages. Nine unidentified bodies had been discovered in Jaipur in August alone. Of these, two were children, both suffocated and dumped in a ditch; four were hit-and-run victims found dead on the sides of various roads; one was an old man who fell down a manhole and drowned (he was not discovered for a month); another was a teenager whose headless torso turned up one morning on the railway tracks.

The ninth was a young woman.

Her naked body had been found on the side of the Ajmer Road on August 22.

According to the coroner's report, she had been raped and brutally murdered and her hands had been hacked off.

A grainy, out-of-focus photograph showed extensive bruising around her face.

"Why only one photograph?" Puri asked C. P. Verma.

"Sir, budget restrictions." It was evidently a phrase he was used to parroting.

"What happened to this woman's body?"

"Sir, it was held in Sawai Mansingh Hospital for the requisite twenty-four hours, and after no claim was made upon it, cremation was done."

"Give me a photocopy of this report and the photo, also."

"Sir, I'll need authorization." He ventured a smile.

"Authorization is there!" shouted Puri, showing him his badge. "Don't do obstruction!"

Within a matter of minutes, the photocopies were in Puri's hands.

C. P. Verma saw the detective to the door personally.

"Sir, anything else from me?" he asked.

"Nothing," snapped Puri as he left.

"Thank you, sir. Most welcome, sir," C. P. Verma found himself saying to the detective's back.

The incharge then returned to his cubicle, pleased with himself for having assisted such a highly ranked detective. He was even more senior than the other investigating officer Rajendra Singh Shekhawat, who had asked to see the same file the day before.

Eight

Ajay Kasliwal couldn't tell whether the girl in the coroner's photograph was Mary.

"So much of bruising is there," said the lawyer, grimacing at the image when Puri showed it to him in the evening.

Mrs. Kasliwal studied it for a few seconds and then said in a tone that might have been born of caution or confusion, "These people look so much alike."

"You can make out any distinguishing marks?" the detective pressed her.

"How should I know?" she answered brusquely.

Puri decided to show the photograph to the servants and asked that they be brought into the sitting room one by one.

Bablu, the cook, came first. A fat, greasy-faced Punjabi with bloated fingers, he gave the photocopy a cursory glance, said, yes, it could be Mary and then returned to his kitchen. Jaya, the shy girl who'd answered the front door for the detective in the morning, was next. She held the piece of paper with trembling hands, looked at the image, squealed and closed her eyes. Puri asked her if she recognized the girl, but she just stared back at him with wide, frightened eyes.

"Answer him," Mrs. Kasliwal instructed.

"Yes, madam . . . I . . . I . . . ," Jaya said, her eyes darting between the Kasliwals and Puri.

"Don't be afraid," urged Puri gently. "Just tell me what you think."

"I don't . . . couldn't . . . say, sir," she said after further coaxing. "It . . . well, it could be . . . Mary, but then . . ."

Puri took back the picture and Jaya was dismissed.

Kamat, cook's assistant, was equally nervous and no clearer on whether the woman in the photograph was his former co-worker. But he seemed remarkably unmoved by the shocking nature of the image and, with a shrug, handed it back to the detective.

That left the mali.

Mrs. Kasliwal would not allow him to enter the house, so he had to be brought to the kitchen door, which opened into the back garden.

The gardener was evidently stoned and stood there with a silly grin and dopey eyes, swaying from side to side in time with a tune he was humming to himself.

Puri handed him the photograph and he stared at it for thirty seconds with his head moving back and forth like a rooster's.

"Do you recognize her?" he asked.

"Maybe, maybe not," replied the mali. "My eyesight is not what it used to be."

All this went to confirm why Puri rarely bothered asking servants—or most people, for that matter—direct questions. Getting at the truth, unearthing all the little secrets that people buried deep down, required a subtler approach.

Which was why, later that evening, the detective made a few phone calls to Delhi, putting into motion the next stage of his investigation.

• • •

The detective spent the night in one of the guest rooms in his client's house Raj Kasliwal Bhavan and, after breakfast, announced his intention to return to Delhi.

Ajay Kasliwal looked taken aback by this news. "But, Puri-ji, you just got here," he said.

"Don't have tension, sir," the detective assured him. "Vish Puri never fails."

Soon, he and Handbrake were on the highway to Delhi, traveling at a legal and responsible speed that was not of the driver's choosing and certainly not to his liking.

By now, Handbrake was burning with curiosity about the detective's latest case. The servants at the house had been talking about little else and the driver had been privy to their theories. Subzi-wallah had told him that the lawyer Sahib had many lady friends and he had got Mary pregnant and had sent her away with a payoff. The cook had whispered that the mali, whom he hated, had raped the maidservant, killed her and buried the body under the spinach. And the Muslim who sold carrot halva on the pavement had been adamant that the girl had fallen in love with a fellow Muslim, converted to Islam and, consequently, been abducted by her family and murdered.

Puri smiled when Handbrake related all this to him.

"Did they ask about me?"

"All of them, Boss."

"And what did you tell them?"

The driver looked suddenly unsure of himself. "I told them that . . . you are . . . that you are an . . . idiot, Boss."

Puri looked pleased. "You told everyone?"

"Yes, just like you asked me to. I said that you forget everything from one day to the next because you are a drunkard and you spend all your mornings sleeping."

"Excellent! Very good work!" said Puri.

Handbrake grinned, grateful for the compliment. But he was still confused by Puri's motive. It showed clearly in his expression.

"Vish Puri's third rule of detective work is to always make all suspects believe you are a fool," explained the detective. "That way they are caught unawares."

"What is the second rule, Boss?"

"Pay no attention to gossip."

"What is the first?"

"That I will tell you when you are ready."

With that, Puri lay back against the seat and went to sleep. He did not wake until they reached the halfway point and Handbrake pulled into the Doo Doo Rest Raunt and Rest Stop car park.

The detective went into the air-conditioned dining room, where he sat at a clean table and enjoyed a cup of chai served in a china cup by a waiter.

Handbrake, meanwhile, went to the open-air dhaba, where he sat among the flies and the truck and bus drivers, and the same tea was served in clay cups.

Puri had good reason for returning to Delhi: he had received a summons. Not the sort of summons issued by the courts (although he had been handed more than his fair share); this was from a potential client, a man whom the detective could not ignore or put off, a childhood hero no less.

Brigadier Bagga Kapoor, retired, was a decorated veteran of the 1965 Pakistan war. He had commanded a tank battalion during the legendary advance over the Ichhogil Canal, which marked the western border with India. In September of that year, he and his men destroyed eighteen enemy tanks, coming within range of Lahore International Airport. When his own tank was hit by enemy fire and two of his men were killed, Brigadier Kapoor pulled his unconscious gunner from the burning vehicle and carried him to safety. For this action, he was awarded the Ati Vishisht Seva Medal.

Puri had never had the pleasure of meeting the legendary Brigadier, although he'd heard him lecture at the Indian Military Academy in Dehradun in 1975. Naturally, he was thrilled at the opportunity to be of service to the great man. But when Brigadier Kapoor had telephoned Most Private Investigators the day before and spoken to Elizabeth Rani, he had not specified the nature of the case. He'd simply left instructions for Puri to meet him in Lodhi Gardens at four in the afternoon.

"I tried telling him that you are out-of-station, but he insisted," Elizabeth Rani told Puri on the phone while he was still in Jaipur. "He also asked that you must go alone."

The detective stopped off at home in time for lunch to discover that Mummy had been trying to find witnesses to the shooting in the neighborhood. According to Rumpi, she had spent all of yesterday and most of this morning knocking on doors.

"By God!" exclaimed Puri angrily. "I told her not to get involved! Why she always insists on doing such interference I ask you?"

"She's just trying to help," said Rumpi as she and Malika prepared rajma chawal for lunch. "Shouldn't you be out there doing the same—asking people what they saw?"

"My dear, I'm totally capable of running my investigations. Already I've got my own people doing the needful."

This was true: Tubelight and one of his boys had been making discreet inquiries in the neighborhood since yesterday; so far, though, they had come up with nothing.

"Mummy will only make a mess of things and put people on guard. It could be dangerous, also. Detective work is not child's play. Now, please, when Mummy returns from doing her chitchat, tell her I want a word tonight. She's to stop this nonsense."

After lunch Puri drove to his office, caught up with the latest developments in the other cases on his books, which included some run-of-the-mill matrimonial investigations, and then drove the short distance to Lodhi Gardens.

The car park at the Prithviraj Road entrance was full of Hindustan Ambassadors with official license plates and red emergency lights on their roofs—just some of the thousands of courtesy cars assigned to India's senior babus, judges and politicians for conducting the business of the state. These days that included taking wives and their lapdogs for their afternoon walks, or so the ruling bureaucratic elite had come to believe.

Puri crossed the Athpula Bridge and followed the path through the gardens. He passed lawns where families sat enjoying picnics, groups of young men played cricket with tennis balls and toy sellers hawked balloons and kazoos. Cheeky chipmunks darted between the boughs of trees, and long-tailed green parakeets with red beaks perched in branches overhead, shrieking noisily. The detective passed an old man practicing his yoga exercises, breathing alarmingly heavily through his nostrils; and a bench half hidden between the bushes where two young sweethearts sat stealing furtive kisses.

Brigadier Kapoor was already waiting for Puri on the steps of the Sheesh Gumbad mausoleum, checking his watch impatiently and looking none too pleased that the detective was three minutes late. The war hero was a year short of eighty and his big military moustache, sideburns and correspond-ingly bushy eyebrows had turned white. Nonetheless, he was still remarkably fit. In American sneakers, socks drawn up to his knees, khaki shorts and a woolly ski hat, he was dressed for exercise.

"Puri, I've heard good things about you," said Brigadier Kapoor, who had attended Dehradun and Sandhurst and spoke with an accent that reminded Puri of bygone days.

"It's a great honor, sir," replied the detective with a salute, then a handshake.

"I do brisk walking for forty-five minutes every day at four o'clock without fail," said Brigadier Kapoor, who carried a military baton with an ivory handle tucked between his chest and the upper part of his left arm. "We'll talk along the way."

Puri was hardly dressed for brisk walking; as usual, he was wearing a safari suit and Sandown cap. But without further ado, the older man set off along on the jogging circuit at three times the pace of the detective's usual gait.

"I need you for something, Puri," said Brigadier Kapoor, sounding as if he might ask him to parachute behind enemy lines. "I don't have to tell you it's for your eyes only."

"Understood, sir."

"It's my granddaughter, Tisca." They passed some copses of giant bamboo, which arched forty feet above them. "She's to be married in two months. There's a big wedding planned here in Delhi. I was introduced to the boy two days ago. Mahinder Gupta's his name. He won't do. He won't do at all!"

The detective groaned inwardly. He had hoped that Brigadier Kapoor was going to offer him more challenging work than another matrimonial. But he still managed to sound interested. "I understand, sir."

"I blame my son, Puri," continued Brigadier Kapoor as

they approached the footbridge that led to Mohammed Shah's tomb. "He's never been a good judge of character. His wife's even worse. Hopeless woman."

By now, Puri had broken into a sweat and had to wipe his brow with his handkerchief.

"What sort of family the boy is from?" asked Puri.

"They do commerce; they're Guptas. Bania caste."

"So this boy's occupied in the family business, is it?"

"He's working at some place called BPO. You've heard of it?"

"BPO stands for Business Process Outsourcing. Such companies operate call centers and all."

"I see," said Brigadier Kapoor with a frown that suggested Puri's explanation did not make things any clearer to him.

"There's anything specific you have against this boy?" asked the detective.

"He's not a man, Puri. He hasn't served his country."

The detective was developing a stitch in his left side. The direction of their conversation was also making him feel uncomfortable. Matrimonial investigations had become his bread and butter (he often dealt with several a week), but usually his clients came to him seeking reassurance about a prospective bride or groom. Brigadier Kapoor, by contrast, had it in for the boy and wanted to scupper the wedding.

Unfortunately, turning the case away was out of the question. The detective could not say no to a man of such stature; to do so would damage his own reputation.

"What else can you tell me, sir?" panted Puri, growing ever shorter of breath.

"The boy has spent a good deal of time in Dubai. God knows what he could have got up to there. The place is a hotbed of Jihadists, Pak spies, dons—every kind of shady character."

"He's here in Delhi these days, sir?"

"I believe so. Plays a lot of golf. Shoots four under par—or so they say."

Much to Puri's relief, they got stuck behind three over-weight society women in Chanel sunglasses, sun visors and unflattering leggings, and had to slow down.

Brigadier Kapoor soon lost patience and barked at the women to give way. With a collective tut, they moved to one side of the path and he marched past them, muttering to himself.

"Sir, tell me," said Puri, struggling to catch up again. "Your granddaughter's what age exactly?"

"Thirty-four or thereabouts." His tone betrayed not a hint of embarrassment, but she was ancient to be getting married.

"And the boy's age, sir?"

"Three years her junior."

"Sir, it's the first time Tisca's getting engaged?"

"That's not the point, Puri," said Brigadier Kapoor sharply. "I want to know about this Gupta boy."

The two men passed Sikander Lodhi's tomb and reached the car park, where Rumpi's rajma chawal was threatening to make another appearance.

"Sir, with your permission, I'll take my leaves," said Puri somewhat sheepishly.

Brigadier Kapoor looked unimpressed. "As you like, Puri," he said. "I'll have my file on Mahinder Gupta sent over to your office tomorrow morning. Report back to me within a week. Get me all the dirt on him. I'll take care of the rest."

"Yes, sir."

"And get yourself in shape, man," chided Brigadier Kapoor, wagging his baton. "At your age I used to run five miles every day before breakfast."

"Yes, sir."

Before the detective could mention his fee and explain his usual policy of a down payment for expenses, his new client marched off with his arms pumping like pistons, as if he was charging an enemy position.

Puri waited until he was out of sight and then sat down on a wall to catch his breath and wipe his brow.

"By God, thirty-four," he said to himself, shaking his head from side to side disapprovingly. "Well past her sell-by date. Off the shelf, in fact."

At home that evening, Mummy was waiting for Puri in the sitting room.

"Chubby, I've something most important to tell you. One big development is there," she said.

"Mummy-ji, if it's about the shooting, please save your breath," he said, as he went through the motion of bending down to touch her feet but only reaching the halfway point.

"Chubby, you must listen, na. It's most important. One servant boy—"

"Sorry, Mummy-ji, but I won't listen," interrupted the detective. "I told you before, you're not to do investigation. It's not a mummy's role, actually. You'll only make things more complicated. Now please, I respectfully request you not to go sticking your nose where it doesn't belong."

"But, Chubby, I—"

"No, Mummy-ji, that is final, no discussion. Now, I'm going to wash and take rest."

Puri went upstairs, leaving Mummy on her own in the sitting room to think things over.

Chubby had inherited his father's pride and stubbornness, she reflected. Om Chander Puri, too, had always been adamant that she should stay out of his investigations. Only on a few occasions, when he'd been completely stumped by a case, had he deigned to discuss the details with her. Although, each time, she'd been able to help him unravel the clues, he'd never been able to bring himself to openly acknowledge her assistance. Similarly, when Mummy had had one of her dreams, Om Chander Puri had rarely taken heed of them.

As a wife, Mummy had always felt compelled to obey her husband. But as a mother, she did not feel constrained to ignore her natural instincts—especially now that her son was in grave danger.

Graver than he knew.

That morning, Mummy had met a young servant boy called Kishan, who worked in house number 23, a few doors down. When she'd asked him if he'd seen anything suspicious on the day of the shooting, he'd looked panicked and blurted out, "I was nowhere near the back of the house!"

"What happened at the back of the house?"

"Nothing!"

"How do you know if you weren't there?"

Eventually, after being plied with a couple of Big Feast ice creams having been assured of Mummy's trustworthiness, Kishan admitted that he had been behind the Puris' home at the time of the shooting.

"What were you doing there?" Mummy had asked.

"Um, well, Auntie I . . ." he'd replied, looking embarrassed.

"Let us say you went to the market to buy milk and took the long way back," Mummy had suggested helpfully.

"Yes, exactly. I'd forgotten."

"What did you see?"

"I was behind a wall waiting for . . . um, well . . ."

"You had to do toilet?"

"Yes, that's right and, well, I heard the shots. They

sounded like firecrackers. Then two minutes later, I saw a man hurrying out of that building site."

Kishan had caught only a fleeting glimpse of the man's face. But there had been something distinct about him.

"He was wearing red boots."

Upon hearing this, Mummy had instructed Kishan not to mention what he'd seen to another soul. It was the kind of information that could get someone killed.

Chubby of all people would understand the significance of the red boots if only he would listen to her. But for now she would have to carry on with the investigation on her own.

"I'll show him mummies are not good for nothing," she told herself.

Nine

Few men failed to notice the young peasant woman walking down Ramgarh Road three mornings after Puri left Jaipur. Her bright cotton sari might have been of the cheapest quality and tied jauntily in the style of a laborer, but it did justice to the firm, shapely body beneath. The demure manner in which she wore her dupatta over her head—the edge gripped between her teeth and one tantalizing, kohl-rimmed eye staring out from her dark features—only added to her allure.

The more lecherous of the men she passed called out lustily.

"I will be the plow and you my field!" bawled a fat-gutted tonga-wallah from the front of his horse-drawn cart.

Farther on, two laborers painting white lines on the concrete divider in the middle of the road stopped their work to stare and make lewd sucking noises. "Come and be my saddle! You will find me a perfect fit!" cried one.

The Muslim cobbler who sat on the corner surrounded by heels and soles, gooey pots of gum and a collection of hammers and needles was more discreet. But he could not take his eyes off her ample bosom or the flash of alluring midriff beneath her blouse. Thoughts passed through his head that, as a married man blessed with three healthy sons, he knew he would have to ask Allah to forgive.

Despite her coy embarrassment, the young woman understood the licentious and perfidious nature of men only too well. She ignored their comments and stares, continuing along the uneven pavement with her small bag toward the entrance to Raj Kasliwal Bhavan. There, just beyond the gate, she spotted a mali crouched on the edge of one of the flower beds, a scythe lying idle by his side. His clothes were old and tatty and he went barefoot. But his pure white hair was a biblical affair. It began like the crest of a wave, sweeping back from his forehead and cascading down around his ears in a waterfall of licks and curls, before finally breaking into a wild, plunge pool of a beard.

The mali was staring into space with a dreamy, far-off expression, which at first the young woman assumed was a manifestation of old age. Drawing nearer and smelling distinctive sweet smoke trailing up from the hand-rolled cigarette, she realized that his placid state was self-induced.

"Namashkar, baba," she greeted him from a few feet away.

The old man stirred from his reverie and, as his drowsy eyes focused on the vision in front of him, his mouth broadened into a wide, contented grin.

"Ah, you have come, my child," he said, drawing his beard through one hand. "Good. I have been waiting."

"We know each other, baba?" asked the woman with a bemused frown, her voice deeper than her youthful looks suggested.

"No, but I have seen you in my dreams!"

"I'm sure you have!" she mocked.

"Why not come and sit with me?" he suggested.

"Baba! If I wanted a corpse I would go to the graveyard!"

Her pluckiness caused the mali to laugh. "Spend a little time with me, my child, and I will show you that I am no corpse!"

"I have no time, baba. I must find work. Is there any available here?"

He patted his thighs. "There is work for you here!"

"Enough, baba. I am no grave robber! I was told Memsahib is hiring."

"Memsahib is always hiring. She demands hard hours and pays little. No one stays for long."

"But you are here."

"Yes, I am content. I have a roof over my head and I can grow everything I need. What I don't smoke, I sell. But for you there is no charge. Make me feel young again and I will give you as much as you like for free."

"Later, baba!" she said impatiently. "I have mouths to feed."

"What kind of work can you do?" he asked, sounding doubtful.

"Baba! Are you the sahib of the house? Are you the one to ask the questions? I'll have you know that I can do many things. I can clean, do laundry and cook. I even know ironing."

The mali took another drag of his joint and gently exhaled, the smoke dribbling from his nose and trailing up his face.

"Yes, I can see that you have been many things," he said.

His words caused the woman to chuckle, but the true reason was lost on the mali.

"A lady in the market told me Memsahib is looking for a maidservant," she said.

"The last disappeared a few months ago."

"What happened to her?"

"She was murdered."

"How do you know?"

"I know."

"Who did it?"

"It could have been one of many men."

"She had lovers?"

The mali laughed again. "That one was known as the 'Little Pony,' " he continued. "There can't have been a man in Rajasthan who hadn't ridden her! I took my turn! So did the driver, the subzi-wallah, Sahib—"

"Sahib?" interrupted the woman with alarm.

"You sound surprised?"

"I've heard it said he's a good man," she added quickly.

"People are not all that they seem. Whenever Memsahib was away, Sahib would knock on the Little Pony's door. He made a feast of her on many nights! You could hear them from miles away. But it wasn't the sahib who killed her."

"How do you know?"

"He was not here when she disappeared."

"Then who is the murderer, baba?"

The mali shrugged and drew the last from his joint, dropping the still-smoking end into the flower bed. The woman turned away from him and looked up at the house.

"Where should I ask for work?" she asked.

"At the back. Go to the kitchen door."

She started up the drive.

"Wait! You didn't tell me your name," called the mali, admiring the way her silver anklets jangled around her slim, brown ankles.

"Seema!" she shouted over her shoulder without stopping.

"I will be dreaming of you, Seema!"

"I'm sure you will, baba!"

Seema made her way up the sun-dappled driveway and

along the right side of the whitewashed villa. A redbrick pathway led through flower beds planted with marigolds and verbena. Beyond, where the path led behind the house, finches gathered around a stale roti, chirping as if catching up on local news.

She reached the door of the kitchen and pulled out the letter of recommendation she had been carrying tucked into her waist. It was from a senior bureaucrat and his wife in Delhi, Mr. and Mrs. Kohli, and stated in English that Seema had worked for them for three years. They had found her "to be an employee of the highest reliability, honesty, loyalty and integrity, also." The letter bore Mrs. Kohli's phone number. Prospective employers were welcome to call her and ask for further details.

Seema's knock was answered by the cook's assistant, Kamat, who, judging by the wisp of hair on his upper lip, was not a day over fifteen. He was carrying a knife with which he'd been chopping ginger. Kamat in turn called the cook, Bablu, whose thick, wide nose flared when he frowned.

"Where are you from?" he asked, drying his hands on a cloth and eyeing her suspiciously.

Seema was careful to strike just the right tone when she answered—not too shy, but not overly confident either. She said, "Sir, my village is in Himachal."

Seema knew that everyone preferred servants from the hills; they were considered more reliable and trustworthy than those from the plains of the Hindi belt. Furthermore, hill people were not traditionally rag pickers, so they were allowed to handle food.

"What can you do?" asked Bablu.

Seema listed her skills and some of her work experience.

"Wait there," said the cook, snatching the letter out of her hand and shutting the door in her face.

Seema anticipated a long wait and it was nearly thirty minutes before the door opened again. This time it was Madam who appeared. Her hair was piled up on her head and covered in a thick, green mud; she was having it dyed with henna.

"You are married?" Mrs. Kasliwal asked Seema, looking her up and down.

"No, madam."

"Why not?"

"My father doesn't have the dowry."

"How old are you?"

"Twenty-six."

Madam handed Seema's letter back to her.

"I made a call to Delhi," said Mrs. Kasliwal, without elaborating on her conversation with Mrs. Kohli. "I need one laundry-cum-cleaner maidservant. Can you start right away?"

Seema nodded.

"The pay is three hundred per month with meals. You must be live-in."

The amount was below the market rate, especially for a live-in position, which meant a seven-day week.

"Madam, that is low," stated Seema, eyeing the woman's diamond wedding ring and her matching earrings, which were worth several lakh rupees. "I want five hundred."

Mrs. Kasliwal tutted impatiently. "Three hundred is fair."

"Four hundred and fifty?"

"Three hundred and fifty. No advance."

Seema considered the offer for a moment and then, with a reluctant wobble of her head, assented.

"Very good," said Mrs. Kasliwal. "Sunday will be your day off and you can leave the house, but otherwise you must be here. I don't want any sneaking out, and no visitors. Is this understood?"

Seema nodded again.

"Bablu will give you your duties. Any stealing and I will not hesitate to call the police. If, in three days, I am not satisfied, then you must leave."

Mrs. Kasliwal led Seema into the kitchen, where she instructed Bablu to put her to work immediately.

It was a long, hard day. First Seema helped out in the kitchen chopping onions, kneading roti dough, picking out the grit from the moong daal and boiling milk to make paneer. Then she had to mop the hardwood floors in the corridors and the dining room. She was allowed thirty minutes for lunch, some subzi, which she ate on her own, crouched outside the kitchen. Afterward, she was sent to a nearby market to pick up three heavy bags of pulses, as well as a packet of cornflakes for Sahib's breakfast. The rest of the early afternoon was spent doing laundry.

As she worked, Seema was left with little opportunity to interact with her co-workers, let alone get to know them. Bablu said little and when he did speak, it was to curse. Mostly this was on account of Kamat, who was clumsy and forgetful and overcooked the chawal and poured fat down the drain. The driver, Sidhu, who had been working in the house for only a month, spent the morning in the driveway chatting on his mobile phone while wiping, waxing and polishing Mrs. Kasliwal's red Tata Indica, which he treated as if it was the Koh-i-Noor. Sahib's driver, Arjun, who had been hired to replace Munnalal, appeared at around twelve o'clock and, although there was no missing his reaction to the sight of Seema, he barely had enough time to eat his khana before returning to the office with his master's tiffin.

Seema found little opportunity to speak with any of the casual staff, either. The dishwasher girl who came for an hour to scrub all the pots and pans before continuing on to a number of other neighboring households was evidently intimidated by Bablu and kept her head down at the sink. The beautician who came to give Madam threading and maalish had airs and didn't deign to say so much as a please or thank-you for a cup of tea. And as for the dalit toilet cleaner, who came from a rag pickers' colony on the edge of Jaipur, she was a mute.

The only person Seema managed to talk to properly was Jaya, the other young maidservant, who had been working in the house since early August.

In the late afternoon, when Madam went out visiting friends, the two of them worked together sweeping and mopping the veranda. Given that Jaya was intensely shy and evidently unhappy, Seema broke the ice by telling her about some of her adventures. She talked about her days with a travelling theater troupe in Assam; the year she spent working as an ayah to a couple of Delhi socialites' children; and her experiences as a Mumbai bar girl and how a crorepati businessman had fallen in love with her and proposed.

These stories were all true, even though many of the mitigating circumstances surrounding them were adapted for the audience.

Jaya liked listening to them and quickly took to her new friend. On a couple of occasions, she even had cause to smile.

That evening, when all the day's chores were done, Jaya led Seema to the servant quarters at the back of the compound.

There were five rooms in all. The mali occupied the first (starting from the left); the next belonged to Kamat; the third was empty; the fourth, which had posters of the Virgin Mary and Hrithik Roshan on the wall, was vacant as well; and the last room belonged to Jaya.

Jaya warned against staying in the fourth room because the door was warped and did not close properly. But Seema said she liked the idea of the two of them being neighbors. Besides, the door could be fixed.

Together they cleaned the room, taking down the posters. And afterward, Seema took her idols from her bag. Having arranged them on the narrow windowsill of the front window, she lit an incense stick and said a prayer.

The two maidservants spent the rest of the evening chatting some more and sharing a few dates. Seema related more stories about her adventurous past and, now and again, asked Jaya about the other servants.

Soon, she had learned that the mali was stoned all the time and always passed out in the evening. Bablu was gay, but pretended to be straight even though there wasn't a Salman Khan movie he hadn't seen. Kamat often drank and turned extremely aggressive and there was a rumor going around that he had raped a girl working in another house.

At ten o'clock the two decided to turn in and Seema went back to her room.

She heard Jaya close her door and turn the key in the lock and it was with some effort that she managed to do the same.

An hour later, Seema was woken by the sound of a whistle. And then someone tried opening her door.

She called out, "Who's there?" But there was no reply and she heard footsteps running away.

Cautiously, Seema got out of bed, went to the door, opened it and looked outside. It was pitch dark and there was no one in sight.

In her right hand, she held the four-inch Nepali Khukuri knife that she always kept under her pillow at night.

Ten

There were fifteen phone lines running into the Khan Market offices of Most Private Investigators Ltd., only six of which were used, officially, by the company. The rest were for undercover operations.

Each of these nine lines had its own dedicated handset, answering machine and a voice-activated tape recorder arranged on a long table in the "communications room" across the hallway from Puri's office. In front of each phone lay a clipboard with notes detailing how the line was being used and precisely how it should be answered.

These notes were for the benefit of Mrs. Chadha, whose job it was to answer the nine phones in a variety of voices.

It was vital, but mostly uncomplicated work. Much of the time, all she had to do was pretend to be a receptionist or a phone operator and then connect the call to either Puri or one of his operatives.

Recently, for example, lines one to four had been assigned to "Hindustan Pharmaceuticals" (as part of the investigation on behalf of the state of Bihar into the illicit sale of legally grown opium). Mrs. Chadha had been required to pick up all calls to those numbers with the words, "Hindustan

Pharmaceuticals, your health is our business, how may I be of assistance?" before connecting them to Puri, a.k.a. Ranjan Roy, CEO.

But at other times, Mrs. Chadha, who was a member of the South Extension Amateur Theatrical Society and a gifted impressionist and liked her job because she could spend most of the day knitting, had to play more complicated roles.

During one of the latest matrimonial investigations, line seven had been dedicated to the "Hot and Lusty" escort service, and for that Mrs. Chadha had had to adopt a husky voice and arrange bookings for a certain Miss Nina.

For the foreseeable future, line nine was allocated to a Chinese takeout called "Hasty Tasty" and for this Mrs. Chadha sounded harried and impatient and asked questions like, "How hot you want chili chicken?"

To help make things sound authentic, the communications room was equipped with a multideck sound system. This had been set up by Flush and worked automatically. Whenever a call came though, the machine would start playing appropriate background noise.

For Hindustan Pharmaceuticals the ambience was nothing special, just general office sounds: typing, murmuring, the distant ringing of other phones. Calls to the Hot and Lusty line triggered a Muzak version of the theme to *Love Story*. And when anyone rang Hasty Tasty, Mrs. Chadha found herself speaking over the clatter of pots and pans, gushes of steam and the cries of irate chefs.

Usually Puri was able to give Mrs. Chadha a rough timing for when a call was expected.

The same morning that Seema applied for work at Raj Kasliwal Bhavan in Jaipur, the detective told Mrs. Chadha to expect line six to ring at around nine o'clock.

When the call came, it was closer to 9:30.

Putting aside the sweater she was knitting for her youngest grandson, Mrs. Chadha answered the phone with a polite "Ji?"

The woman on the other line asked for a certain Mrs. Kohli.

"Yes, it is she," she said in English, sticking to her own voice for once.

The conversation that ensued panned out just as Puri had predicted. The caller, a well-spoken lady called Mrs. Kasliwal, divulged during a two-minute preamble that she had a large house in Jaipur, that her husband was a well-respected lawyer, and that her handsome son was studying in London.

Eventually she came to the point. Had a servant girl called Seema worked for the Kohlis?

"For three years or thereabouts," answered Mrs. Chadha. "A most satisfactory worker she was."

"Might I ask why she was terminated?" asked Mrs. Kasliwal.

"Actually, my eldest son and his family returned from posting in Kathmandu and he brought back one ayah, so there is no need for the girl."

"But you had no complaints?" asked Mrs. Kasliwal, sounding as if she would need convincing.

"Not at all," said Mrs. Chadha. "One can say she's a cut above the riffraff."

The conversation drifted on to other matters, with Mrs. Kasliwal dropping a few names and extending an invitation to tea the next time the Kohlis were in Jaipur.

After she hung up, Mrs. Chadha logged the call on the appropriate clipboard and called Puri to tell him that the conversation had gone well. Then she got back to her knitting while she waited for the next scheduled call. A young, prospective groom was expected to call on line seven and ask for the services of Miss Nina.

Puri did not expect to hear from Facecream for at least 24 hours. She had not carried a mobile phone with her so she would have to go to a pay phone out in the street to call him.

Getting away from the house could prove difficult, but after working with the Nepali beauty on several dozen operations, the detective was in little doubt that she would find a way.

At Puri's request, Tubelight had sent two of his boys to Jaipur as well. Shashi and Zia had arrived in the Pink City yesterday and been tasked with trying to locate Kasliwal's former driver, Munnalal, and locating the spot on the Ajmer Road where the unidentified woman had been dumped on August 22.

Meanwhile, there was one other lead to follow: the stones Puri had found in Mary's room. He had arranged to have them sent to Professor Rajesh Kumar at the geology department of Delhi University.

"Perhaps Doctor-sahib can provide me with a clue to where they came from," Puri told Elizabeth Rani, who was waiting in front of Boss's desk as he placed the little stones, one by one, inside an envelope.

"We must leave no stone unturned, isn't it, Madam Rani?" said Puri, chuckling at his own pun. "It's a long shot, no doubt, but then no clue is ever insignificant, no?"

"Yes, sir," she answered efficiently before returning to her desk to make the arrangements for the envelope to be dispatched to Professor Kumar's office—Professor Kumar for whom, secretly, Elizabeth Rani had a soft spot.

Puri, who likened himself to a spider at the center of a web with silky tendrils branching out all around him, eased back into his chair, confident that all the little secrets of the Kasliwal household would soon be his. There wasn't another detective in India, private or otherwise, who could have handled it better. And (as Puri acknowledged, begrudgingly) there was only one to equal him.

The young hotshots straight out of detective school (like that bloody Charlie, Harun what's-his-name, who always wore a silk suit and gelled his hair so every goonda could spot him coming a mile off) certainly offered little in the way of competition. The problem with such Johnny-come-lately types was that they watched too much American television and imagined every case could be solved by turning up at a crime scene and using an ultraviolet light.

Not that forensics didn't have its place. As Puri had told a class of cadets at the Delhi headquarters of the Central Bureau of Investigation (the Indian equivalent of the FBI) during one of his recent lectures, Indians had been pioneers in the field.

"In the fifteenth century, one Delhi court investigator, Bayram Khan, solved the most brutal murder of the Great Mughal's courtesan by matching a hair he located floating in the baths where she was drowned by the eunuch Mahbub Alee Khan," the detective had read from a speech that had been typed—and of which the English grammar had been greatly improved—by Elizabeth Rani. "Also let us not forget the Tamil alchemist, Bhogar, who led the way in substance testing. For example, he made extensive comparisons of tobacco ashes. This achievement came a full one and a half centuries before British detective Sherlock Holmes wrote a monograph on the same subject without so much as acknowledging the earlier work."

Puri had gone on to talk about the great Azizul Haque and Hem Chandra Bose, who developed the fingerprint classification system and opened the first Fingerprint Bureau in Calcutta in 1897—although Sir Edward Richard Henry took the credit for their pioneering industry.

"So, as we can see, forensics certainly has its uses," he'd added. "But there is no substitute for good, old-fashioned intelligence gathering. The microscope cannot match the power of the human eye, we can say."

Naturally, in this field, India had also led the world.

"Some two thousand and three hundred years ago, Mr. James Bond's ancestors were living in caves," he'd said. "In those dark, distant days, there was no Miss Moneypenny, no Mr. Q, and the only gadgets were flints to strike together to make fire."

This point had got a gratifying laugh from his audience.

"But in India at this time, we were having the great Maurya Empire," the detective had continued. "The founder of our greatest dynasty was, of course, the political genius Chanakya. It was he who established what we can call the art of espionage. He was, in fact, the world's first spymaster, establishing a network of male and female secret agents. These satris, as they were thus known, operated throughout the empire and its neighboring kingdoms."

Puri had not needed to remind the cadets that it was Chanakya who had written the world's first great treatise on statecraft, the *Arthashastra*, an extraordinarily practical guide to running and nurturing a fair and progressive society—one that India's modern rulers, and indeed the world's, would have done well to study. But he had drawn their attention to the section on running a secret service and read an excerpt:

" 'Secret agents shall be recruited from orphans. They shall be trained in the following techniques: interpretation of signs and marks, palmistry and similar techniques of interpreting body marks, magic and illusions, the duties of the ashramas, the stages of life, and the science of omens and augury. Alternatively, they can be trained in physiology and sociology, the art of men and society.' "

Chanakya, Puri explained, had recommended numerous disguises to be adopted while conducting clandestine operations.

"Brothel keepers, storytellers, acrobats, cooks, shampooers, reciters of puranas, cowherds, monks, elephant handlers, thieves, snake catchers and even gods, to name just a few," he said. "For agents planning to infiltrate a city, Chanakya suggested adopting the cover of a trader; those working on the frontiers should pose as herdsmen. When a secret agent needed to infiltrate a private household, he urged the use of—and I quote—"hunchbacks, dwarfs, eunuchs, women skilled in various arts and dumb persons.' "

Nowadays of course, dwarfs were no longer easy to recruit since many of them had found work in Bollywood. The wealthy classes were no longer inclined to hire hunchbacks as servants. Disguising yourself as a nun was no longer a guaranteed way of gaining access to the home of a high official. And, ever since one-rupee shampoo sachets had become available at paan stalls, shampooing had ceased to be a viable profession.

But the *Arthashastra* remained the basis of Puri's modus operandi. The section on the recruitment, training and use of assassins aside, the treatise remained as instructive today as it had proven to the rulers of the great Maurya Empire.

In all that time, human character had changed little.

"Nowadays," he'd concluded, "a man can fly from one end of the planet to another in a few hours only. Achievements in science are at a maximum. But still, there is more mischief going on than ever before, especially in overpopulated cities like Delhi."

Puri believed this was because the world was still passing through Kali Yuga, the Age of Kali, a time of debauchery and moral breakdown.

"More and more, people's moral compass is turning 180 degrees. So you must be vigilant. Remember what Krishna told Arjuna at the battle of Kurukshetra. 'The discharge of one's moral duty supersedes all other pursuits, whether spiritual or material.' "

Eleven

With Facecream now inside the Kasliwal household, Puri decided to turn to Brigadier Kapoor's case.

He spent a few hours on the phone checking into the prospective groom's background and soon learned that Mahinder Gupta was to be found at the Golden Greens Golf Course most evenings.

The club was in NOIDA, the North Okhla Industrial Development Area to the east of Delhi, which, despite its clumsy acronym, had become one of the most elegant addresses for Delhi's wealthy, image-conscious elite. To reach it, Handbrake took the road that passed the magnificent Humayun's Tomb and frenetic Bhogal market with everything from toilets and bamboo ladders to cotton mattresses for sale on the sidewalks.

At around seven o'clock the Ambassador passed east on the toll bridge that spanned the Yamuna River.

Handbrake had recently overheard Puri bemoaning the fate of the holy river to someone. Apparently, he and his friends had swum in its waters when they were young. On summer weekends, they had crossed by ferry to buy watermelons from the farmers on the other bank. But now, as the

106

terrible stink that filled the inside of the car attested, the Yamuna was a giant sewer—three billion liters of raw waste went into it each year.

On the other side, Handbrake found himself in unknown territory; he had never been to NOIDA before. He had hoped there might be "signage" to point the way to the golf course, but none appeared. Risking a telling-off, he told Puri he didn't know the way.

"Sir, any directions for me?"

Such honesty did not come naturally to Handbrake. His instinct as a former Delhi taxi driver was never to admit ignorance of an address. Partly, this was an issue of pride. Behind the wheel was the one place in the world where he felt like a king. And what king likes to show weakness?

But mostly it was because his former boss, Randy Singh, owner of the Regal B Hinde Taxi Service, and Handbrake's mentor, had always insisted that if a passenger didn't know the way to their chosen destination, then it was a driver's God-given right to fleece them royally.

This philosophy had been instilled in Randy Singh by his father, old Baba Singh, who'd made his fortune rustling water buffalo. Thus the Singh family credo ran: "They have it; why should we not take it?" Indeed, Randy Singh believed that it was the duty of every taxi driver to find ways and means of ripping off all his customers. In his office, he kept an up-to-date map of the current roadworks and diversions across Delhi. Every morning, he briefed his boys on the hot spots where they were sure to run into long delays. He also bribed the men from the Department of Transport whose duty it was to install the government-issued fare meters, which were meant to protect passengers from fraud, to charge an extra three paisa for every mile. This extra profit he split with them seventy-thirty in his favor.

Not surprisingly, Regal B Hinde Taxi Service received a good many complaints from its customers. But Randy Singh never showed remorse. And he prepped his drivers on how to react to disgruntled passengers. Play the dumb villager newly arrived in the big city, he instructed. "Sorry, sir! No education, sir! Getting confusion, sir!"

Handbrake's new employer saw things very differently. If you weren't completely honest and tried to bluff your way around; if you set off in any old direction hoping for the best and then stopped to ask the way from ignorant bystanders only to find yourself performing half a dozen U-turns, the detective was liable to get extremely hot under the collar.

"Oolu ke pathay! Son of an owl!" he'd shouted recently when Handbrake had pretended to know his way around Mustafabad and they'd ended up going round and round in circles in Bhajanpura instead.

Given the respect Handbrake was developing for Boss, such cutting insults hurt. But for all his great deductive powers, Puri was just as lost in many areas of New Delhi's newest suburbs. His map, which was the most up-to-date available in the market, had been printed two years earlier and did not include many of the roads and developments that had "come up."

It didn't help that, throughout Delhi, "signages" were rare. Or that the many "sectors"—which sounded like planetary systems in a Hollywood science fiction film—were just as mysterious as new galactic frontiers. A driver might reach Sector 15 expecting to find Sector 16 nearby, but to his frustration turn a corner and find himself in Sector 28 instead.

Recently, when Handbrake had been sent to Apartment 3P, Block C, Street D, Phase 14, Sector 17 in Gurgaon, it had taken him well over an hour to find it.

As for the Golden Greens Golf Course, Puri had never

been there either. So when Handbrake came clean about not knowing the way, the detective told him to ask someone for directions. But not just anyone.

Migrant laborers were a no-no. According to Puri, they weren't used to giving directions because they came from villages where everyone knew everyone else and roads didn't have names.

"Ask them where anything is and they will tell you 'over there.'"

As for fellow drivers, they were not to be relied on, because half of them were probably lost themselves.

Puri sought out real estate brokers and bicycle-rickshaw-wallahs as good sources because they had to be familiar with the areas in which they worked. Pizza delivery boys could also be trusted.

Soon after turning off the NOIDA expressway, Handbrake·spotted a Vespa moped with a Domino's box on the back and pulled up next to it at a red light.

"Brother, where is Galden Geens Galfing?" he shouted in Hindi to the delivery boy over the sound of a noisy, diesel-belching Bedford truck.

His question was met with an abrupt upward motion of the hand and a questioning squint of the eyes.

"Galden Geens Galfing, Galden Geens Galfing," repeated Handbrake.

The delivery boy's puzzlement suddenly gave way to comprehension. "Aaah! Golden Greens Galf Carse!"

"Ji!"

"Sectorrr forty-tooo!"

"Brother! Where is forty-tooo sectorrr?"

"Near Tulip High School!"

"Where is Tulip High School?"

"Near Om Garden!"

"Brother, where is Om Garden?"

The delivery boy scowled and shouted in an amalgam of English and Hindi, "Past Eros Cinema, sectorrr nineteen! Turn right at traffic light to BPO Phase three! Enter farty-too through backside!"

Some time later, Handbrake delivered Boss to the front door of the clubhouse and drove to the parking lot. He expected a long wait. But for once, he wasn't bothered and sat back in his seat to enjoy the view.

It occurred to him to take a few photographs of the manicured landscape with the new mobile phone Puri had given him. How else would he be able to prove to the people in his village that such an empty, beautiful place existed?

Puri was not a member of the Golden Greens Golf Course, although he would have liked to be. Not for the sake of playing (secretly he couldn't stand the game—the ball was always ending up in those bloody ponds), but for making contacts among India's new money, the BPO (Business Process Outsourcing)-cum-MNC (Multi-National Corporation) crowd.

Such types—as well as many politicians, senior babus and Supreme Court judges—were often to be found on these new fairways to the south and east of the capital. In Delhi, all big deals were now being done on the putting greens. Playing golf had become as vital a skill for an Indian detective as picking a lock. In the past few years, Puri had had to invest in private lessons, a set of Titleist clubs and appropriate apparel, including argyle socks.

But the fees for the clubs were beyond his means and he often had to rely on others to sign him in as a guest.

Rinku, his closest childhood friend, had recently joined the Golden Greens.

He was standing in reception wearing alligator cowboy boots, jeans and a white shirt embroidered with an American eagle.

"Good to see you, buddy! Looks like you've put on a few more pounds, yaar!"

"You're one to talk, you bugger," said the detective as they embraced. "Sab changa?"

Rinku's family had been neighbors of the Puris in Punjabi Bagh and they had grown up playing in the street together. All through their teenage years they had been inseparable. But in their adult lives, they had drifted apart.

Puri's military career had exposed him to many new people, places and experiences, and he'd become less parochial in his outlook. By contrast, Rinku had married the nineteen-year-old girl next door, whose main aspiration in life had been to wear four hundred grams of gold jewelry at her wedding. He had followed his father into the building business and, during the boom of the past ten years, made a fortune putting up low-cost multistory apartment blocks in Gurgaon and Dwarka.

Few industries are as dirty as the Delhi construction business, and Rinku had broken every rule and then some. There was hardly a politician in north India he had not done a shady deal with; not a district collector or senior police-wallah to whom he hadn't passed a plastic bag full of cash.

At home in Punjabi Bagh, where he still lived in his father's house with his mother, wife and four children, Rinku was the devoted father and larger-than-life character who gave generously to the community, intervened in disputes and held the biggest Diwali party in the neighborhood. But he also owned a secret second home, bought in his son's name, a ten-acre "farmhouse" in Mehrauli. It was here that he entertained politicians and bureaucrats with gori prostitutes.

It greatly saddened Puri to see how Rinku had become part of what he referred to as "the Nexus," the syndicate of politicians, senior bureaucrats, businessmen and crime dons (a good many of whom doubled as politicians) who more or less ran the country. Rinku stood for everything that Puri saw as wrong with India. The disease of corruption was slowly eating away at his friend. You could see it in his eyes. They were paranoid and steely.

And yet Puri could never bring himself to break the bond between them. Rumpi said it was because he had spent his childhood trying to keep Rinku out of trouble.

"So, saale, when did you get membership, huh?" asked Puri.

They had gone to the bar and sat down at a table that provided a panoramic view of the Greg Norman–designed course.

"I'll let you in on a little secret, buddy," answered Rinku. "I'm a silent partner in this place."

He put a finger to his lips, the gold chains around his wrist shifting with a tinkle.

"Is it?" said Puri.

"Yah! And as a gift to you, I'm going to make you a member. No need to pay a farthing. No bloody joining fee. Nothing! You just come and go as you like."

"Rinku, I—"

"No argument, Chubby! This is final! On the house!"

"It's very kind of you, Rinku. But really, I can't accept," said Puri.

" 'Very kind of you, Rinku, I can't,' " echoed Rinku mockingly. "What the hell's with all this formal bullshit, Chubby, huh? How long have we known each other? Can't a friend gift something to another friend anymore, huh?"

"Look, Rinku, try to understand, I can't accept that kind of favor."

"It's not a favor, yaar, it's a gift!"

Puri knew he could never make Rinku see sense; his friend couldn't accept that he did not live by his so-called code. He would have to accept the offer and then, in a few weeks, after Rinku had forgotten about the whole thing, renounce his membership.

"You're right," said the detective. "I don't know what I was thinking. Thank you."

"Bloody right, yaar. Sometimes I don't recognize you any more, Chubby. Have you forgotten where you're from or what?"

"Not at all," replied the detective. "I just forgot who I was talking to. It's been a long day. Now, why don't you buy me a drink, you bugger, and tell me about this man I'm interested in."

"Mahinder Gupta?"

Puri nodded.

"He's a Diet Coke," said Rinku dismissively.

"A what?"

"Bloody BPO type, yaar. Got a big American dick up his ass but thinks he's bloody master of the universe. Just like this lot."

Rinku scowled at the young men in suits standing around the bar. With their degrees in business management and BlackBerries, they were a different breed from Puri and Rinku.

"You know what's wrong with them, Chubby? None of them *drink*!"

The suits all turned and stared and then looked away quickly, exchanging nervous comments.

Their reaction pleased Rinku.

"Look at them!" He laughed. "They're like scared sheep because there's a wolf around! You know, Chubby, they go in for women's drinks: wine and that funny colored shit in fancy bottles. I swear they wear bloody bangles, the lot of them. The worst are the bankers. They'll take every last penny from you and they'll do it with a smile."

The waiter finally arrived at their table.

"Why the hell have you kept us waiting so long?" Rinku demanded.

"Sorry, sir."

"Don't give me sorry! Give me a drink! For this gentleman one extra-large Patiala peg with soda. For me the same. Bring a plate of seekh kebab and chicken tikka as well. Extra chutney. Got it? Make it fast!"

The waiter bowed and backed away from the table like a courtier at the throne of a Mughal conqueror.

"So what's this Diet Coke been up to, huh? Giving it to his best friend's sister or what?"

Puri tried to answer but he only got out a few words before Rinku interrupted.

"Chubby, tell me one thing," he said. "Why do you bother with these nothing people? After all these years, you're still chasing housewives. What's your fee—a few thousand a day, maximum? I'm making that every minute. Round the clock. Even sitting here now my cash till is registering. Ching!"

"Don't worry about me. I'm doing what I'm meant to be doing. This is my dharma."

"Dharma!" scoffed Rinku. "Dharma's for sadhus and sanyasis! This is the modern world, Chubby. Don't give me that spiritual shit, OK?"

Puri felt a flash of anger and shot back, "Not everyone is a . . ."

But he stopped himself speaking his mind, suddenly

afraid that if he did, it would bring an end to their relationship once and for all.

"Not everyone is what? A bloody crook like me? Is that what you were going to say?"

They sat in silence for nearly a minute.

"Listen, I didn't come here to argue," said Puri eventually. "I'm not one to tell friends how to live or what to do. You've made your choices; I've made mine. Let's leave it at that."

The Patiala pegs arrived, both tumblers filled to the brim.

Puri picked up his and held it above the small round table that separated them. After a moment's hesitation, his friend did the same and they clinked glasses together.

Rinku downed half his Scotch and let out a loud, satisfied gasp, followed by a belch.

"That's a proper drink," he said.

"On that, we agree." Puri smiled.

"So this Sardaar-ji gets married and on his first night he has his way with his new wife. But the next morning he gets divorced. Why? Because he notices a tag on her underwear that says: *Tested by Calvin Klein!*"

Puri roared with laughter at the punch line to Rinku's latest Sikh joke.

The two men were on their second drink.

"I heard another one the other day," said the detective when he had wiped the tears from his cheeks.

"Santa Singh asked Banta Singh, 'why dogs don't marry?' "

"Why?" asked Rinku gamely.

"Because they're already leading a dog's life!"

Only a slick of grease and some green chutney remained on their snack plates by the time Puri broached the subject of Mahinder Gupta again.

"Your Diet Coke comes here most nights after work—

around eight thirty, usually," Rinku told him. "Sometimes his fiancée joins him. She's as bloody nuts about golf as he is. I played a round with him just one time. He wouldn't take my bet. Said gambling was against the club rules! I tell you, Puri, these guys are as stiff as—"

"Anything else?" interrupted the detective.

Rinku drained his glass, eyeing his friend over the brim.

"He's got a place in a posh new block near here, Celestial Tower. All bought with white.* Can you believe it, Chubby? The guy's got a mortgage from the bank! What kind of bloody fool does that, I ask you? So you want to meet him— your Diet Coke?"

"Where is he?"

"In the corner."

There were three men sitting at the table Rinku indicated. They had arrived a few minutes earlier.

"A thousand bucks says you can't guess which one," said Rinku.

"Make it three thousand."

"You're on."

It took Puri less than thirty seconds to make his choice.

"He's the one in the middle."

"Shit yaar! How did you know?" said Rinku, fishing out the money and slapping it down on the table.

"Simple yaar!" He pronounced it "simm-pull." "The man on the right is wearing a wedding ring. So it shouldn't be him. His friend on the left is a Brahmin; I can see the thread through his vest. Guptas are banias, so it's not him. That leaves the gentleman in the middle."

Puri looked more searchingly at Mahinder Gupta. He was

* White money is legitimate, not derived from the "black" economy.

116

of average height, well built and especially hairy. His arms looked as if they had been carpeted in a shaggy black rug, his afternoon shadow was as swarthy as the dark side of the moon, and the many sprigs poking out from the neck of his golfer's smock indicated that even the tops of his shoulders were heavily forested. But Gupta did not strike Puri, who always made a point of sizing up a prospective bride or groom for himself, as the macho type. If anything, he seemed shy. When he spoke on his BlackBerry—he was using it most of the time—his voice was quiet. Gupta's reserved body language was also suggestive of someone who was guarded, who didn't want to let go for fear of showing some hidden part of his character.

Perhaps that was why he didn't drink.

"What did I tell you?" said Rinku. "Guy doesn't touch a drop of alcohol! Saala idiot!"

"What time will he play?"

"Should be any time."

A few minutes later, Gupta's golf partner arrived and the two of them headed off to the first tee.

"Chubby, you want to play a round?" asked Rinku.

"Not especially," said the detective.

"Thank God! I hate this bloody game, yaar! Give me cricket any day! So you want to come to the farmhouse? I've got some friends coming later for a party. They're from Ukraine. They've got legs as long as eucalyptus trees!"

"Rumpi is expecting me," said Puri, standing up.

"Oh, come on, Chubby, don't be so bloody boring, yaar! I'll make sure you don't get into trouble!"

"You've been getting me into trouble ever since we were four, you bugger!"

"Fine! Have it your way. But you don't know what you're missing!"

"I know exactly what I'm missing! That's why I'm going home."

Puri playfully slapped Rinku on the shoulder before making his escape.

On his way home, the detective considered how best to proceed in the Brigadier Kapoor case.

Mahinder Gupta struck Puri as somewhat dull—one of a new breed of young Indian men who spent their childhoods with their heads buried in books and their adult lives working fourteen-hour days in front of computer terminals. Such types were generally squeaky clean. The Americans had a word for them: "geeks."

Being a geek was not a crime. But there was something amiss.

Why would a successful, obviously fit and active BPO executive agree to marry a female four years his senior?

To find out, Puri would have to dig deeper.

First thing tomorrow morning, he would get his team of forensic accountants looking into Gupta's financial affairs. At the same time, he'd assign Flush to find out what the prospective groom was up to outside office hours and see what the servants knew.

Twelve

Puri did not reach home until ten o'clock, an hour later than usual.

The honk of the car's horn outside the main gate marked the start of his nightly domestic routine.

The family's two Labradors, Don and Junior, started barking, and, a moment later, the little metal hatch in the right-hand gate slid open. The grizzled face of the night-watchman, Bahadur, appeared, squinting in the bright glare of the headlights.

Bahadur was the most conscientious night watchman Puri had ever come across—he actually stayed awake all night. But his arthritis was getting worse and it took him an age to open first the left gate, then the right, a process that Handbrake watched restively, grinding the gears in anticipation.

Finally, the driver pulled inside, stopped in front of the house and then jumped out quickly to open the back door. As Boss stepped onto the driveway, Handbrake handed him his tiffin.

The dogs strained on their ropes, wagged their tails and whined pathetically. Puri petted them, told Handbrake (who was renting a room nearby) to be ready at nine sharp and then greeted Bahadur.

The old man, who was wearing a stocking cap with earflaps and a rough wool shawl wrapped around his neck and shoulders, was standing at attention with his back to the closed gates. He held his arms rigid at his sides.

"Ay bhai, is your heater working?" asked Puri, who had recently installed an electric heater in the sentry box in anticipation of the cold, damp smog that would soon descend upon Delhi.

"Haan-ji! Haan-ji!" called out Bahadur, saluting Puri.

"You've seen anything suspicious?"

"Nothing!"

"Very good, very good!"

Puri entered the house, swapped his shoes for his monogrammed slippers and poked his head into the living room. Rumpi was curled up on the couch in a nightie with her long hair down around her shoulders. She was engrossed in watching *Kaun Banega Crorepati*, India's version of *Who Wants to Be a Millionaire?*, but turned off the TV, greeted her husband and brought him up to date with what was going on in the house.

There were no visitors or guests, she told her husband. Radhika, their youngest daughter, who was studying in Pune, had called earlier. Malika had gone home to her children, alcoholic husband and impossible mother-in-law. And Monica and Sweetu had gone to bed in their respective quarters.

"Where's Mummy?" asked Puri, perching on the arm of the armchair nearest the door.

"She went out a few hours ago. I haven't heard from her."

"Did she say where she was going?"

"She mumbled something about visiting some auntie."

"Mumbled? Mummy doesn't do mumbling. I asked you to keep an eye on her, isn't it?"

"Oh please, Chubby, I'm not one of your spies. I can't be expected to keep track of her all the time. She comes and goes as she pleases. What am I supposed to do? Lock her in the pantry?"

Puri frowned, hanging his head reflectively. His attention was drawn to the stain on the white carpet in the living room made by some prune juice Sweetu had carelessly spilled recently. It reminded him that he needed to have another word with that boy.

"I'm sorry, my dear, you're right of course," he conceded. "Keeping up to date on Mummy is not your responsibility. I'll try calling her myself. First I'm going upstairs to wash my face." This was code for: "I'm hungry and I'd like to eat in ten minutes."

After he'd freshened up and changed into a white kurta pajama and a cloth Sandown cap, Puri went up onto the roof to check on his chilies. The plants that had been caught in the cross fire appeared to be making a full recovery.

The detective was little closer to finding out who had shot at him. His sources inside Tihar jail had heard nothing about a new contract on his life. Tubelight's boys had not been able to find any witnesses to the shooting, either.

All the evidence pointed to the shooter being an amateur, an everyday person, who would have passed unnoticed in the street.

There was only one lead and it was tentative at best: Swami Nag had apparently returned to Delhi, but his whereabouts remained unknown.

Puri picked a chili to have with his dinner and made his way downstairs. Rumpi was busy in the kitchen chopping onions and tomatoes for the bhindi. When the ingredients were ready, she added them to the already frying pods and stirred. Next, she started cooking the rotis on a round tava, expertly holding them over a naked flame so they puffed up with hot air like balloons and became nice and soft.

A plate had already been placed on the kitchen table and Puri sat down in front of it. Presently, Rumpi served him some kadi chawal, bhindi and a couple of rotis. He helped himself to the plate of sliced tomato, cucumber and red onion, over which a little chat masala had been sprinkled, and then cast around the table for some salt.

"No salt, Chubby, it's bad for your heart," said Rumpi without turning around from the cooker.

Puri smiled to himself. Was he really that predictable?

"My dear," he said, trying to sound charming rather than patronizing but not proving entirely successful, "a little salt never did anyone any harm. It is hardly poison, after all. Besides, you've already cut down on the amount you're using, and we don't even have butter on our rotis any more."

"Dr. Mohan has ruled out butter and said you have to cut down on salt. This is your life we're talking about. You want to leave me a widow so I have to shave my head and live in a cell in Varanasi and chant mantras all day long?"

"Now, my dear, I think you're being a little overdramatic. You know full well that well-to-do middle-class widows don't have to sing mantras for a living. Besides, are we going to allow Doctor-ji to ruin every last little pleasure? Should we go through life living in fear?"

Rumpi ignored him and carried on preparing the rotis.

"All I require is a one small pinch to have with my chili," he continued. "Is that really going to kill me?"

Rumpi sighed irritably and relented.

"You're impossible, Chubby," she said, spooning out a

little salt from one of the sections of her dabba and putting it on the side of his plate.

"Yes, I know," he replied playfully. "But more important, now I am also happy!"

He bit off the end of the chili, dipped it in the salt and took another bite.

For most people this would have been equivalent to touching molten lead with the tip of their tongue. The Naga Morich chili is one of the hottest in the world, two to three times as potent as the strongest jalapeño. But Puri had built up an immunity to them, so he needed hotter and hotter chilies to eat. The only way to ensure a ready supply was to propagate them himself. He had turned into a capsicum junkie and occasional dealer.

"So how is my Radhika?" asked the detective, who ate with his hands, as did the rest of the family when at home. This was a convention he prided himself on; Indians were supposed to eat that way. Somehow a meal never seemed as satisfying with cutlery. Feeling the food between your fingers was an altogether more intimate experience.

"Very fine," answered Rumpi, who made sure her husband had everything he needed before taking her place next to him and serving herself a little kadi chawal. "She found a good deal on one of those low-cost airlines so as to come home for Diwali. It's OK with you, or should she take the train?"

More family news followed during the meal. Their second grandchild, four-month-old Rohit, the son of their eldest daughter, Lalita, had recovered from his cold. Jagdish Uncle, one of Puri's father's four surviving brothers, had returned home from the hospital after having his gall bladder removed. And Rumpi's parents were returning from their vacation "cottage" in Manali.

Next, she brought Puri up to date on local Gurgaon news. There had been a six-hour power cut that morning (it had been blamed on fog). An angry mob of residents had stormed the offices of the electricity company, dragged the director out and given him "a good thrashing." Eventually, the police had intervened using lathis and roughed up a lot of people, including many women.

Finally, Rumpi broached the delicate subject of a vacation; she wanted to go to Goa.

"Dr. Mohan said you need a break. You never stop working these days, Chubby," she said.

"I'm quite all right, my dear. Fit as a fiddle, in fact."

"You're not all right at all. All this stress is taking its toll. You're looking very tired these days."

"Really, you're worrying over nothing. Now what about dessert? There's something nice?"

"Apple," she replied curtly.

After Puri had finished eating, he washed the residue of kadi chawal from his hands in the sink, ladled out a glass of cool water from the clay pot that sat nearby and gulped it down.

Afterward in the sitting room, he turned on his recording of *Yanni Live at the Acropolis*, relaxed into his favorite armchair and dialed Mummy's number.

She answered on the sixth ring, but there was a lot of static on the line.

"Mummy-ji, where are you?" he asked her.

"Chubby? So much interference in there, na? You're in an auto or what?"

"I'm very much at home," he said.

"You've not yet reached home! So late it is? You've had your khana outside, is it?"

"I'm at home, Mummy!" he bawled. "Where are you?"

The static suddenly grew worse.

"Chubby, your mobile device is giving poor quality of connection. Listen, na, I'm at Minni Auntie's house. I'll be back late. Just I need rest. Some tiredness is there."

She let out a loud yawn.

"This line is very bad, Mummy-ji! I'll call you back!"

"Hello, Chubby? My phone is getting low on battery and no charger is here. Take rest. I'll be back later, na—"

The line went dead.

Puri regarded the screen suspiciously.

"Who is Minni Auntie?" he shouted to Rumpi, who was still in the kitchen.

"Who?"

"Minni Auntie. Mummy said she's at her house."

"Might be one of her friends. She has so many, I can't keep track."

Rumpi came to the door of the sitting room, wiping her hands on a tea towel.

"Who are you calling now?" she asked Puri.

"Mummy's driver."

He held the phone to his ear. It rang and rang, but there was no response and he hung up.

"She's out there looking into the shooting—I know it," he said wearily.

Rumpi made a face. "Oh, Chubby, I'm sure she's just trying to help," she said.

"It's not her place. She's a schoolteacher, not a detective. She should leave it to the professionals. I'm making my own inquiries about the shooting and will get to the bottom of it."

"If you ask me, I think Mummy's a natural detective," said

Rumpi. "If you weren't being so stubborn and proud, you might give her a chance. I'm sure she could be very helpful to you. It doesn't sound like you've got any clues of your own."

Puri bristled at this last remark.

"My dear, if you want your child to learn his six times table, you go to Mummy," he said brusquely. "If you want a mystery solved, you come to Vish Puri."

As her son had rightfully surmised, Mummy was not at Minni Auntie's (although such a lady did exist; she was one of the better bridge players among the nice group of women who played in Vasant Kunj); she was on a stakeout.

Her little Maruti Zen was parked across the street from the Sector 31 Gurgaon police station, five minutes from Puri's home.

With her was her driver, Majnu, and Kishan, the servant boy, whom she'd persuaded to come with her. She'd also brought along a thermos of tea, a Tupperware container packed with homemade vegetarian samosas and of course her handbag, which, among other things, contained her battery-operated face fan.

This had come in extremely useful when her son had called earlier. By holding it up to her phone, she had created what sounded like interference on the line, which helped her avoid having to give away her location. This was an old trick she'd learned from her husband, who had occasionally used his electric razor to the same effect.

During forty-nine years of marriage, she'd picked up a number of other useful skills for a detective and a good deal of knowledge as well.

Take red boots, for example.

Mummy knew that they were part of a senior police officer's dress uniform and were supposed to be worn only during parades. Occasionally cops were known to wear them for their day-to-day work when their other boots went for repairs.

If the shooter was indeed an officer—who else would wear such footwear?—then the most logical place to start looking for him was the local "cop shop."

Of all the stations in Gurgaon, the one in Sector 31 had one of the worst reputations. Stories abounded about police-wallahs arresting residents of the bastis and forcing them to cook and clean for them; of beatings, rapes—even murders.

"We might be here for hours," moaned Majnu, who was always whining. They had been outside the station for an hour already and he was annoyed at having to work late.

"We have no other choice," Mummy told him. "Everyone else is being negligent in this matter. Some action is required."

At around 10:40, a man in plain clothes emerged from the station. Kishan recognized him as the person he'd seen leaving the scene of the shooting.

"Madam, please don't tell anyone it was me who told you! The cops will kill me!" he said when he realized that the shooter was a police-wallah.

"Your secret is safe," Mummy reassured Kishan, giving him a couple of hundred rupees for his trouble. "Now go home and we'll take it from here."

The servant boy did not have to be told twice. He hurriedly exited the car and rushed off into the darkness.

On the other side of the road, Red Boots got into an unmarked car, started the ignition and pulled into the road, heading west.

Mummy and Majnu followed behind. But the driver kept getting too close and she had to scold him more than once.

"There's a brain in that skull or just thin air or what?"

Twenty minutes later, they found themselves pulling up outside a fancy five-star Gurgaon hotel.

Red Boots left his car with the valet and went inside.

"I'm going to follow him. You stay out here in the car park," Mummy told Majnu.

"Yes, madam," sighed the driver, who was by now in a sulk.

Puri's mother passed through the hotel doors—they were opened by a tall Sikh doorman with the kind of thick beard and moustache that appealed to tourists—into the plush lobby. Red Boots had turned left, past the bellboy's desk and the lifts. Mummy saw him disappear inside a Chinese restaurant, Drums of Heaven.

Outside the entrance, she stopped for a moment and looked down at what she was wearing in alarm; her ordinary chikan kurta and churidaar pajamas were hardly appropriate for such a fancy place.

"But what to do?" she said to herself, continuing her pursuit.

Beyond a kitsch dragon and pagoda, Mummy was greeted by an elegant hostess, who looked Tibetan. Would Madam like a smoking or nonsmoking table?

"Actually I'm meeting one friend, only," replied Mummy. "Almost certainly she's arrived. Just I'll take a look. So kind of you."

The hostess escorted Mummy to the back of the restaurant, where Red Boots was sitting with a fat-throated man in a white linen suit. They were both smoking cigarettes and drinking whisky.

Behind them there was a vacant table for two; Mummy made a beeline for it, sitting directly behind her mark.

"Must be my friend has yet to arrive," she told the Tibetan lady. "Her driver's always getting confusion."

The hostess placed a menu on the table and went back to her podium.

Mummy pretended to peruse the dim sum section while trying to eavesdrop on Red Boots's conversation with Fat Throat, gradually inching her chair backward as close as she dared.

The Muzak and the general murmur from the other tables drowned out most of their words. So Mummy asked the waiter to turn off the music—"Such a headache is there"—and, after turning up her hearing aid to full volume, she was able to grasp a few clear sentences.

"You'd better not fail again. Get him out of the way or the deal won't go through," Fat Throat was saying in Hindi.

"Don't worry, I'll take care of him," replied Red Boots.

"That's what you said before and you missed."

"I told you I'll get it done and I'll get—"

Just then Mummy felt a searing pain in her head.

The waiter had returned and asked to take her order. The effect was like having a screaming megaphone put up to her ear.

"Madam, are you all right?" asked the waiter.

Again his words boomed through her head and Mummy flinched in pain, managing to turn her hearing aid down to normal before he could ask anything else.

"Yes, yes, quite all right," she said a little breathlessly. There was a loud ringing in her right ear and she felt dizzy. "I think I'd better step outside. Some air is required."

Gathering up her handbag, Mummy made her way out of the restaurant and the hotel.

She found Majnu lying back in his seat fast asleep.

"Wake up, you duffer!" screeched Mummy, banging on the window. "What is this, huh? Dozing off on the job. Think I'm paying you to lie around? You're supposed to be keeping an eye out and such."

"For what, madam?"

"Don't do talkback! Sit up!"

Mummy got into the back of the car and waited.

Forty minutes later, Red Boots and Fat Throat came out of the hotel, shook hands and parted ways. The latter got into a black BMW.

"You follow that car," instructed Mummy. "And pay attention, na!"

Soon they were heading through Sector 18. But Majnu had grown overly cautious and stayed too far back. When the BMW turned left at a light, he got stuck behind two trucks. By the time the light changed and the trucks had given way, Fat Throat's car was nowhere in sight.

"Such a simple thing I asked you to do, na! And look what happens! Ritu Auntie is doing better driving than you and she can't do reverse!" cried Mummy.

Having his driving compared to a woman's was the worst insult Majnu could imagine and he sulked in silence.

"Now, drive me back to my son's home," she instructed. "Tomorrow we'll pick up the trail. Challo!'"

Thirteen

"Mr. Puri, they've taken him!" shouted Mrs. Kasliwal without so much as a hello when the detective answered his phone the next morning. She sounded more irate than panicked. "Fifteen minutes back they came knocking without warning. There was such a scene. Media persons were running around hither and thither, invading our privacy and trampling my dahlias!"

"Please calm yourself, madam, and tell me who it is who is taking who!" said Puri, never at his most patient or sympathetic when dealing with a hysterical or melodramatic woman (and even less so at 7:45 when he was in the middle of shaving).

"My husband, of course! The police arrested him! Never could I have imagined it could happen here! Some upstart police-wallah arresting Chippy like a . . . a common criminal for the whole world to see."

"On what charge?" asked the detective. But she was still talking.

"Have these people no respect for privacy, Mr. Puri? I've seen animals at the zoo behaving with more dignity!"

Mrs. Kasliwal started berating someone in the room with

her. One of the servants, evidently. Puri wondered if it could be Facecream. Then suddenly, she was back.

"How this can happen, Mr. Puri? Is it legal? Surely the police can't just go around arresting respectable people and casting clouds over family reputations whenever they fancy? There has to be some cause."

It was true that before the age of 24-hour television news, the police would never have made a show of arresting a man of Kasliwal's status. But nowadays, high-profile arrests were public spectacles. This was the cops' idea of PR—to give the impression that they were doing something other than extorting bribes from drivers.

"Madam, please tell me, with what is he charged?" asked Puri again. But Mrs. Kasliwal still wasn't listening.

"I want to know what you're going to do about this, Mr. Puri," she continued, barely pausing for breath. "Thus far, I must say the quality of your service is most unsatisfactory. I can't see you're getting anywhere. You came here for a few hours, asked some questions and then did a disappearing act. Have you made any progress at all?"

"Madam, will you *please* tell me with what your husband's charged?" said the detective.

Mrs. Kasliwal let out an irritated tut. "Pay attention, Mr. Puri. I told you already. Chippy has been charged with murder. Police are now saying he killed that silly servant girl Mary. But it is all lies. They're trying to cook the case."

"Have they a body?" asked Puri calmly.

"They're saying she and the bashed-up girl in your photograph are one and the same. But it's not her. I know it."

"Forgive me, madam, but you were not so certain when I showed it to you before," said Puri.

Mrs. Kasliwal tutted again. "Most certainly I was!" she said. "I told you categorically it was not Mary. Your memory is faulty. Now, I'm going to ask K. P. Malhotra to represent Chippy. They are old friends and he's one of the best lawyers in India. He'll get him off for sure. The charges are all spurious. I'll talk to him about whether your services are still required. It could be he has his own detective."

Puri kept the phone up to his ear, saying, "Hello, Hello," but realized she had hung up and that the dial pad of his mobile was now covered in shaving foam.

The detective hastily finished his ablutions and got dressed.

Had he let his client down, he wondered? Should he have seen this development coming?

Puri searched his conscience and found it clear. It was quite normal for people to lose confidence in his abilities in the middle of an investigation. To be fair, their lack of faith was understandable.

From the Kasliwals' perspective, Puri appeared to be doing nothing. They hadn't seen him down on his hands and knees scrutinizing the floors with a magnifying glass. He hadn't threatened and cajoled the servants as most other private investigators and police detectives would have done. He hadn't even stuck around in Jaipur.

But Puri's methodology, suited as it was to the Indian social environment, had always proven infallible. And it could not be rushed. As he often told his young protégés, "You cannot boil an egg in three minutes, no?"

Nonetheless, the situation was urgent. If convicted, Kasliwal would face life imprisonment.

The detective considered an air-dash to Jaipur, but given his fear of flying and the fact that it would gain him at the most an hour, he opted instead for the "highway."

By eight o'clock, he and Handbrake were on the road again.

Puri sat on the backseat calling his contacts to find out more on the charges brought against his client.

A source inside the Chief Prosecutor's Office (one of his uncle's daughter's husband's brothers) told him that the arresting police officer was called Rajendra Singh Shekhawat.

Shekhawat was a "topper"—one of the most successful detectives in the state. He was said to be young, bright, ambitious and highly adept at keeping his superiors happy.

"So where did he find the body?" Puri asked his uncle's daughter's husband's brother.

"She was found on the Ajmer Road," he said.

"Recently?"

"No, no! Long time back. August, I think."

Puri hung up and called Elizabeth Rani, who had access to the World Wide Web on what she called "whif-ee." She soon located a transcript of the comments Inspector Shekhawat had made to the press in front of Raj Kasliwal Bhavan minutes after the arrest. He'd claimed that the investigation into Mary's disappearance had been "of the utmost professionality." Furthermore, "substantive evidence" had been "unearthed by the use of modern detective methodology." Ajay Kasliwal was, according to the inspector, "a cold-blooded killer" who had "raped and strangled the maidservant girl until dead."

When Inspector Shekhawat had been asked by a reporter about the motive for the murder, he'd replied, "Clearly, the accused and the victim were having intercourse of one sort or another—who is to say?—and he was endeavoring to conceal his misdeed."

Elizabeth Rani also told Puri that the story was running

number two (after India's comeback against the West Indies) on the bulletins of the 24-hour news channels. Evidently all of them had been tipped off about the arrest and dispatched live uplink trucks.

"Sir, the scene was quite chaotic," said Elizabeth Rani.

"Yes, I can well imagine," said the detective before hanging up.

Puri had developed an intense disdain for India's news media. All that the burgeoning American-style news channels peddled was sensationalism. Standards in journalism had been thrown out the window; a new breed of editors would stop at nothing to attract "eyeballs."

"The three Cs now dominate the news agenda," a senior commentator had written last month in a respectable newsmagazine. "Crime, cricket and cinema."

Recently, Puri had been watching one of the most popular channels in the middle of the afternoon and been shocked to see live pictures of a man committing suicide. He had jumped off the top of a building while journalists excitedly commentated below.

Last week, another so-called award-winning news outfit had aired one of their "stings." They had placed hidden cameras in the office of a university professor and caught him canoodling one of his students.

But nothing caught the headlines in India like murder in a middle-class family.

Such cases—and the "National Crime Region" supplied a goodly number nowadays—became orgies of speculation.

"Trial by media circus" was how the detective referred to it.

Halfway to Jaipur, Puri stopped at a dhaba and ordered sweet chai and a gobi parantha. The TV was tuned to Action

News and, just as the detective had feared, their mid-morning bulletin was dominated by what a computer-generated graphic described as the "Maidservant Murder."

BREAKING NEWS . . . PINK CITY SHOCKED BY BRUTAL MURDER OF HELP . . . HIGH COURT LAWYER CHARGED . . . POLICE SAY VICTIM WAS FIRST RAPED . . . MOUNTAIN OF EVIDENCE AGAINST ACCUSED ran the ticker tape along the bottom of the screen.

Simultaneously, the channel was running video of what an anchorman described as "chaotic scenes" outside Raj Kasliwal Bhavan during the arrest.

It did indeed look like bedlam—but only because of the scrum of cameramen and reporters who mobbed the accused as he was led from his house. In the middle of the fray, Puri spotted his client being helped into the back of a Jeep. Cameramen surrounded the vehicle, trying to stick their lenses through the windows, but were repelled by the police. Then the Jeep sped away with some of the rabid pack chasing after it on foot.

The report then cut to a close-up of a pretty young lady reporter whose urgent demeanor suggested that the world might be about to end.

"The cops have intimated they've got a steel-tight case against High Court lawyer Ajay Kasliwal," she said in an adolescent, nasal voice. "Earlier today, he was taken from here under police escort to the local cop shop, where he'll be held until charge sheeting. Arun."

A suave, urbane young man sitting in a slickly lit studio appeared and in a voice that sounded like an Indian version of an American game-show host said, "Extraordinary developments there in the Pink City, Savitri. Tell us what are the charges against Kasliwal exactly?"

"Well, Arun, the High Court lawyer stands accused of

raping and murdering his maidservant Mary. Her body was discovered in a ditch on the Ajmer Road. I understand her face was very badly beaten, so it took some time to identify her.

"Now, sources inside the police department have told me"—for this read Inspector Shekhawat, Puri thought—"that a number of witnesses saw Ajay Kasliwal dump the body in the middle of the night. I've also been told that the police have impounded his Tata Sumo and they'll be carrying out tests on it today. Arun."

The anchor in the studio, who shared the screen with a little box which replayed the pictures of the arrest on a continuous loop, said, "I take it the police wouldn't have made such a high-profile arrest if they weren't pretty sure they'd got their man. What was Ajay Kasliwal's response to the charges?"

"Kasliwal refused to say *anything* at all when he was arrested this morning. Not one word left his mouth. I'm told he'll be held for twenty-four hours while the cops make further inquiries. They'll be focusing on his relationship with the maidservant Mary. What exactly went on between them? We should have more answers later today. Back to you in the studio, Arun."

"Thanks Savitri. Savitri Ramanand there reporting live from the scene of the arrest of Jaipur High Court lawyer Ajay Kasliwal. We'll be bringing you more on the Maidservant Murder throughout the day. In the meantime let us know what you think. Email us at the usual address on the screen. We want to hear from you.

"Next, the latest on Team India's triumph in the second test. We'll be back after these messages. Don't go away."

Film star Shahrukh Khan then appeared on the screen, endorsing Fair and Handsome, one of the dozen or so different products he was currently advertising, and Puri, who had unconsciously been grinding his molars for the past five minutes, told the waiter to switch off the TV.

Soon, the detective was enjoying his parantha and a fresh bowl of curd.

He was almost finished when his private phone rang. It was Professor Rajesh Kumar at Delhi University calling.

"Hello, sir! Haan-ji, sir! Tell me!" bellowed the detective.

The pleasantries over, Professor Kumar informed Puri that he'd got the test results back on the stones from Mary's room.

"There's something most unusual about them," he said. "Where did they come from?"

"Jaipur, sir," Puri told him.

"That's most peculiar," said the professor. "We found unusually high traces of uranium."

"Did you say uranium?" asked Puri.

"Yes, Chubby, that is exactly what I said."

Fourteen

The Jaipur police station where Ajay Kasliwal was being held was depressingly typical. The building was a concrete square, two floors high with steel supports jutting out of the roof in case a third floor was ever required.

Red geraniums spilled onto the well-swept pathway but did little to soften its charmless architecture. Puri wondered how people elsewhere in the world could view police stations as sanctuaries. For Indians, they were lions' dens.

Seeing a well-fed man in a smart grey safari suit, polished leather shoes and a Sandown cap, the duty officer immediately stood up from his chair, looking as alert as if the prime minister himself was making an impromptu visit.

"How may I be of assistance?" he asked in Hindi with a convivial jiggle of the head.

Puri explained his credentials and his purpose for visiting the station: he wanted to see Ajay Kasliwal.

The duty officer took the detective's card and explained that he needed to refer the matter to his "senior," who was in the next room.

A few minutes later the officer in question entered.

139

"It will be our pleasure to help you in any way. Some cold drink? Some tea?" he asked.

For the sake of diplomacy, Puri sat with the police-wallah for ten minutes, dropping a few names into the conversation and leaving him in no doubt that he was someone with contacts at the pinnacle of power in Delhi. The detective also complimented the officer on the tidy appearance of the station.

"Our Indian police are most cooperative," he said, in a deliberately loud voice with a grin.

Such flattery always went down well. "Thank you, thank you, so kind of you, sir." The officer beamed.

A stern-looking woman constable escorted Puri to the cells.

They were at the back of the station, three in total, each twelve-feet square with a squat toilet positioned behind a low concrete wall that offered little privacy. There were no windows and no ventilation of any kind. The stench of sweat, piss and acrid bidi smoke hung heavily in the air. The bars and the doors were antiquated and the clunky locks required six-inch keys, which jingled from the constable's belt like reindeer bells.

The first cell contained seven prisoners. They were racing captured cockroaches across the floor on a course delineated by empty cigarette boxes. Crouching over the contenders, the prisoners' voices alternated between cheers of encouragement, howls of disappointment and whoops of victory.

At the back of the second cell, a half-naked sadhu with dreadlocks sat in apparent comfort on the hard concrete floor, while two old men with long white beards passed the time over a game of cards. Another man with a cadaverous appearance leaned up against the bars, staring through them with a blank, melancholy expression.

Ajay Kasliwal had the last cell to himself. It was devoid of furniture and proper lighting. He was sitting in the semi-darkness against the back wall with his face buried in his hands.

When he looked up, Puri was shocked to see how exhausted he appeared. Deep creases had developed along his forehead. Bags the color of storm clouds had gathered beneath his eyes.

"Thank God!" he exclaimed. Standing up, he rushed to the front of the cell and clasped the detective's hands. "Thank you for coming, Puri-ji! I'm going out of my mind!"

For a moment, it seemed as if the lawyer would break down in tears, but he managed to regain his composure.

"I tell you, I never laid a finger on that poor girl," he said, his grip still tight. "You do believe me, don't you, Puri-ji? These charges are bogus. I'm a gentle giant, actually. Ask anyone and they'll tell you the same. Ajay Kasliwal could not and would not hurt a fly. I'm a Jain, for heaven's sake! We people don't like to kill anything, not even insects."

The lady constable, who had been standing behind Puri, interrupted. "Ten minutes only," she said coldly and withdrew farther down the corridor.

"Of course I believe you, sir," said the detective. "One way or other, we'll get you out of this pickle. You have Vish Puri's word on that."

He let go of Kasliwal's hands and reached into his trouser pockets, taking out a packet of Gold Flake cigarettes.

"These are for you," he said, passing them through the bars.

Kasliwal thanked him, tore into one of the packets and, with trembling hands and fumbling fingers, put a cigarette to his lips. Puri lit a match and Kasliwal pushed the end of the cigarette into the flame. The detective surveyed his client's features in the flickering light, searching for clues to his mental state. He was concerned to see that he had developed a tic above his left eye. Such a spasm could be the first indicator of more serious problems to come. The detective had seen other men—confident, successful men like Kasliwal—reduced to blubbering wrecks after being put behind bars.

Ashok Sharma, the "Bra Raja," who had hired Puri to investigate the bizarre set of events that had led to the death of his brother (the Case of the Laughing Peacock), had suffered a nervous breakdown after spending just one night in Delhi's notorious Tihar jail.

Of course, Kasliwal's cell was positively five-star compared to Tihar. But tomorrow morning, he had a date in front of a magistrate at the District and Sessions Court, where he would be charge sheeted. And if bail was denied—and in the case of a "heinous crime" it often was—he would be remanded into judicial custody and sent to the Central Jail. There, Kasliwal would be forced to share a dormitory with twenty convicted men. If he wished to remain unmolested, he would have to pay them protection money.

"The first thing I must know, sir, is who is representing you?" asked Puri.

"My wife was here two hours back and says K. P. Malhotra has agreed to take the case. I haven't talked to him yet; my mobile ran out. He's meant to come this afternoon."

"He's someone you trust?"

"Absolutely. We've known each other for twenty-odd years. He's a good attacker and adept at defending his wicket, also."

"Badiya—that's good to hear," said Puri. "But, sir, if I'm to continue, there can be no other private detective. It will make things too hot in the kitchen."

Kasliwal stole a furtive glance at him; Puri guessed that the lawyer's wife had already sown the seeds of doubt about the detective's abilities.

"You're not satisfied with my work, is it?" he prompted.

"Well, Puri-ji, frankly speaking, so far I've not seen much evidence of progress," admitted Kasliwal. "Now I'm behind bars charged with rape and murder. Can you blame me for shopping elsewhere? My life and reputation are at stake."

"Sir, I assure you everything and anything is being done. But my methods are my business. It is for the client to place his trust in my hands. Not once I have failed in a case and I'm not about to start now. Equally, Rome wasn't built in the afternoon. These things can't be rushed."

Kasliwal pursed his lips as he weighed his options over the last of the cigarette.

"I'll make sure you're the only one on the case, Puri-ji," he said eventually.

"Good," said the detective. "Now let us waste no more time. Tell me exactly and precisely what occurred when you were brought in. Inspector Shekhawat read you the riot act, is it?"

"He says he's got witnesses who saw me dump the body."

"Police-wallahs can always find witnesses," said Puri. "A good lawyer will deal with them in court. What else?"

"He says a former servant is ready to testify that I raped her."

"Who is she?"

"How should I know, Puri-ji? I kept quiet during the interview, refused to say a word, so naturally I didn't ask who this woman is."

"Did Shekhawat mention any hard evidence?"

"No, but I'm sure he must be searching for something to spring tomorrow."

Kasliwal took a last drag on his cigarette, let the stub fall on the floor and ground it under his heel.

"Tell me one thing, Puri-ji. In your opinion, the girl they found on the side of the road . . . she is Mary?"

"Seems that's what your Inspector Shekhawat is intimating."

Kasliwal's chin sank to his chest. "So, someone murdered her after all," he sighed. "But who?"

"You have some idea?" asked the detective.

"No, Puri-ji, none."

"What about Kamat? Your wife told me he's a drunkard and was having relations with the female. It's true?"

"I've no idea."

"Tell me about your movements the night that body was discovered. August twenty-second. Can you recall?"

"I was in court come the afternoon. In the evening, I freshened up at home and . . ." Kasliwal flushed with embarrassment. Puri could guess what he had been up to.

"You had 'takeout,' is it?"

The lawyer nodded. "My usual order."

Howls of excitement came from the first cell. Evidently another cockroach race was reaching a thrilling climax. When the noise had died down, Puri asked about Kasliwal's hearing.

"It's set for tomorrow at eleven o'clock," he told the detective. "I'm trying to get it heard by one of the few honest judges. But seems no one's willing to lift a finger to help. My enemies have made sure of that."

Kasliwal cast a look over his shoulder.

"Looks like I'll be spending a night in the penthouse suite, huh." He laughed sardonically. "Thank God there's a couple of cops in here I helped out some years back, so I shouldn't be facing harassment. But, Puri-ji, a few hundred bucks wouldn't go amiss. That way at least I can get some outside food brought in."

"You'll find five hundred stuffed inside the cigarette packet, sir," whispered Puri.

Kasliwal nodded gratefully as the woman constable called out, "Time's getting over!"

The two men shook hands.

"I'll be in court tomorrow for sure," said the detective. "In meantime, don't do tension, sir. Rest assured, everything is being done to secure your release. The responsibility is on my head. Already some very promising clues are there. Now take rest."

As Puri was making his way out of the station, the duty officer informed him that Inspector Shekhawat wanted "a word."

"By all means," said the detective, who was anxious to get the measure of his adversary.

Puri was led upstairs straight into his office.

Shekhawat was in his late thirties, stocky, well built, with a thick head of black hair, an equally thick moustache and dark, deep-set eyes. He was the embodiment of the supremely confident Indian male who is taught self-assurance within the extended family from day one. The kundan studs in his ears did not indicate a hip, arty or effeminate man; he was a Rajput of the Kshatriya or warrior caste.

"Sir, it's a great honor to meet you," he said in Hindi in a deep, booming voice. Shekhawat offered Puri his hand with a big politician's grin. "I've been an admirer of yours for quite some time. Thank you for taking the time to see me. I know that you are a busy and important man."

Puri was not altogether immune to flattery, but he doubted Shekhawat's sincerity. Behind the smile and friendly handshake, he sensed a calculating individual who had invited him into his office with the sole purpose of ascertaining whether he posed a threat.

"I was hoping we would meet," said Puri, replying in Hindi, his tone perfectly amicable. "It seems we're working on the same case but from different ends. We might be able to help each other."

Shekhawat seemed bemused by this suggestion. He smiled with slow deliberation as he resumed his place behind his desk and Puri sat down in a chair opposite him.

"It's my understanding that Ajay Kasliwal is your client, is that correct?" asked the inspector.

"That's right."

"Then I'm not sure how we can help each other, sir. I want to see Kasliwal convicted; you on the other hand want to see him walk free. There is no middle ground."

One of the phones on the inspector's tidy desk rang. He picked up the receiver. Hearing the voice on the other end prompted a subtle change in the man's bearing. He stiffened and his eyebrows slowly slid together until they were almost joined.

"Sir," he said. There was a pause as he listened. Then he said again, "Sir." He met Puri's gaze, held it for a second and then looked down. "Sir," he repeated.

While the detective waited, he looked up at the photographs and certificates that hung on the wall behind the desk. From these he was able to piece together much of Shekhawat's life. He'd gone to a government school in Jaipur, where he'd been a hockey champion. He'd married extremely young; his wife could not have been a day over sixteen.

146

They'd had four children together. He'd attended the Sardar Vallabhai Patel National Police Academy in Hyderabad and studied to be an officer. Three years ago, he'd been awarded a Police Medal for Meritorious Service.

"Must have been for a big case," said Puri when Shekhawat hung up the phone after a final "Sir." "The Meritorious Service award, I mean."

"I caught the dacoit, Sheshnag," he bragged. "He'd eluded our forces for thirteen years but I personally tracked him down to his hideout and arrested him."

"I read about it in the papers. So you were the one," said Puri. "Many congratulations, Inspector! It was a fine piece of detective work. Must have been very satisfying."

"Yes, it was. But frankly, sir, I take far greater satisfaction from arresting a man like Ajay Kasliwal. He is the worst kind of criminal. For too long, men like him have roamed free. Money and influence have kept them safe from prosecution. But thankfully times are changing. Now the big cats must face justice for their crimes like all the animals in the jungle. We are living in a new India."

"I admire your principles," said Puri. "I'm all for even-handedness. But my client is a good man and he's innocent."

"Sir, with respect, Kasliwal is as guilty as Ravan," said Shekhawat with an arrogant smirk. "I have all the evidence I need to put him away forever. He raped and murdered that young woman."

"You're certainly confident," said Puri, hoping to coax the inspector into showing all of his hand.

"I've three witnesses who saw Mr. Kasliwal dump the body by the roadside."

"So I understand, but why was no charge brought against my client for two months?"

Shekhawat answered decisively. "The witnesses took time to come forward because they were scared of intimidation from the client, who threatened them at the scene."

Puri allowed himself a chuckle.

"I very much doubt that will hold up in court."

"I have hard evidence as well."

"How can there be more evidence when the accused is innocent?"

"For that, sir, you will have to wait until tomorrow. I am not at liberty to divulge anything more."

The detective held up his hands in a gesture of defeat.

"Well, I can see I'm going to have my work cut out proving my client's innocence," he said. "Obviously you are determined to see this thing through, so I suppose I'd better get back to my work."

Puri lingered for a moment by the door, looking down absentmindedly as if he'd forgotten something.

"There's something else I can help you with?" asked Shekhawat in the patient tone reserved for children and the senile.

"There is one thing, actually," said Puri, suddenly sounding unsure of himself.

He took out his notebook and flipped through the pages until he came to one in the middle crammed with illegible writing.

"Yes, that's it," he said, as if reading from it. "From what I'm told, the girl's body was cremated after no one came to claim it. Is that correct?"

"That's true."

"And the photograph taken by the coroner was out of focus and extremely grainy."

Shekhawat eyed Puri suspiciously, no doubt wondering how he had come by this information.

"If you say so," he said.

"Also," continued the detective, "her face was all bashed up, bloody and swollen. She'd obviously been given a severe beating."

The inspector's nod was vague encouragement to go on.

"Given this, I'm curious to understand how you can be sure she is the maidservant Mary."

"That's not in dispute. Two witnesses have identified her from the coroner's photographs."

"Former or current employees of the Kasliwals, no doubt."

"The defense will be informed at the appropriate time," said Shekhawat officiously.

Fifteen

Facecream had discovered a gap in the perimeter wall behind the servant quarters just large enough for a person to squeeze through. She'd made use of it a couple of times in the past two days, sneaking out undetected to go to a pay phone booth a few streets away.

But Facecream was not the only person using this secret gateway: the earth between it was well trodden.

This raised the alarming possibility that an outsider was entering the property unseen and unchallenged—perhaps the same person who had tried to open her door that first night.

Determined to find out who was coming and going through the wall, she had set a trap, stringing a tripwire—or rather a trip-thread—across the gap. Anyone passing through it would now inadvertently tug a bell hanging inside her room.

In the past two days, she'd had just one bite—a stray pye-dog. But the line remained taut. And now, as she set off for a midnight rendezvous with Puri, she was careful not to fall victim to her own ruse. Treading carefully over the thread, Facecream passed through the gap in the wall.

On the other side lay an abandoned property, an old bungalow with broken windows surrounded by a large garden overgrown with vines and long grass. She stopped, surveying the shadowy terrain ahead for any sign of movement. Nothing stirred in the undergrowth save for grasshoppers. The only sounds were distant ones: the hum of an autorickshaw, the screech of an alley cat. Up above, bats darted through the air. In the moonlight, she caught glimpses of them swooping above the tree line, where their black wings appeared momentarily, stretched against a hazy backdrop of stars.

Jaya feared the bats and the owl that lived in one of the khejri trees. She had warned her new friend Seema not to go into the garden at night.

The bungalow, she believed, was inhabited by malicious djinns. They had driven out the owners and guarded their territory jealously. At night, lying in her room, she claimed to be able to hear their terrible, mocking laughter and the cries and screams of those they had entrapped in the spirit world.

Djinns, Jaya told Seema, often possessed people. Just recently, one had attached itself to her aunt, forcing her to speak in strange tongues. It was only thanks to a travelling hakim that she had been cured. He'd taken her to the tomb of a Sufi saint and exorcised the malicious fiend.

But Facecream did not fear djinns. Parvati, the mountain goddess, whose magic talisman she wore around her neck, had always protected her against attacks from both ghoulish and human assailants. Living rough on the streets of Mumbai when she'd first come to India had also given her a sixth sense for recognizing danger. And just in case, her Khukuri knife was tucked into her waist.

Facecream set off across the garden and made her way

down the side of the bungalow, nimbly avoiding the odd bits of rusting metal hidden under the tall grass and weeds, and stopping now and again like a deer testing the air.

When she reached the front of the property, she passed through the leaning iron gate that stood at the entrance to its neglected driveway, tugged her shawl over the back of her head so that it framed her face, and turned left into the quiet lane.

The security guards in the sentry boxes positioned outside the other neighboring properties were all snoring loudly and she slipped past them unnoticed. The drivers at the bicycle rickshaw stand were all asleep as well, slumped on the seats of their vehicles with their legs stretched out across their handlebars.

Further on stood a large house surrounded by a high wall and a pair of gates mounted with bright lights. Soon after she had passed these lights, Facecream noticed a shadow creep along the ground in front of her. Then, gradually, it began to shrink.

She was being followed.

The distinctive sound of rubber chappals scuffing against the ground told her that her stalker was no djinn.

For a moment, Facecream considered turning around, drawing her Khukuri and charging. But then she remembered Puri's advice about controlling her reckless streak and decided to wait for better attack terrain.

She continued to the next junction, turned right and broke into a sprint. Reaching the first parked car, she hid behind it, lying flat on the ground, and watched to see who came around the corner.

A few seconds later a pair of hairy male legs appeared. They stopped, shifted from left to right indecisively and then hurried on in her direction. Facecream could see from the man's skinny ankles that he was no match for her. She drew herself up on all fours like a cat and prepared to spring at him. But at the last moment, she held back and let out a loud "Boo!"

Tubelight staggered back in shock, looking as if he might keel over.

"What are you doing? Trying to give me a heart attack?" he cried.

"Ssssh! Keep your voice down! You'll wake the guards!" hissed Facecream. "What are you doing here?"

"Boss is running late and asked me to let you know."

"So why were you following me?"

"I knew you wouldn't want to be seen with me behind the house."

"You weren't trying to sneak up on me?"

"Don't be ridiculous. If I'd wanted to do that, I could have easily taken you by surprise."

Facecream laughed. "You were making more noise than a buffalo in heat."

"Listen, if I'd been on my guard you would never have been able to surprise me."

"Whatever you say, bhai."

Puri picked them both up and drove them to the Park View Hotel, where he was staying. It was nowhere near a park (his room provided a view of a car park), though it was a modern affair with air-conditioning, clean sheets, and Western-style toilets.

The trio sat at a table in the otherwise empty restaurant. The night manager placed a bottle of Scotch, some bottles of soda, ice and glasses on the table before returning to the front desk.

Puri poured a peg for himself and Tubelight and a plain

soda for Facecream, who strongly disapproved of alcohol. He'd once heard her describe it as "a curse on women."

"So, Miss Seema," he said. "Your message said 'urgent.' "

In Puri's presence, Facecream was always serious, calm, respectful and, although it rarely showed, affectionate. She seemed totally removed from the party girl or cheeky village damsel she often played.

The detective surveyed her appraisingly. He found himself wondering who the real Facecream was. And whether she knew herself.

"Yes, sir, I have important information for you," she said. Her soft, eloquent pronunciation was unidentifiable as Seema's coarse village burr.

"I've spent the past few days working side by side with Jaya. We've cleaned together and, in the evenings, cooked and shared all our meals. I've told her many stories about my—Seema's—past. She loves hearing them and a bond has formed between us.

"Last night, Jaya started telling me about herself and the many difficulties she's faced. She was married off to her second cousin at fifteen. They had a son, but he died after two years. Cause unknown. It sounds to me like jaundice. Then two years ago, her husband was killed in a train accident. Her in-laws said she was cursed and threw her out of the house. When she tried to return to her parents' home, they refused to take her back.

"Jaya was taken in by her eldest sister here in Jaipur. This sister got her the job with the Kasliwals. Things started to go better for her. But one evening, when her sister was out working, her brother-in-law forced himself on her. Somehow the sister found out and blamed Jaya. After that, she had to come and live in the servant quarters."

Puri nodded encouragement to go on.

"Jaya is extremely shy and nervous," Facecream continued. "She also gets very frightened at night and hates to sleep on her own. This evening, I discovered why."

Tubelight lit a cigarette and squinted in the haze of smoke that swirled in front of his face.

"When the police arrived this morning and arrested Mr. Kasliwal, Jaya became extremely distressed," Facecream recounted. "I found her making up the beds in tears. When I asked her what was wrong, she refused to answer. I sat with her for a while as she cried. And then she said, 'He didn't do it.'

" 'Who didn't do what?' I asked.

" 'Sahib is a good man. He didn't kill Mary. It was somebody else.'

"I couldn't get anything more out of her after that. For the rest of the day, she looked grief stricken. At teatime, she dropped a cup. Mrs. Kasliwal shouted at her and called her stupid. Jaya went to her room and in the evening she refused to eat.

"After I had finished my duties, I took her some food and sat with her and combed her hair. Then she asked me if we were friends. I told her, 'Yes, we are good friends.' She took both my hands in hers and asked me if I could keep a secret. She said it was a very big secret and that if I told anyone, we would both be in danger. I assured her that I would help her in any way I could. Then, Jaya told me in a whisper that she knew who had killed Mary. She said she'd seen the murderer disposing of the body."

"Go on," said Puri, shifting in his chair in anticipation.

"On the night Mary disappeared, Jaya was fast asleep. But at around eleven o'clock, she was woken by a commotion in Mary's room. She opened her door a crack and saw Munnalal, the driver, carrying away Mary's body in his arms.

Jaya caught a glimpse of Mary's face. She says it was ghostly pale. Her eyes were wide open, but frozen.

"Munnalal carried her to Sahib's Tata Sumo, laid her on a big piece of plastic in the back, shut the door quietly and then quickly drove away with his headlights off."

"What did Jaya do next?" asked Puri, sipping his drink.

"She crept out of her room. On the ground, she says she noticed some drops of blood leading to the spot where the Sumo had been parked. She found the door to Mary's room half open and looked inside. The thin cotton mattress was soaked with blood. On the ground next to it lay one of the kitchen knives from the house, also covered in blood."

"By God," said Puri.

"Jaya ran back to her room and bolted the door behind her. She sat there for hours in the darkness, crying, terrified. Eventually, she fell asleep. In the morning, the trail of blood on the ground had vanished."

"Did she look inside Mary's room again?"

"Yes. She says the door was wide open. All Mary's belongings, apart from the posters on the wall, had gone."

"The mattress?"

"That too. The floor had also been washed."

Puri thought for a moment, gently rubbing his moustache with an index finger.

"Munnalal must have come back and gotten rid of everything," suggested Tubelight.

"Might be," said Puri. "Let's put ourselves in his chappals. In the dead of night, he returns to clean up his misdeed. He's got to get rid of her paraphernalia and all. So what next? Could be, he takes it all away. Gets rid of it elsewhere. Or he tosses it over the back wall."

"That's the likeliest possibility," Facecream ventured.

Puri shot her a look.

"You found something?" he said eagerly.

She grinned and pulled up the leg of her baggy cotton trousers. Taped to her ankle was something wrapped in a plastic bag. She placed it on the table and opened it. Inside was a four-inch kitchen knife. The blade was rusted.

Tubelight let out a low whistle.

"I found it in the undergrowth," she said.

"Absolutely mind-blowing!" exclaimed Puri with a big, fatherly smile.

"I've got other good news," said Tubelight.

"Munnalal?"

"My boys found him today. He's living in the Hatroi district of Jaipur."

"First class!" said the detective. "Tell them to watch him round the clock and I'll pay him a visit tomorrow."

"Any more instructions for me?" asked Facecream.

"Spend time with Kamat," instructed Puri. "Find out if Mrs. Kasliwal was correct and he was doing hanky-panky with the female."

Sixteen

Mummy, like so many Indians, had a gift for remembering numbers. She didn't need a telephone directory; the Rolodex in her mind sufficed.

The late Om Chander Puri had often made use of her ability.

"What's R. K. Uncle's number?" he would call from his den in the back of their house in Punjabi Bagh as she made his dinner rotis in the kitchen. Seeing the digits floating in the air before her eyes she'd reply automatically, "4-6-4-2-8-6-7."

Mummy had no difficulty remembering the numbers of "portable devices" either, despite their being longer.

Jyoti Auntie, a senior at the RTO (Regional Transport Office), was on 011 1600 2340.

It was this lady, with whom Mummy had partnered at bridge on many a Saturday afternoon in East of Kailash, who she called now to ask about tracing Fat Throat's BMW numberplate.

"Just I need one address for purposes of insurance claim," she told Jyoti Auntie when she called her the morning after Majnu had lost him in Gurgaon.

"Oh dear, what happened?" asked Jyoti Auntie.

"The owner was doing reckless driving, bashed up my car and absconded the scene," she lied. "Majnu gave chase but being a prime duffer, he got caught in a traffic snarl."

Jyoti Auntie sympathized. "Same thing happened to me not long back," she said. "A scooter scratched my Indica and took off. Luckily I work at RTO, so after locating the driver's address, Vinod paid the gentleman a visit and got him to reimburse me for damages done."

"Very good," said Mummy.

"You have a note of the numberplate?" asked Jyoti Auntie.

"No need, just it's up in my head. D-L-8-S-Y-3-4-2-5. One black color BMW. It is Germany-made, na?"

Her friend tried to look up the numberplate in the system, but the computers were "blinking," so Mummy had to call back after an hour.

"The vehicle belongs to one Mr. Surinder Jagga, three number, A, Block Two, Chandigarh Apartments, Phase Four, Home Town, Sector 18, Gurgaon," divulged Jyoti Auntie.

Mummy wrote down the details (she did not have a head for remembering addresses) and thanked her.

"You're playing bridge on Saturday, is it?" asked Jyoti Auntie.

"Certainly, if not totally," said Mummy. "Just my son, Chubby, is facing some difficulty and requires assistance."

"Nothing serious, I hope."

"Let us say it is nothing I cannot sort out," said Mummy.

Less than two hours later, Mummy and Majnu pulled up outside Block Two, Chandigarh Apartments, Phase Four, Home Town, Sector 18, Gurgaon.

Fat Throat's black BMW was parked in front of the building.

"You wait here and don't do sleeping," instructed Mummy. "Just I'm going to check around. Should be I'll revert in ten minutes. But in case of emergency, call home and inform my son's good wife. You're having the number, na?"

"Yes, madam," sighed Majnu, who was only half listening and privately lamenting the fact that he had missed his lunch.

Mummy let herself out of the car and made her way to the entrance to Block Two.

Chandigarh Apartments was not one of the high-end superluxury developments. It housed call center workers and IT grunts, most of whom hailed from small towns across the subcontinent and had flocked to Delhi to live the new Indian dream.

Like so much of Gurgaon's new housing, which had been sold for considerable sums amid a blitz of slick marketing and—false—assurances of round-the-clock water and electricity supplies, Block Two was beginning to crumble. Less than two years after its "completion," tiles had started falling off its façade; the monsoon rains had left enormous damp stains on the walls and ceilings; and the wooden window frames were warped.

The lift was out of order and Mummy had to climb the stairwell where the builders (who had cobbled together the structure with substandard bricks) had failed to remove blobs of plaster from the bare concrete stairs. Here and there, wires hung incongruously from the walls as if the very innards of the building were spilling out.

Mummy, bag in hand, soon reached the third floor landing.

Flat 3A was on the immediate left.

A pair of a men's black slip-on shoes lay in front of the door. On the wall to one side of it hung a plaque that read:

TRUSTWORTHY PROPERTY DEALERS LTD.
OWNER: SHRI SURINDER JAGGA

This was all the information Puri's mother required for the time being.

Now that she knew Fat Throat was a property broker, Mummy would ask around and find out more about him. With any luck, someone might be able to tell her what Jagga and his co-conspirator, Red Boots, were up to.

Mummy turned to head back downstairs. But just then, the door swung open.

Standing there in the doorway, eclipsing a good two-thirds of the frame, was Fat Throat, no longer dressed in his white linen suit but a black cotton kurta pajama. Behind him in the poorly lit interior she could make out another, smaller figure.

Surinder Jagga narrowed his eyes and stared at Mummy suspiciously, as if he recognized her, and said, in the same deep, chiling voice she remembered from the Drums of Heaven restaurant, "Yes, madam? You're lost?"

Mummy, caught off guard and intimidated by the sheer size of the man and his thuggish bearing, stuttered, "I . . . see . . . well . . . just I'm looking for, umm, Block Three."

"This is Block Two," answered Fat Throat abruptly.

"Oh dear, silly me. Thank you, ji. So confusing it is, na?" she said and started down the stairs.

Mummy had taken only a few steps when Fat Throat called after her.

"Wait, Auntie!"

She stopped, feeling her heart beat a little faster. Without turning around, she reached inside her handbag and wrapped her fingers around her can of Mace.

Could be, he spotted us following him home, Mummy

said to herself. Curse that idiot driver of mine. It's all his fault, na.

"Which apartment you want?" Fat Throat asked.

"Um . . . a . . . apartment six number, A," she ventured. There was a pause.

"The Chawlas, is it?" he asked.

"That's right."

"OK, auntie, it's across the way," he said. "You want I should send someone with you?"

"No, no, it's quite all right," she said, breathing a sigh of relief.

Mummy continued on her way. As she made the first turn in the stairs, she heard another voice coming from the landing above her. Looking up, she saw a second man emerge from Fat Throat's apartment.

He stooped to put on his black shoes and, in the shaft of light coming in through a window in the stairwell, Mummy got a good look at his face.

She recognized him instantly.

It was Mr. Sinha, one of Chubby's elderly neighbors. And he was carrying two thick briefcases. One in each hand.

Seventeen

Pandemonium broke out when Ajay Kasliwal arrived at the Jaipur District and Sessions courthouse at eleven o'clock the following morning.

But it was carefully orchestrated.

Rather than being brought in through the building's back entrance, away from the eye of the media storm, he was escorted through the main gate in a police Jeep.

Twenty-five or so constables made a show of trying to hold back the baying pack of "snappers" (which had grown significantly in number). But the determined press-wallahs quickly surrounded the vehicle. And as the accused stepped down from the back of the Jeep with the police around him, he was accosted by lenses and microphone-wielding reporters all screaming questions at once.

A couple of burly constables then took Kasliwal by his arms. With some of their colleagues acting like American football linebackers, they tunneled a passage through the crowd, frog-marching him inside the courthouse.

Inspector Shekhawat—plenty of starch in his spotless white shirt; comb grooves etched in his wavy hair—stood to one side of the steps, watching the "chaotic scenes" that he knew would play so well on TV.

After the media tidal wave crashed violently against the entrance and was successfully repelled, he answered some of the reporters' questions.

"Is it true you've discovered some bloodstains?"

"Our forensics team put Ajay Kasliwal's Tata Sumo under the scanner and came up with dramatic results. Dried blood was found on the carpet at the back. There was so much, it had soaked through."

"Anything else you can tell us?"

"We also found a number of women's hairs. These also we are analyzing. Also, we found a woman's bloody fingerprint on the bottom of the backseat. So there's no doubt in my mind her body was placed there and driven to its final destination."

"Can you confirm that Kasliwal refused to answer questions yesterday?"

"Yes, under interrogation he refused to answer any and all questions."

"Why he chose to be silent?"

"It's his right, actually. But it's unusual. An innocent man has nothing to hide."

Puri slipped past Shekhawat unnoticed and made his way inside. He found the corridor outside Court 6 crowded with defendants, plaintiffs, witnesses and a disproportionately large number of advocates in white shirts and black jackets. The court crier appeared, calling out the names of those to be summoned before the judge in the same affected, nasal voice that Indian street vendors use to advertise their wares. The presiding judge, Puri discovered, had an extremely busy day ahead of him.

Kasliwal's arraignment, although the most high-profile case, was only one of twenty slated to be heard.

Some would require only a few minutes of His Honor's time: a deposition would be taken and then the case would have to be adjourned because a key piece of evidence had gone missing and the police needed time to track it down (a classic delaying tactic). Others might drag on for thirty or forty minutes while the lawyers wrangled over a precedent in law established in a landmark case dating back to Mughal times.

Puri chatted to an advocate he met while waiting in the corridor for Kasliwal's arraignment to begin. The young man was representing himself against a former client who had paid him with a bad check.

"How long has your case been going on?" asked Puri.

"Nearly two years," replied the advocate. "Every time I want to get a court date, I have to pay a bribe to the clerk. But then my client feathers the judge's nest and he adjourns the case, and so it goes on and on."

"Judge Prasad has a sweet tooth, is it?" asked Puri.

The advocate smiled wryly, evidently surprised by the detective's apparent naïvete.

"His shop is always open for business," answered the young man. "You can pay at the bench as easily as you buy milk from Mother Dairy."

It was another twenty minutes before the court crier stepped out into the corridor and summoned Ajay Kasliwal.

Soon, the accused was brought from the holding room where he'd spent the past thirty minutes consulting his lawyer.

Puri clipped into the courtroom ahead of him and, finding it packed to capacity, stood by the door. The gallery was cluttered with a hodgepodge of benches and old rickety cane chairs, some with holes in their seats. Before them, stretching across the breadth of the room, rose the bench, a solid wooden structure that looked like a dam designed to hold back floodwaters. In the center, wearing a black cape, thick glasses and a bomb-proof countenance, presided Judge Prasad. Two clerks and a typist sat on either side of him.

When Kasliwal was led inside, every head in the gallery strained to watch him escorted to the dock, a little platform surrounded by a waist-high grille. It might well have dated back to the sepoy trials following the Indian mutiny against the British in 1857.

Puri's client had clearly not slept a wink on the hard concrete floor of his cell. The bags under his eyes had darkened to the hue of ink and the tic in his eyelid had grown more pronounced, causing him to wink with perturbing frequency.

The detective could only imagine how humiliated Kasliwal must feel. But he retained a dignified and defiant pose, standing erect with his arms behind him and chin held high. When he looked into the gallery and saw his immediate family sitting there, including his son, Bobby, who had flown in from London the night before, his expression conveyed confidence and courage.

"State versus Ajay Kasliwal!" announced the court crier.

Silence fell over the gallery as the print and wire service journalists readied their pens and notebooks.

Judge Prasad was not one to stand on ceremony. His impatient manner suggested he would much rather be somewhere else (from what Puri had been told, his preferred location was the Jaipur golf course). This was not the Rajasthan High Court. There were no computers or microphones, no air-conditioning, no coffee machines dispensing sweet, frothy cups of Nescafé.

This was a place of business.

The more hearings Judge Prasad could pack into a single day, the more he could enrich his growing property portfolio. Thus, he did not allow lawyers to stand at their desks and engage in tedious examinations and cross-examinations. That was another luxury only the High Court could indulge. Here in Court 6, trials were conducted with all those gathered directly in front of him. This way, monetary bargaining and transactions could be conducted without anyone in the gallery overhearing.

"Approach!" he instructed Kasliwal's lawyer and the state prosecutor, Veer Badhwar.

Both men stepped forward and stood shoulder to shoulder in front of the bench.

The hearing, conducted in Hindi, took all of ten minutes.

First, Judge Prasad asked Mr. Badhwar to present the charges and he gladly did so. The prosecutor then called Inspector Shekhawat, who explained that bloodstains had been discovered in the back of Kasliwal's vehicle.

The accused was then read the charges of rape and murder and asked how he pleaded.

"Not guilty, Your Honor."

His plea was entered into the record. Mr. Malhotra then asked that his client be granted bail.

"Does the accused have an alibi for his location on the night of the murder?"

"Sir, I respectfully submit the police have not provided ample proof that the murdered girl is my client's former maidservant. The body was cremated twenty-four hours after it was discovered and was not properly identified at the time."

"Answer the question," said the judge impatiently as the typist hammered away at his keys, recording their verbal exchange.

"He was at a friend's house, Your Honor," said Malhotra.

"Is this *friend* willing to come forward?"

"We have not been able to locate the friend at the present time, but we are confident we will do so within a few hours."

"Does the police have any objection to the court granting bail?"

"We do, Your Honor," answered Inspector Shekhawat. "The crime is a heinous one. The accused is a danger to the public."

Judge Prasad scribbled something on the file that lay in front of him, checked his watch and then said, "Bail is denied. The accused is to be remanded into judicial custody. Constables, take him away."

"Your Honor, I object. My client has no criminal record and is an upstanding member of the community."

"Bail is denied. You are welcome to appeal the court's decision."

The judge asked the clerk to search for a date for the trial to begin.

Files and papers were moved back and forth across the bench; ledgers were opened and closed. The clerk ran his index finger over pages and columns until it came to rest on a spare slot nearly five months away. "April ninth at three forty-five," he said.

Badhwar and Malhotra were dismissed and Kasliwal was led from the courtroom to be taken to the Central Jail. Within seconds, the gallery emptied as his family and the newspaper hacks went in pursuit of him.

By the time he left the courtroom, another group of file-toting advocates and their clients had gathered in front of the bench.

Puri lingered behind, not wanting to get caught in the crush at the door.

• • •

The detective caught up with Bobby Kasliwal on the steps of the courthouse, where he was waiting for his mother and Malhotra, who had gone to bribe the appropriate clerk to set a date to appeal the bail verdict and bring forward the start of the trial.

Puri was struck by how much Bobby took after his father—nose, chin and height were almost identical. He combed back his black hair in the same style. And he had adopted some of Ajay Kasliwal's mannerisms—the way in which he stood, for example, back straight and fingers laced together in a cradle.

But Bobby's youthful mien betrayed his lack of experience. His life was lived through books. This was evident to Puri from the small indentations on the sides of his nose, the ink stain on his middle index finger and his pullover's threadbare elbows, which he'd worn down during long hours leaning on his desk studying his textbooks. Fidgeting constantly, he appeared to be inwardly grappling with fear and some form of regret.

"Quite a journey you must have had," said Puri after introducing himself.

"Yes, sir, the flight was nearly ten hours and then three more hours on the road," said Bobby, who was polite but made little eye contact. His right leg quivered nervously as if he was busting to go to the toilet.

"By God! Must have been exhausting, no?" said Puri.

"It was OK, sir, thank you, sir," he said automatically.

"So tell me, how is England? Must be cold."

"Very cold, sir. It rains too much."

"But you're enjoying? London, that is?"

"Very much, sir. It's a wonderful opportunity."

Bobby looked over Puri's shoulder, evidently searching for any sign of his mother.

"So your mummy is doing all right, is it?" asked the detective.

"She's not been sleeping well, sir. She's getting migraines."

Puri shook his head gravely.

"It is only right and correct that you have come home," he said in a sympathetic, avuncular tone. "Your mummy and papa need every last drop of support they can get."

He took Bobby gently by the arm and, pulling him toward him, added, "I can only imagine what anxiety you and your near-or-dear are experiencing. Must be something akin to hell. But rest assured everything is being done to clear your papa's good name. By hook or crook we'll get these fraudulent charges reverted. I give you my word on that. Most Private Investigators never fails."

He released Bobby's arm.

"Thank you, sir. I'm very grateful to you. There's no way my father could have done this thing. How they can even suggest it, I don't know. He never broke one law in his entire life."

"I understand you're planning to work with him after your studies are complete?"

"Certainly, sir. It's always been my dream to work with Papa. There's so much I can learn from him. I want to make a difference the way he has."

Puri fished out a copy of his business card and handed it to him.

"Call me if any assistance is required. I can be reached night or day. If there's anything you wish to discuss—anything at all—dial my number. Confidentiality is my watchword."

"Right, sir," said Bobby.

Puri turned to leave, but twisted around on his left foot and exclaimed, "By God, so forgetful I'm getting these days! One question mark is there, actually."

"Sir?" Bobby frowned.

"Your whereabouts on the night of August twenty-first of this year? You were where exactly?"

"In London, sir."

"Acha! You already reached, is it?"

"I flew two weeks earlier."

"That is fine. Just I'm ticking all the boxes."

"No problem, sir."

Puri lingered for a moment, looking down at the ground, apparently lost in thought. Bobby put his hands in his pockets, took them out again and then folded them in front of his chest.

"Did you get to know her—Mary, that is?" asked the detective after a long pause.

"Know her, sir?"

"Must be you talked with her?"

"Not really, sir, she was, well, a servant. I mean, she made me tea and cleaned my clothes. That's about it. I was studying mostly."

"Can you tell me her last name or where she came from?"

"No, sir, I wouldn't be able to tell you that. My mother should know."

Puri reached inside his safari suit and took out a folded piece of paper, a photocopy of the coroner's photograph of the murder victim.

He handed it to Bobby without telling him what it was.

The young man unfolded it and grimaced at the gruesome image.

"Is that Mary?" asked the detective.

"I think so. It looks like her, sir," said Bobby, still staring down at the image. And then he suddenly pushed the photocopy back into Puri's hands, ran to the side of the steps and threw up.

Eighteen

Brigadier Kapoor called while Puri was on the way to see Munnalal. It was his third attempt in as many hours, but the detective had been too busy to pick up earlier.

"Puri! I've been trying to reach you all day! What is your present location?" he demanded as soon as the detective answered.

"Sir, I'm out-of-station, working on a most crucial and important case—"

"More important than mine, is it?" scoffed Brigadier Kapoor indignantly.

"Sir, honestly speaking, my commitment and dedication to your case is one hundred and ten percent. Just an emergency-type situation was there and it became necessary for me to leave Delhi right away for a day or two."

Puri sounded unreservedly conciliatory. He was, after all, in Brigadier Kapoor's employ, albeit temporarily, and it was expected that an employer would periodically berate his or her employees to keep them in line. If the detective had been in his client's shoes, he would have probably done the same. How had the Marathi poet Govindraj put it? "Hindu society is made up of men who bow their heads to the kicks from above and who simultaneously give a kick below."

"I don't want to hear excuses!" barked Brigadier Kapoor, sounding as if he were back on the parade ground. "An entire week has passed without a word. I've not received one piece of intelligence! Now report!"

In fact, it had only been five days since Puri had agreed to take on the case, and in that time, the Most Private Investigators team had been anything but idle. As he explained, his top two researcher-cum-analysts had been doing the initial footwork: getting hold of Mahinder Gupta's financial statements and phone records and analyzing all the data for anything suggestive or suspicious. At the same time, Puri's operative Flush had been ingratiating himself with the target's servants and neighbors.

He had also been going through the subject's garbage.

"Trash Analysis" was standard procedure in any matrimonial case, "Waste not, know not!" being one of the detective's catchphrases. The stub of an airline boarding pass or a cigarette butt smeared with lipstick had, in the past, been enough to wreck the marriage plans of more than a few aspirants.

Fortunately, getting hold of people's garbage was a cinch. Indian detectives were much luckier than their counterparts in, say, America, who were forever rooting around in people's dustbins down dark, seedy alleyways. In India, one could simply purchase an individual's trash on the open market.

All you had to do was befriend the right rag picker. Tens of thousands of untouchables of all ages still worked as unofficial dustmen and women across the country. Every morning, they came pushing their barrows, calling, "Kooray Wallah!" and took away all the household rubbish. In the colony's open rubbish dump, surrounded by cows, goats, dogs and crows, they would sift through piles of stinking muck by hand, separating biodegradable waste from the plastic wrappers, aluminium foil, tin cans and glass bottles.

Flush had had no difficulty whatsoever scoring Gupta's garbage, even though he lived on his own in a posh complex called Celestial Tower, which, according to a hoarding outside the front gate, provided a "corporate environment" in which residents could "Celebrate the New India!" But so far, Puri's promising young operative had discovered nothing incriminating.

"No condom, no booze, no taapshelf magazine," he'd told his boss the day before on the phone.

Gupta subscribed to publications such as *The Economist* and *The Wall Street Journal Asia*. He was strictly veg and ate a lot of curd and papayas. His only tipple apart from Diet Coke was Muscle Milk, a sports drink. He also used a number of different hair- and skin-care products.

Socially, he mixed in corporate circles and attended conferences with titles like BPO in the Financial Sector— Challenges & Opportunities. He visited the temple once a week and kept a small puja shrine in his bedroom, complete with photographs of his parents, who lived in Allahabad, and a number of effigies, including Ganesh, Hanuman and the goddess Bahuchar Mata.

Gupta employed a cook, who came for two hours in the afternoon; a sweeper, who, along with the floors, was charged with washing the three bathroom-cum-toilets every day; and a cleaner who was responsible for wiping everything the sweeper wasn't assigned to do.

The latter had told Flush that her employer was a private man who was meticulously tidy. Her only gripe was that he had recently purchased a "dhobi machine," which she resented because it had robbed her of the income she had been earning from washing his clothes.

The sweeper had grumbled about the low pay and the fact that Gupta shed a lot of hair, which blocked the shower drain in the master-bathroom-cum-toilet. She'd also had plenty to say about the memsahib down the hallway, who was apparently carrying on with another housewife in flat 4/67.

Gupta's driver had not divulged any salacious secrets about his employer either. The two bottles of Old Monk rum with which Flush had plied him had elicited no stories of "three-to-the-bed" orgies, nights of cocaine-fueled debauchery or illicit visits to secret love children. Apparently, Gupta spent most evenings either playing golf or watching golf on ESPN.

"He's an oversmart kind of guy," Flush had concluded.

Ordinarily at this stage in a matrimonial case, Puri would have advised his client against any further investigation. But he wasn't leaving anything to chance and had his team go to phase two.

Flush had been charged with tapping the subject's phone lines and tailing him. And that very evening, assuming he could make it back to Delhi, Puri was planning to gate-crash a premarriage party Gupta was having in his apartment, to plant a couple of bugs.

Puri explained the plan to Brigadier Kapoor, but he still sounded dissatisfied.

"What about his qualifications? Have you checked on them?" he asked.

"Gupta attended Delhi University as advertised. That much is confirmed."

"Any girly friends?"

"We did interviews with two batchmates. Both told that Gupta kept himself to himself. A very studious fellow, it seems. Didn't so much as talk to females. No reports of hanky-panky. Equally, he was strictly teetotal. Never touched so much as one drop of alcohol or bhang."

"Other marriages?"

"We're getting on top of the registers, sir."

"What about his time in Dubai? What was he doing there?"

"Working for a U.S. bank. I've contacted my counterpart in West Asia. A highly proficient fellow. He's asking around."

"Any affairs?"

"With females, sir?"

"Males, females—anything?"

"No indication, sir."

Brigadier Kapoor let out an exasperated sigh.

"Listen, Puri, I want you on the case around the clock," he reiterated. "Time is running short. The marriage is only three weeks away. I'm more convinced than ever that something is not right with this man. He came for tea the other day to meet my dear wife and I could see it in his eyes. As plain as day. There's something missing.

"Now," Brigadier Kapoor carried on, after clearing his throat. "I know a thing or two about men, Puri. When you've fought alongside them, sent them into battle, seen them felled by enemy fire and bleeding to death in front of your very eyes, you become a good judge of a man's character. This man is hiding something and I want to know what it is. I'll expect to hear from you day after."

Munnalal lived at the far end of a long, dirty lane overhung with a rat's nest of exposed wires and crisscrossing cables. Caught within these tendrils, like bugs in a spider's web, forlorn paper kites and plastic bags floundered.

The lane and its narrower tributaries, which branched off into a seemingly endless warren, were lined with terraces of tall, narrow brick houses. Their diminutive front doors were overlaid with iron latticework and daubed with red swastikas to ward off the evil eye.

Puri had to abandon the Ambassador at the far end of the lane and proceed on foot.

He was acutely conscious of how conspicuous he appeared in such impoverished surroundings. Many of those he passed eyed him with apprehension, assuming, no doubt, that he was a plainclothes cop, government official or rich landlord.

A woman sitting on the front step of her home, picking lice from her daughters' hair, dropped her gaze when she spotted Puri drawing near. Farther on, three old men crouched on their haunches against a wall, turned, looked him up and down through narrowed eyes and then muttered surreptitious comments about him to one another.

Only the neighborhood's squealing children, who ran back and forth playing with all manner of makeshift toys— metal rims of bicycle wheels, inflated condoms—were not intimidated by the detective's official bearing. Grinning from ear to ear, they cried with outstretched hands, "Hello, Mister! One pen!"

Fortunately, no one paid any attention to Tubelight, who led the way, walking ten steps ahead of the detective without giving any indication that they were together. Dressed in the simple garb of a laborer, he had spent the past few hours in one of the neighborhood eateries, playing teen patta with a group of local men.

Gleaning information about Munnalal, who was not well liked in the neighborhood, had proven easy. Word was that he had come into a good deal of money in the past few months and gone from driving the cars of rich sahibs to owning a Land Cruiser of his own. He hired out the vehicle in the local transport bazaar, mostly to "domestic tourists" visiting Rajasthan from elsewhere in India.

"They say he's got a new plasma television, too," Tubelight had told Puri when the two had rendezvoused on the edge of the Hatroi neighborhood twenty minutes earlier and the operative had reported all he'd learned. "It's his Koh-i-noor. Spends his days sitting and staring at it."

Cricket was Munnalal's main staple, along with Teacher's Fine Blend.

"He's completely tulli most days," Tubelight had added. "A heavy punter as well. Into the bookies for twenty thousand."

The local lassi-wallah had also proven a mine of information. Over a couple of glasses of his refreshing yogurt drink, he'd told Tubelight that Munnalal was a wife beater. On a number of occasions the vendor had spotted bruises on Munnalal's wife's face and around her neck.

The man sitting on the side of the lane, selling padlocks, combs and wall posters of Hindu and Bollywood deities, had confirmed this. He'd also told Tubelight that Munnalal often fought with his neighbors. Recently there had been a dispute over a wall shared with the Gujjar family. It had resulted in a punch-up. Munnalal had put his neighbor in the hospital with a concussion and a broken arm.

"Sounds like quite a charmer, isn't it?" Puri had commented.

"Want me to keep an eye on him, Boss?" Tubelight had asked. "See what he gets up to?"

"Such a fool will provide his own rope," the detective had replied sagely. "I'm going to shake his tree and see what falls to earth."

"You're going to do a face-to-face?"

"Why not? I'm feeling sociable! Let us pay Shri Munnalal a visit. Lead the way."

Puri soon reached the house and banged on the door. It was answered by a harried-looking woman with a bruise on her cheek, who looked him up and down suspiciously and demanded to know what he wanted.

"You're Munnalal's wife?" asked the detective in Hindi in a deep, authoritative voice.

"What of it?"

"Go tell him he has a visitor."

"He's busy."

"Go tell him. Don't waste my time."

The woman hesitated for a moment and then let Puri in.

"Wait here," she said as she went to fetch her husband.

By now Puri, who was wearing his aviator sunglasses, was standing on the edge of a small courtyard scattered with a few children's toys and bucket of wet laundry waiting to be hung on the clothesline. In one corner, a charpai leaned against the dusty wall.

TV cricket commentary blared from an open door on the other side of the enclosure. A moment later, it suddenly stopped and Puri could make out the woman's scolding voice followed by a man's. He was speaking Rajasthani, which the detective didn't understand, but his tone was suggestive of someone less than pleased at being interrupted.

A moment later Munnalal appeared at the door to inspect his visitor.

One look at Puri caused him to stand a little straighter and to thrust the bottom of his vest into the top of his loose-fitting trousers. There was no hiding the fact, however, that he was a man loath to shift from his favorite mattress. Fat-faced, with a gut spilling over his waist, he had not shaved in days. Stubble had taken root on his bloated throat like black fungus, spreading over his chin and cheeks and threatening to engulf the rest of his features. His sunken eyes were bloodshot. And his vest, which failed to contain the great bunches of hair that protruded from his armpits, was dotted with spots of grease.

Still, what Munnalal lacked in looks and appearance, he evidently made up for in shrewdness. In Puri, he instantly recognized a threat. Rather than demanding to know his visitor's identity and purpose, he turned on the charm.

"Welcome to my home, sir," he said in Hindi with a smarmy smile.

"You're Munnalal?" asked Puri with a perfunctory handshake, almost overcome by the stench of booze on the man's breath.

"Yes, sir."

"I've come to offer you some help."

"Help? Me, sir?" he said, surprised. "How can I refuse?"

"You can't," said Puri.

With a half-quizzical look, Munnalal offered the detective a plastic deck chair in the shade on the east side of the courtyard.

"Make yourself comfortable, sir," he said before disappearing back into his room and calling his wife to bring the two of them refreshments.

When Munnalal reemerged a few minutes later, he had put a comb through his greasy hair and changed into a clean white salwar.

"So, sir, what can I do for you?" he asked Puri, drawing up a chair opposite his guest. He offered Puri a cigarette and then lit one of his own.

"I need some information," replied the detective.

"Ask me anything," he said grandly with a broad grin and a flourish of his hands.

"I understand you used to drive for Mr. and Mrs. Ajay Kasliwal."

"That's right," replied Munnalal. "I was with Sir and Madam for a year or so."

"So you knew the maidservant Mary?"

Munnalal's grin froze.

"Yes, sir. I knew her," he said, cautiously. "Is that what this is about?"

"You knew her well?"

"Not well—" Munnalal broke off, clearing his throat nervously. "Sir, why all these questions? Who are you—sir?"

Puri explained that he was a private detective from Delhi working for Ajay Kasliwal. Munnalal digested this information for a moment with a troubled frown, drawing on his cigarette a little harder each time.

"They're saying on the TV that Sahib murdered the girl," said Munnalal, exhaling a cloud of smoke.

"Ajay Kasliwal is innocent. Someone set him up. I'd like to know what you know about it."

Munnalal forced a laugh.

"Me? What could I know? I'm just a driver, sir."

"You *were* a driver. But from what I hear you've gone up in the world. They say you're a rich man these days."

"Who says that?" Munnalal asked skeptically.

"Your neighbors, mostly," said Puri. "They say you live like a maharaja. Munnalal-sahib they call you. Apparently, you drink Angrezi liquor. You bet big sums on cricket. Seems you've come into a lot of money recently."

Munnalal shifted uneasily in his chair. "It's my business how I live."

"Where did the money come from?"

"An uncle died and left me his house," he said defiantly.

"An uncle?"

"He was childless. I was his favorite."

Puri surveyed Munnalal with patient eyes.

"What can you tell me about the night Mary disappeared, August twenty-first?"

"Nothing, sir."

"Nothing at all?" Puri smiled. "Come now, you must know something. Where were you that evening?"

"I took Sahib to a hotel and waited for him in the car park."

"You didn't go back to the house?"

"Not until later when I dropped him home—that was around one in the morning."

Munnalal stubbed out the end of his cigarette and quickly lit another one.

"That's strange," said Puri, whose hands were folded neatly in his lap. "I'm told you were at the house at around eleven o'clock and carried Mary's body from her room to the back of the vehicle."

"Who told you that?" exploded Munnalal, his eyes filled with venom.

"That's not important," answered the detective coolly. "What is important is that you tell me exactly what happened at Raj Kasliwal Bhavan on August twenty-first. Otherwise I might have to pass on what I already know to Inspector Rajendra Singh Shekhawat. Perhaps you know him? No. Well, he's a very energetic young officer. I'm sure he's good at getting people to talk."

Abruptly, Munnalal pushed back his chair and stood up. For a moment the detective thought he might lunge. But instead, he began to pace back and forth, regarding Puri like a caged tiger.

"You were there that evening, weren't you?" said the detective.

"I never left the hotel car park. The other drivers will back me up."

Puri slipped his sunglasses down the bridge of his nose and stared at Munnalal over the top of them.

"I have a witness who saw you carry the body from Mary's room to Mr. Kasliwal's Tata Sumo."

"I never murdered anyone!" shouted Munnalal.

Puri held up a calming hand. "There's no need to get angry. As long as you cooperate you've got nothing to worry about."

Just then, Munnalal's wife emerged from the kitchen bearing two metal cups of water on a tray. She served Puri first and then her husband. Munnalal downed the contents in big gulps. Then he handed the empty cup to his wife, fished out a few rupees from his shirt pocket and sent her out to buy him another packet of cigarettes.

"What do you want?" asked Munnalal when they were alone again.

Puri placed the cup of water on the ground untouched.

"What any person wants? To be comfortable."

Munnalal's lip twisted into a knowing sneer.

"How comfortable?"

"That depends. First I want to know what happened at Raj Kasliwal Bhavan that night."

"What if I refuse to talk?"

"I don't need to tell you what the police will do to you to get a confession."

Munnalal grunted knowingly and sat down again. A long silence ensued as he weighed his options.

"Sir, I never killed that girl," he said, sounding conciliatory. "She tried to kill herself."

His words were met with an expression of cold skepticism.

"That's the truth," insisted Munnalal. "I went to her room and found her lying on the floor. There was blood everywhere. She'd cut her wrists."

"What business did you have going to her room?"

Munnalal faltered. "I . . . she . . . she owed me money. I went to collect it."

Puri sighed. "Don't lie to me or it will be the worse for you. Now tell me: why did you go to her room?"

"I already told you, sir!" protested Munnalal. "I went to her room to collect the five hundred rupees she'd borrowed from me. She was lying there covered in blood. She'd used a kitchen knife. But she was still alive. So I tied her wrists with cloth to stop the bleeding, carried her to the Sumo and drove to the clinic."

"Then what?"

"The nurse took her in. That was the last I saw of Mary."

"What was the name of the clinic?"

"Sunrise."

Puri took out his notebook and wrote down the name.

"Then what did you do?" he asked.

"I returned to the hotel to pick up Sahib."

There was a pause.

"You had blood on your clothes?"

"A little but I washed it off."

"And the knife? How can you explain it ending up in the garden behind the house?"

Munnalal shrugged.

"Someone else must have thrown it there."

"You never touched it?"

"When I first entered the room, I picked it up. But I didn't return to the room after that."

"Did you inform anyone the next morning?"

"No."

"Why not?"

Munnalal looked cornered. He took another long, hard drag on his cigarette and said, unconvincingly, "It could have meant trouble for me."

Puri pushed his sunglasses back up the bridge of his nose.

"Let me tell you what I think *really* happened," he said. "You went to that room to have your way with Mary. Probably it wasn't the first time. She turned a knife on you. There was a scuffle and you stabbed her. Maybe she died then and there. Or, like you say, she was still alive. Either way, you carried her to the Sumo and drove away. Later, you came back to the house and cleaned up the blood, got rid of her things and threw away her knife. Probably you also went into the house and took a silver frame to make it look like she'd stolen it and run away."

"I told you, I didn't murder her and I never stole anything either," objected Munnalal. "Go to the Sunrise Clinic and they'll tell you she was brought in alive."

Puri stood up.

"I'll do that," he said. "But there is still the matter of the knife and the witness who saw you remove the body."

"Sir, I'm sure we can come to some arrangement," Munnalal said. "I'm a reasonable man."

"When you're ready to tell me the whole truth, then we'll find out how reasonable you can be," said the detective. He handed Munnalal his card. "You've got until tomorrow morning. If I don't hear from you before then, I'll tell Inspector Shekhawat everything I know."

Nineteen

Puri and Tubelight sat together on the backseat of the Ambassador as Handbrake drove to Jaipur airport.

"How many of your boys have you got watching Munnalal?" asked the detective.

"Zia and Shashi are on the job, Boss."

"They're experienced enough? I don't want anything going wrong."

"They're good boys," said Tubelight. "Want me to check on this Sunrise Clinic?"

"Make it your top priority. I want to know if that bloody Charlie took the female there. Ask the doctors and all. They must be knowing. Could be they'll tell us what became of her."

"Think she tried suicide, Boss?"

"Munnalal is so used to telling lies he wouldn't be knowing the truth if it landed in his channa. But why he would concoct a cock-and-bull story about a clinic?"

"You think he killed her?"

Puri shrugged. "We're still only having some of the facts. So many open-ended questions remain. There's been no satisfactory verification of the body. I'm certain the police are barking up the wrong tree. Let us be sure not to do any barking of our own."

Puri's mobile rang and, after scrutinizing the number on the screen, he answered it.

By the time he hung up, Tubelight had formulated his own theory about what had happened at Raj Kasliwal Bhavan on the night of August 21.

"Munnalal rapes the girl," he said. "Gets trashed and abuses her. She pulls a knife and there's a tussle. Mary gets stabbed and expires. Then he carries the body to the vehicle and dumps it on Ajmer Road."

He looked triumphant, but Puri sighed.

"Baldev," he said, using Tubelight's real name, "why you're always insisting on doing speculation?" Puri's tone was not patronizing. Tubelight was, after all, one of the best operatives he had ever worked with, even if he was prone to jumping to conclusions.

"A pen cannot work if it is not open. Same with the human mind. Let us stick to what facts there are. According to police estimates, the body was dumped on twenty-second night. So if Munnalal did the killing, seems odd he would hang on to the body for twenty-four hours."

"He had to move it, Boss."

"He's a fool, but not so much of a fool. Either Mary and the dead girl are *not* one and the same, or something else transpired after Munnalal removed Mary from her room."

Puri took off his sunglasses and rubbed his sore eyes.

"Ask yourself this: why a common driver should be opting to take the female to the private clinic who'll be charging a hell of a lot when the state hospital is near to hand? Number two, what's he doing hanging around the house so late in the first instance? Not doing the dusting, that is for sure. Should be Jaya and other servants have the answers. Let us hope

Facecream finds out. Three, if Munnalal didn't return to the scene, who cleaned away the blood and all?"

Tubelight nodded, impressed. "I hadn't thought of that," he said.

"Deduction is my specialty, actually. But deduction cannot be done with thin air. That is where you come in. After the Sunrise Clinic, find out where this bugger got so much money. Must be he's doing blackmail. Question is, to whom he's giving the squeeze?"

Puri checked his watch as Handbrake pulled up outside the airport terminal. The last flight was due to depart for Delhi in thirty minutes. That was just enough time to buy a ticket and get through security.

"You're coming back tomorrow, Boss?" asked Tubelight as Puri got out.

"Handbrake's to proceed from here directly to Gurgaon. Tomorrow morning we'll revert at first light. Should be we'll reach by eleven, eleven-thirty."

"You've got airsickness pills, Boss?"

Puri gave him a resigned look.

"Bloody lot of good they did me last time," he said.

Puri didn't get airsick. It was a myth he perpetrated to disguise the real reason he avoided planes: being up in the air terrified him.

Over the years, he had tried all manner of treatments to cure his phobia, but so far nothing had worked. Not the Ayurvedic powders. Not the hypnosis. And certainly not the Conquer Your Worst Fears workshop run by that charlatan "Lifestyle Guru" Dr. Brahmachari, who'd taken him up in a hot air balloon and only succeeded in giving him nightmares for weeks.

To make matters worse, Mummy was forever reminding him about the prophecy made at his birth.

According to the family astrologer (a complete bloody goonda if Puri had ever met one), the detective was destined to die in an air crash.

"Don't do flying," Mummy had been telling him for as long as he could remember. "Most definitely it will be your doom."

Puri considered himself a spiritual man, but in keeping with his father's belief system, he was not superstitious. To his mind, astrology was so much mumbo jumbo and had an adverse effect on people's thinking.

Rumpi did not altogether agree with him, of course. She couldn't help herself. But the detective had always told his three daughters that no good had ever come from sooth-saying.

"Imagine some seer predicts you will marry a rich babu," he'd told them one day when they were all teenagers. "It will create a bias and get your thinking into an almighty jumble. You and your mother will pass over boys with greater quali-ties who are more compatible. Ultimately, you will not find contentment."

"But I want to marry a prince, Papa!" Radhika, the youngest, who'd been twelve at the time, had told him.

"Perhaps one day, chowti baby," the detective had told her, "But only the God knows. Trust to your fate and don't do second-guessing."

Of course, it is always easier to preach such credos than to live by them. Indeed, whenever Puri laid eyes on an airplane, he heard that voice in his head asking, "What if?"

This was why, despite the three hundred deaths every day on India's roads, he still felt safer traveling by car. It was also why, given the option of a three-hour flight or a 36-hour journey on a Rajdhani train, he opted for Indian railways whenever he could.

But today Puri had no choice. The only way he was going to make it to Mahinder Gupta's party was by flying to Delhi.

And so it was an uncharacteristically nervous and skittish Vish Puri who made his way through security, having bought himself a business-class ticket (if he was going to meet his doom he might as well do it with extra legroom).

What his fellow passengers and the pretty young air hostess made of him can only be imagined.

Upon entering the cabin, Puri, who was by now feeling strangely disoriented, sat down in someone else's empty seat. When its rightful occupant arrived, the detective refused to budge and only did so when the air hostess intervened.

Next, Puri had to be asked to move his suitcase out of the aisle and place it in the overhead locker. When he complied, the case sprang open and his Sexy Men aftershave and a pair of VIP Frenchie chuddies fell into the aisle.

By now, Puri's hands were trembling so much, his seatbelt had to be buckled for him. During takeoff, he sat as rigid as a condemned man in an electric chair. His hands gripped the armrests, his fingernails sank deep into the soft plastic and he found himself muttering a mantra over and over.

"Om bhur bhawa swaha tat savitur varay neeyam . . ."

Once the plane was in the air, he began sweating profusely and built up a considerable amount of gas in his stomach. This he vented periodically—to the intense displeasure of the Australian lady tourist sitting on his right: "Jesus! Do you mind?"

When Puri tried to calm his nerves with the remains of a quarter-bottle of Royal Challenge he'd brought on board, the air hostess informed him that it was illegal to consume alcohol on domestic flights and he had to put it away.

During the landing, Puri held his breath and closed his eyes.

The moment the aircraft left the runway, he unclipped his seat belt and staggered to his feet. Once again, he found the air hostess by his side, this time ordering him to sit down until the plane had come to a complete halt and the overhead seat-belt light was switched off.

Puri complied. But the moment he saw the gangway through the window, he was again up out of his seat and, suitcase in hand, pushing his way to the exit.

"We look forward to seeing you again soon," said the air hostess cheerily as he left the plane ahead of all the other passengers.

"Not if I can help it," mumbled the detective.

Puri had hired a brand-new S Class Mercedes to pick him up at the airport. The driver, who wore a white uniform buttoned up to his neck and a yacht captain's cap embellished with gold-leaf emblems, was standing outside the arrivals gate holding up a whiteboard with the alias the detective had adopted for the evening written upon it: "Monty Ahluwalia."

Mr. Somnath Chatterjee was also waiting for him in the car park.

Mr. Chatterjee, of indeterminable age, had a severe hunch born of a lifetime bent over a sewing machine. His clothes were always too large for him—the sleeves of his shirts came down to his knuckles; his trouser legs were always rolled up around his skinny ankles, giving the impression that he had somehow shrunk inside them.

But anyone who had known him long enough, like Puri,

could testify to the fact that Mr. Chatterjee had always been extremely skinny. His inattention to the proportions of his own apparel was in no way a reflection upon his skills as a tailor. Indeed, he ran Delhi's most successful costume house.

Mr. Chatterjee was, in fact, the scion of a noble line of Bengali tailors who had once fitted the Nawabs of West Bengal. Under the rule of the British East India Company, the family had set up shop in Calcutta and adapted to its European tastes, providing uniforms for the (not-so) Honorable Company's troops, and supplying the British theaters with costumes. It was a source of much interest to Puri that Mr. Chatterjee's great-grandfather had even provided disguises for Colonel Montgomery of the Survey of India—the real-life inspiration for Colonel Creighton in *Kim,* Rudyard Kipling's tale of intrigue and espionage during the Great Game with Russia.

Chatterjee & Sons had moved to Delhi in 1931, following in the footsteps of their British patrons. For the past twenty years, Mr. Chatterjee had been providing Puri with his disguises.

Normally, he went for his fittings at Mr. Chatterjee's premises, which were hidden down a long alleyway off Chandni Chowk in Shahjahanabad, or Old Delhi, as it was now called.

The premises were filled to the rafters with hundreds of costumes and paraphernalia. Hindu deities were stored on the ground floor; Hanuman monkey suits, strap-on Durga arms and Ganapati elephant trunks hung in rows. Uniforms from numerous epochs were to be found one flight up: the military regalia of Macedonian foot soldiers, Maratha warriors, Tamil Tigers, Vedic Kshatriyas and Grenadier Guards. The third floor was home to traditional garb of hundreds of different Indian communities: from Assamese to Zoroastrian. There was a special room set aside for headgear of all sorts, including the woven bamboo ceremonial hats worn by Naga tribesmen, the white mande thunis of the Coorg and British pith helmets. And the fourth floor was the place to go to find all the props, including mendicant and beggar accoutrement: swallowable swords, snake charmers' baskets (complete with windup mechanical cobras), and attachable deformed limbs.

Crucially for Puri, Mr. Chatterjee also provided a variety of Indian noses, wigs—his Indira Gandhi one was especially realistic—beards and moustaches. These he kept in the cool of the basement, where dozens of wooden boxes were itemized: "Sikh Whisker," Rajasthani Handlebar," "Bengali Babu."

What Mr. Chatterjee didn't have in stock he could have made. Twenty-seven tailors worked in a room on the top floor, sitting cross-legged in front of their sewing machines surrounded by swathes of silk, cotton and chiffon.

On a few occasions in the past, when Puri had come to Mr. Chatterjee and requested something out of the ordinary at short notice, these men had worked late into the night to accommodate him—like the time he had needed an Iraqi dishdasha to attend a polo match.

Tonight, however, Puri required nothing as exotic. He had asked Mr. Chatterjee to supply him with a standard Sikh disguise.

Puri clambered into the back of the tailor's worn-out van, where assistants with stage glue and a makeup kit gave him a quick makeover. Ten minutes later, he emerged wearing a large red turban, fake moustache and beard, a pair of slip-on black shoes and unflattering brown glasses with thick lenses. Puri slipped on several gold rings and put a ceremonial kirpan around his neck.

Mr. Chatterjee inspected him from head to toe, craning

his neck upward like a tortoise peeping out of his shell, and made an approving gesture with his head.

"Most realistic, sir!" said the old man in Hindi, his voice wheezy and high-pitched. "No one will ever recognize you! You would have made a great actor!"

Puri puffed his chest with pride.

"Thank you, Mr. Chatterjee," he replied. "Actually, as a young man, I did a good deal of amateur theater. In the ninth grade I won the Actor of the Year award for my portrayal of Hamlet. Often, I considered joining the stage. But duty called."

"What is the case this time?" whispered Mr. Chatterjee, who always got a thrill from aiding the detective. "Has someone been murdered?" he asked conspiratorially, his eyes lighting up with enthusiasm. "Are you after that bank robber—the one in the paper who stole fifty crore?"

The detective did not have the heart to tell him that he was involved in a straightforward matrimonial investigation.

"I'm afraid it's top secret," Puri whispered in English.

"Aaah, taap secret! Taap secret!" repeated the old man, giving a delighted giggle as he accompanied the detective to his car.

"I trust my secret is safe with you, Chatterjee-sahib?" asked Puri, laying a fond hand on one of the old man's hunched shoulders.

"I would rather die than tell them anything, sir!" he cried with watering eyes. "Let them pull out my fingernails! Let them blind me! Let them cut off my—"

Puri gave him a reassuring pat.

"I'm sure it won't come to that," he interrupted. "Now, you'd better go. It's best if we're not seen together. I'll come to your office in a few days once the case is resolved and settle my account."

"Yes, thank you sir, be careful sir," said Mr. Chatterjee, returning to his van.

Puri watched him climb inside and pull away, certain that, on his way back to Chandni Chowk, the old tailor would check in his rearview mirror to make sure he wasn't being followed and, no doubt, call him later in the evening to assure him that the coast had been clear.

Puri made a quick stop en route to Mahinder Gupta's apartment to pick up Mrs. Duggal, his escort for the evening.

She was waiting for him in the reception of a five-star hotel. When she saw the Mercedes pull up, she came out to meet it. A moment later she was arranging herself on the comfortable leather seat next to the detective and admiring the swish interior.

"So I take it we'll be sticking to our usual routine," she said to Puri after they had exchanged pleasantries.

"You know the old saying: 'Why fix what isn't broken?' " answered Puri.

Mrs. Duggal, a petite auntie who wore her sporty silver hair pulled back, smiled her innocent smile.

"I must say, I do so enjoy our little forays, Mr. Puri," she said in her quiet, lilting voice. "Retirement is quite all right. It's wonderful seeing the grandkids growing up. Did I tell you Praveen won a silver medal in breaststroke on Friday? I can't tell you how proud we all are. I wouldn't have missed being there for the world. But sometimes I do find myself pining for the old days. I miss that sense of adventure."

No one meeting Mrs. Duggal or passing her in Panchsheel Park where she took her morning walk with her neighbor, Mrs. Kanak, would have imagined that she had worked for RAW, India's secret service. During the 1980s and '90s, Mrs. Duggal and her husband, a career diplomat, had been stationed in some of India's most high-profile foreign high commissions and embassies. Ostensibly, she had worked as a secretary, taking dictation, typing and answering the telephone. But secretly her mission had been to keep tabs on her compatriots—diplomats, bureaucrats, administrative staff and, most important, her fellow spies.

To this day, not even her husband or children knew of Mrs. Duggal's so-called double role and the fact that she was a decorated national heroine.

While based in Dubai, she had identified the traitor Ashwini Patel and prevented him from betraying the identity of the highly placed Indian mole working inside Pakistan's secret service, ISI. During her four-year stint in Washington, Mrs. Duggal had discovered that the Military attaché was having an affair with a Chinese spy and had seen to it that the hussy sent phony naval plans to her superiors in Beijing. And in Moscow she had collected evidence of the High Commissioner's involvement in the Iraq Oil for Food scandal.

For the past four years, though, Mrs. Duggal had been enjoying her well-earned retirement back in Delhi. She passed her days playing bridge, spoiling her grandchildren with home-made ladoos and spending long weekends with her husband, now also retired, by the Ganges in Haridwar.

Occasionally she also did freelance jobs for Puri, whom she had worked with some fifteen years back when she had needed discreet investigation into the Moscow embassy's chef.

Her usual part was that of the detective's wife, for which Mrs. Duggal needed no disguise. She was dressed in the understated style that had worked so well for her during her undercover days: a simple but fetching beige silk sari with gold zari design, a black blouse, a pair of sensible heels and a modest selection of kundan jewelery.

"You're very sober, Mrs. Duggal," commented the detective as the car pulled onto the main road to NOIDA.

"I'm glad you approve," she replied. "You know I'm not one for gaudy colors."

Puri gave her a couple of Flush's ingenious sticky bugs, one of which looked like a wasp, the other a fly, and explained where he wanted them placed.

Mrs. Duggal popped them into her handbag, where she also kept her lock-picking tools: a couple of hair grips and a metal nail file.

"Should be child's play for two old professionals such as ourselves," said Puri.

"Just as long as I'm home by eleven-thirty, Mr. Puri. My husband will be expecting me. Any later, and he'll start thinking I've got a boyfriend."

The two chuckled as the Mercedes sped along the new three-lane toll road.

Half an hour later, they were standing in the elevator heading up to the twenty-second floor of Celestial Tower.

A long, carpeted corridor with wood-paneled walls and air-conditioning vents purring overhead led to the executive penthouse.

Puri rang the bell and the door was promptly opened by a servant, who ushered them into a spacious, dazzling white apartment. He was relieved to find it crowded with members of the Gupta and Kapoor families and their closest friends. Among such a large gathering (the party was at least seventy strong), no one would notice a couple of old gate-crashers, let alone challenge them. Indeed, as the detective and his escort stepped through the door, looking for all the world like a respectable auntie and uncle, they were greeted warmly by Mahinder Gupta's parents. It did no harm that Mrs.

Duggal wobbled from side to side with "arthritic" hips and grimaced each time she put her right foot forward.

"Monty Ahluwalia and my good wife," Puri said in halting English with a deep, provincial drawl as he shook Mr. Gupta by the hand.

"Such a beautiful apartment," commented Mrs. Duggal to Mrs. Gupta. "You must be very proud."

The four of them engaged in small talk for a few minutes. It wasn't long before the Guptas revealed the apartment's whopping price tag: five crore.

"Of course, it's absolutely rocketed up since then," Mr. Gupta told Mr. and Mrs. Monty Ahluwalia. "Our son spent fifteen lakhs on the bathroom alone."

"Seventeen lakhs actually, darling," cooed Mrs. Gupta, going on to describe the Italian Jacuzzi bathtub. "The toilet's also amazing. You know, it flushes automatically, has a heated seat, a sprinkler system and a bottom blow-dryer! You really *must* try it."

As Mr. and Mrs. Monty Ahluwalia began circulating among the other guests (and trying the Japanese hors d'oeuvres, which the detective did not rate, grumbling to a fellow Punjabi that he was a "butter chicken man through and through"), Puri began to understand why Brigadier Kapoor was so against his granddaughter's marriage.

The Kapoors belonged to the refined, elite classes of south Delhi: military officers, engineers, the odd surgeon and one Supreme Court judge. Puri could picture them at cultural evenings at Stein Auditorium or the IIC, wine tastings at the Gymkhana Club and art exhibitions at the Habitat Center.

Indeed, as the detective and Mrs. Duggal mingled, they overheard some of them discussing a retrospective of the Indo-Hungarian artist Amrita Sher-Gil, which had been showing at the National Gallery of Modern Art. Elsewhere, an uncle in a blazer, striped cotton shirt with French cuffs and loafers was telling another uncle, who was dressed almost identically and had a matching greying moustache, about the cruise he and his wife had recently taken around the Great Lakes. And at the far end of the room, Brigadier Kapoor himself, dressed in a three-piece suit and standing with his silver-haired wife at his side, was telling another elderly auntie in a mauve sari about a charity dinner that he and Mrs. Kapoor had attended at Rashtrapati Bhavan.

The Gupta clan, by contrast, was drawn from the Punjabi merchant castes. All the younger men seemed to have salaried positions with IT multinationals and worked twelve-hour, six-day weeks. They wore off-the-rack suits and gold watches, had gelled hair and talked mostly about the markets, Bollywood and cricket. They smoked, drank and laughed raucously, occasionally giving one another matey slaps on the back. Their wives showed a fondness for chunky sequined heels, garish eye shadow and either sequined cock-tail dresses or Day-Glo saris worn with strapless, halter-style blouses. Four of them were clustered in the kitchen admiring the stainless steel extractor fan.

"Wow!" one exclaimed. "So shiny, yaar."

Puri and Mrs. Duggal chatted for a while with Gupta's fiancée, Tisca Kapoor, who seemed like a sensible, articulate woman, if hugely overweight and clearly nervous about how the two families were getting along. As they talked, the detective dropped his napkin on the ground and attached a bug to the underside of one of the faux alligator-skin side tables.

He and his partner in crime then split up. The detective crossed the room to the gas fireplace, where he attached another device to the back of one of the photo frames, and then went in search of a Scotch on the balcony.

Meanwhile Mrs. Duggal hobbled over to the kitchen

(where a few of the older Gupta aunties were discussing the attributes of the front-loading washing machine, which, they all agreed, was worth the money) and attached the magnetic fly under the lip of the extractor fan.

She then made her way to Mahinder Gupta's bedroom. Having attached the wasp to the bottom of the metal bed frame, she stepped into the bathroom and locked the door behind her.

In one corner stood the Jacuzzi bathtub and in another the toilet.

Mrs. Duggal washed her hands in the sink and, as she did so, noticed a metal medicine cabinet on the wall.

It was locked.

Curious, she took out a hair grip and metal nail file and, in a few seconds, popped the cabinet open.

On the shelves inside, she found an unmarked bottle filled with pale yellow liquid and two syringes. She took the bottle and put it into her glasses case in her handbag.

Just then she heard Mrs. Gupta's voice in the bedroom. "Come this way, it's through here."

The handle on the door turned and there was a knock.

"One moment," called out Mrs. Duggal.

She locked the medicine cabinet, sat down on the toilet and quickly stood up again. Sure enough, it flushed automatically.

Mrs. Duggal opened the door to find Mrs. Gupta and three other women who had come to inspect the bathroom waiting on the other side.

"You're quite right, the toilet really is a wonder," she gushed. "So much easier on the hips."

Twenty

At about 10:30 that evening, just as Puri reached home after dropping off Mrs. Duggal, the front door of Munnalal's house in Jaipur suddenly swung open with a thud.

A beggar with a horribly deformed hand who was crouching against a wall ten feet away watched as Munnalal stepped outside. In one hand he was carrying his mobile phone, his thumb working the keypad. From his pocket protruded the wooden butt of a revolver.

Munnalal's wife appeared in the open doorway with an anguished, searching expression.

"Your food is ready!" she screeched to his back as he set off down the lane. "Where are you going? It's late!"

"None of your business, whore!" he bawled over his shoulder. "Go back inside or I'll give you a thrashing!"

The beggar, seeing Munnalal striding toward him, made the mistake of holding out his deformed hand, which looked like a melted candle, and pleaded for alms—"Sahib, roti khana hai."

In return he received a hail of abuse.

"Bhaanchhod!" Munnalal called him as a passing shot,

kicking his begging bowl and the few pitiful coins that it contained into the open drain.

The unfortunate man howled, scrambling on all fours after the receptacle, which had landed upside down in fetid slime.

"Hai!" he moaned after retrieving it and retaking his position against the wall where he had been sitting all evening.

A couple of passing locals, who had seen how cruelly Munnalal had behaved, took pity on the beggar and dropped a few rupees at his feet.

"May Shani Maharaj bless you!" he cried after them, picking up the coins and touching them to his forehead and lips.

The beggar watched his benefactors continue on their way, passing Munnalal's front door, which, by now, had been slammed shut. Then he stood up, collected his pitiful possessions and, when he was sure no one was watching, twisted off his deformed hand. He shoved it under his soiled lungi and set off down the lane.

"Bastard Number One's on the move, heading in your direction," said Tubelight's man Zia into the transmitter concealed in the top of his cleft walking stick.

"Roger that," came back a voice in the clunky plastic receiver in his ear.

The voice belonged to Shashi, his partner, who had watched too many American cop shows and insisted on using the lingo.

"Who is this Roger?" hissed Zia into his communicator.

"Your papa, yaar," quipped Shashi.

"Shut up, OK!"

"Ten-four," replied his colleague.

Munnalal hurried down the lane, stopping briefly at the cigarette stand, where he bought a sweet paan. Greedily he stuffed it into his mouth and tossed a grubby note onto the vendor's counter.

Soon, he reached the busy main road, where he stepped beyond the broken, piss-stained pavement at the edge of traffic. Amid a haze of dust and diesel fumes, with horn-blaring Bedford trucks hurtling past, Munnalal went about trying to hail an autorickshaw.

Zia decided to watch him from the entrance to the lane, staying in the shadows and telling Shashi, who was parked nearby, to keep his engine running.

Much to their shared—and in Munnalal's case, obvious—frustration, all the autos that drove past were occupied. Some carried as many as eight people with six on the backseats and another couple clinging to the sides like windsurfers.

Five minutes passed. A blue Bajaj Avenger motorcycle driven by a man wearing a helmet with a tinted visor pulled up on the other side of the road.

At first, Zia paid the driver cursory attention. But after Munnalal succeeded in hailing an auto and drove away in the direction of the old city, the Avenger made a quick U-turn and set off after him.

Zia and Shashi were not far behind on an old Vespa.

"Someone else is following Bastard Number One," said Zia.

"Roger that. Did you get a pozit-iv eye dee?"

"Huh?"

"Po-zit-iv eye dee! Means did you recognize him?"

"How could I recognize him, you fool? He's got a helmet on and his numberplate is covered in mud."

"Ten-four. Do you think he's a perp?"

"Speak Hindi, will you!"

"A perp means a goonda type."

"I don't know!"

"Think we should get between them?"

"No, but don't fall behind."

"Copy that."

Munnalal's auto buzzed and spluttered its way down M.I. Road, past Minerva cinema. Occasionally, he spat great gobs of paan juice out the side of the vehicle, painting the road's surface with intermittent red streaks.

Ten minutes later, the auto turned down the lane that ran behind Raj Kasliwal Bhavan. Finally it came to halt outside the deserted bungalow with the overgrown garden.

Munnalal got out and paid the driver, who promptly drove off in search of another fare. He looked up and down the street to make sure no one was following him and then slipped through the leaning iron gate. A second later he was lost amid the long grass and shadows.

The motorcyclist, having dismounted and watched Munnalal's movements from behind the corner, took off his helmet and, leaving it on his bike, continued his pursuit on foot.

Zia and Shashi, who had pulled up a safe distance behind him, rounded the corner in time to see the motorcyclist pass through the gate and enter the garden.

"No way I'm going in there," whispered Shashi as they crossed the lane. "I heard an owl!"

"They're harmless, yaar. All they do is sit in trees and go hoo hoo."

"OK, hero, you go in there and I'll wait here and cover you."

"What is this 'cover me' business? Bloody half-wit. Think you're Dirty Hari?"

"It's Dirty *Harry*," corrected Shashi.

"Whatever, yaar. You stay here. Relax. Maybe take a nap."

Cautiously, Zia headed into the garden. Shashi watched him go and, finding himself alone, had a change of heart.

"I thought I'd better watch your back," he whispered when he caught up with his partner.

Together, the two of them crept forward through the long grass and weeds. The owl started hooting again, causing Shashi to grip Zia's arm. And then suddenly a figure ran straight into them, knocked them both to the ground and sprinted off in the direction of the lane. Zia and Shashi were dazed and it took them a few seconds to pick themselves off the ground.

"Go after him! I'll check ahead!" ordered Zia.

"Ten-four!"

Shashi gave chase, but he was too slow. As he reached the lane, the motorcycle kicked into start and, with a roar of the engine, made a 180-degree turn and sped away.

Shashi watched the Bajaj Avenger disappear from sight, knowing that his cousin's Vespa was no match for it, and went to find his partner.

They met outside the gate.

"He got away!" said Shashi in a loud voice.

"Keep your voice down, you fool!"

"Don't call me a fool!"

"OK, half-wit! What happened?"

"He took off. What about Bastard Number One?"

"He's dead."

"What? Are you sure?"

"Yes, I'm sure!" snapped Zia. "He's lying behind that abandoned house with a knife sticking out of his throat."

Shashi's eyes widened.

"What happened?"

"Well, it wasn't suicide!"

Shashi held his hands over his face and kicked at the ground. A pall of dust rose around him.

"That's just our luck!" He cursed. "Bloody fat bastard goes and gets himself terminated while we're on duty. Boss and Tubelight are going to *kill* us!"

"I know! It's all your fault. You should have rubbed the mud off the numberplate and written it down when you had a chance," said Zia.

"What do you mean *I* should have? What about you?"

"It was your turn to do the thinking."

Shashi paced back and forth a couple of times. Then a thought occurred to him.

"What about his mobile phone? Did you get it?"

"It wasn't there."

"Sure?"

"I checked all his pockets!"

"Wallet?"

"Gone as well?"

There was a pause.

"What do we do now? Call the cops?"

"No, you idiot, we get out of here before someone sees us."

"Right . . . I mean Roger that," said Shashi.

"Bloody fools!" was Puri's reaction to news of Munnalal's murder and the events leading up to it.

It was Tubelight who broke it to him at two in the morning.

"Do the cops know?" asked the detective as he tried to shake off the deep, restful sleep he had been enjoying.

"Doubtful. The body is probably lying unnoticed, it being nighttime, Boss. Should I make an anonymous call? Tip off the cops?"

"Not yet. They'll trample the scene. I'll try to get there as fast as I can."

Puri hung up the phone and switched on the light in the panel behind his bed. Rumpi stirred.

"What is it, Chubby?" she asked sleepily.

"Trouble," he answered. "Where's the driver?"

"I put him in with Sweetu."

"Wake him and then pack my things, will you? I've got to return to Jaipur immediately. The case has taken a turn for the worse. Someone has been murdered."

"Who?" she asked.

"The man who held all the answers."

Puri changed and went into his study. Opening the safe, he took out his .32 IOF and slipped it into his trouser pocket.

By the time he went downstairs, his wife was standing by the front door with his packed overnight case, a few cold rotis wrapped in tinfoil and a flask of hastily made "dip tea."

The detective smiled and gently took her cheek in his right hand. "Meri achhi biwi, my good wife," he said.

She could feel the cold metal of Puri's pistol against her thigh as she gave him a fond hug.

"Take care," she said.

The detective chuckled. "Don't worry about me, my dear. When it comes to danger, I've got a sixth sense."

"Danger doesn't worry me," answered Rumpi. "But those deadly pakoras and chicken frankies you like so much do."

Puri managed to get a couple of hours' sleep and reached the Jaipur city limits at dawn. An apologetic and sleepy Tubelight was waiting for him at Ajmeri Gate. They headed straight to the murder scene. But the police had beaten them to it. Three Jeeps and the coroner's wagon, which looked like an armored milk van, were parked outside the gate of the derelict house. Five impassive constables stood nearby, chatting among themselves.

Puri told Handbrake to stop the car across the road, from where he watched and waited. A few minutes later, a procession emerged from the garden. It was led by a couple of orderlies carrying a stretcher with a blanket draped over Munnalal's body. Two more constables with rifles slung over their shoulders followed. Bringing up the rear was Shekhawat, smoking a cigarette.

"Good morning, Inspector," said Puri as he got out of the Ambassador.

"What are you doing here, sir?" he asked, surprised to see the detective.

"Just I was on my way to see my client for an early morning conference," he answered cheerily.

"At this time?" The inspector looked at his watch. "It's not even six."

"What to say? I like an early start."

Puri gave a nod in the direction of the stretcher, which was being slid into the back of the coroner's wagon.

"Who have you got there?" he asked.

"Male, mid-forties, found with this knife sticking out of his throat."

Shekhawat held up the bloody murder weapon, which he'd put in a plastic bag.

"By God," said Puri, feigning surprise. "Any identification?"

"Nothing. So far he's a naamaalum, unknown. He was carrying this."

Shekhawat held up Munnalal's revolver, also now in a plastic bag.

"May I see the body?" asked Puri.

"Why all the interest, sir?"

"The murder occurred behind my client's house. Might be I know the victim, isn't it."

Shekhawat led the detective over to the coroner's wagon and told the orderlies to pull back the blanket.

Munnalal's face was frozen in an expression of sheer horror. The wound was on the left of the neck and the blood had soaked his shirt.

His lips and chin were also stained with paan juice.

"Do you recognize him, sir?" asked Shekhawat.

The detective made a face that suggested ignorance.

"Unfortunately not, Inspector."

The orderlies replaced the blanket back over Munnalal's face. Puri and Shekhawat turned and walked away.

"Any theories?" asked the detective.

"We got an anonymous tip-off in the middle of the night. Someone called and said he saw two men hurrying out of the garden and driving away on a Vespa. He gave us the number-plate. My guess is these two murdered him for his wallet and phone."

"So a robbery then," suggested the detective.

"Seems that way," answered Shekhawat.

Puri was looking down at the dust on the street where a number of vehicles had left tracks, privately cursing the police for being such bunglers. If only he had reached the scene before them.

"Well, Inspector, I can see that you have everything well in hand," he said. "I'll wish you a good day."

The detective got back into his car.

"Go straight to Raj Kasliwal Bhavan," he told Handbrake tonelessly.

As the Ambassador pulled away, Puri watched the reflection of the inspector in the rearview mirror. Shekhawat in turn watched the back of Puri's vehicle. The curious expression on his face made the detective uneasy.

It was only a question of time before he found out that Munnalal once drove for Kasliwal and his murder was bound to reflect badly on his case. Puri could see tomorrow's newspaper headlines already:

HIGH COURT LAWYER'S FORMER DRIVER FOUND DEAD. COPS SUSPECT FOUL PLAY.

"Can your boys' vehicle be traced back to them?" asked Puri, with some urgency.

"No way, Boss, but why?"

"Shekhawat has the numberplate."

"How, Boss?" exclaimed Tubelight.

"Most probably the killer himself gave it to him. Your boys have been most careless. Tell them to go back to Delhi right away. I would want to talk to them once this thing is over."

The Ambassador turned right at the end of the road, then right again and pulled into Raj Kasliwal Bhavan.

After coming to a stop, Puri sat for a moment in a gloomy silence.

"What's wrong, Boss?" asked Tubelight.

"I've come to a theory about what all has been going on. If I'm right, it would not end well for anyone."

Tubelight knew not to ask Puri about his theories. There was no point. The detective always kept his cards close to his chest until he was sure he had solved the case. This secrecy was derived partly from prudence and partly from his controlling nature.

"Any luck at the Sunrise Clinic?" he asked Tubelight.

"I chatted with the receptionist. Says no girl matching

Mary's description was brought in. I think she's lying. I'm going back at seven to meet the security guard on duty the night Mary was murdered."

"Allegedly murdered," Puri reminded him.

"Right, Boss. What's your plan?"

"Just there's some checking up I need to do here. Take the car and send it back for me. I'll pick you up around eight o'clock."

Puri got out of the vehicle, but turned and said through the open door, "Be alert! Whatever miscreant did in Munnalal knew what he was doing."

"A professional, Boss?"

"No doubt about it at all. A most proficient and cold-blooded killer."

Twenty-one

Puri followed the brick pathway that led along the right-hand side of Raj Kasliwal Bhavan, rounded the corner of the house and paused outside the door to the kitchen. It was closed. All was quiet inside.

The detective surveyed the garden to see if anyone was around. Finding the coast clear, he walked over to the servant quarters and edged along the space between the back of the building and the property's perimeter wall.

Facecream's small window was easily identifiable from the thread that went up the wall and disappeared inside. Puri knocked on the glass three times and made his customary signal: the call of an Indian cuckoo.

A moment later, the window opened and Facecream appeared.

"Sir, you shouldn't have come!" she whispered in Hindi. "It won't be long before everyone is up. Memsahib does her yoga at seven on the lawn!"

"Munnalal was murdered last night in the garden right behind this wall," said Puri.

"Last night, sir? Just here? I didn't hear anything." There was a wounded indignation in her tone.

"Could the killer have come from inside?" asked the detective.

"There's no way anyone can come in and out without my knowing, Boss," said Facecream.

Puri brought her up to date with the events of the night before and told her how he had come to examine the knife wound for himself. When he was finished, Facecream said, "Sir, was the motorcycle a blue Bajaj Avenger?"

Puri's eyes lit up with expectation. "Tell me!" he said.

"Sir, Bobby Kasliwal has one. Last night he rode away on it at around eleven-fifteen."

"By God! What time he returned?"

"Past midnight."

Puri let out a long, resigned sigh. "It's what I feared," he said to himself.

"What is, sir?"

He didn't answer, but asked, "Is the motorcycle kept in the garage?"

"Yes, sir."

Puri nodded. "I'll have a look. Anything else you can tell me?"

"Sir, I've been trying to find out what more the servants know about Munnalal. Nobody has a good word to say about him. Jaya claims he constantly harassed her. She says he groped her a number of times. Once, when he was drunk, he tried to force his way into her room."

"Does she know if there was anything going on between Munnalal and Mary?"

"She's not sure, sir. She heard some sounds coming from Mary's room one night. This was soon after she started working here, in late July. But she couldn't say for sure whom Mary was with."

Puri heard a rustling sound coming from the side of the

servant quarters and signaled to Facecream to close the window. Casually, he put his hands behind his back and pretended to be looking for something on the ground so that if anyone appeared asking him what he was doing there, he could claim to be searching for clues.

The rustling grew louder.

Presently, a large black crow hopped into view, turning over leaves with its beak.

"False alarm," he gestured to Facecream, who came back to the window and opened it.

"Can you tell me anything else?"

"Sir, I got the cook's assistant, Kamat, drunk. He liked Mary but I doubt there was anything going on between them. I got him to admit he's a virgin."

"Is he aggressive?"

"Yes, but he's not that tough."

"How do you know?"

"He tried it on and I slapped him. He ran off crying."

It was Facecream's opinion that the mali, too, was no threat. "He's smoking charas all day," she said, "and can no longer differentiate between reality and fantasy. He makes up stories about everyone. He seems to hate Kasliwal. Apparently he's been telling everyone that Sahib has been coming to my room at night!"

"By God," murmured Puri. "Anything more?"

"That's all," she answered. "But, sir, have you considered that after you confronted Munnalal, he figured out that it was Jaya who saw him carrying away Mary's body and he was planning to intimidate her or silence her?"

"That would certainly explain why he was carrying a weapon," said Puri. "But there is one other possibility—"

His words were interrupted by the shrill sound of Mrs. Kasliwal's voice. She was calling from the kitchen door.

"Seema? Seema! Chai lao! This instant!"

"Sir, I'd better go," said Facecream reluctantly. "I'm not in her good books. Yesterday I broke a plate and she's docking my salary forty rupees. That doesn't leave me much to take home!"

Puri laughed. "Just a few more days and we'll have you out of here. Let's talk tonight at the usual time."

The detective remained where he was while Facecream hurried off toward the kitchen.

"Haanji, ma'am. Theek hai, ma'am," he heard her saying to Mrs. Kasliwal.

The two women went inside, closing the door behind them, and Puri stole over to the garage, which was on the other side of the garden to the left of the house. He tried the side door, found it open and stepped inside.

Bobby's Bajaj Avenger was parked at the back.

The numberplate was coated in red mud.

Upon further inspection, Puri found a spot of blood on the accelerator grip. There was another on the helmet.

"He's gone to visit his father in jail," Mrs. Kasliwal told Puri when he asked about Bobby's whereabouts.

She was on the front lawn in the dandasana position, squeezing shut one nostril with her index finger and breathing out hard through the other.

"At what time, madam?"

Mrs. Kasliwal snorted a couple more times and then laid her upturned hands on her knees. "He left at six-thirty or thereabouts," she said.

"You're certain, madam?"

"Of course I'm certain, Mr. Puri!" she snapped.

Puri watched as she moved into the Ardha Matsyendrasana, or Half Lord of the Fishes, pose.

215

"He's carrying a mobile phone, madam?" asked Puri.

Mrs. Kasliwal sat up straight again, exhaling as she did so.

"Certainly he's having one, Mr. Puri. But why the sudden interest in my son?"

"Actually, there's a certain matter I would like to discuss with him."

"Tell me what exactly?"

"Actually, I was hoping he might bring me one or two caps from London next time he's reverting to India. I'm particularly partial to Sandowns. By far the best quality is made by Bates Gentlemen's Hatter of Piccadilly. I hoped Bobby would bring me one or two. Naturally I would make sure he's not out-of-pocket."

She looked at him with a baffled expression.

"Caps, Mr. Puri? Caps are the priority, is it? What about the investigation? What progress is there?"

"Plenty, madam, I can assure you."

"So you keep saying, Mr. Puri! But I see no evidence of it. Thousands are being spent of our money and for what? No progress at all! Frankly speaking, I don't know what it is you're doing all day."

She lowered her chin to her chest.

"Fortunately my lawyer, Mr. Malhotra assures me the police case is shot full of holes. Only the flimsiest of evidence they have. Nothing concrete. He'll be getting Chippy off for sure."

Puri fished out his notebook.

"What is Bobby's mobile number, madam?" he asked, pencil at the ready.

Mrs. Kasliwal rattled off the digits too quickly for the detective, who had to ask her to repeat them three times before he had it written down correctly.

"Very good, madam," he said, putting away his notebook.

"I'll be on my way. One thing is there, though. Your former driver, Munnalal. Last night only, he was most brutally murdered."

Mrs. Kasliwal's body visibly tensed for a moment.

"It happened in the property directly abutting your own, madam, at eleven-thirty. You heard anything?"

"Nothing," claimed Mrs. Kasliwal. "I was fast asleep I can assure you. Such a long, tiring day it was. But how can you be sure he was murdered?"

"He was stabbed in the neck, madam."

Mrs. Kasliwal made a face as if she had smelled something unpleasant and shook her head from side to side.

"Such dangerous times we live in, I tell you," she said. "Most probably he got into an altercation with the wrong sort."

"Anything is possible, madam," said Puri. "But seems odd to me he was murdered here—right behind your house."

"Who knows what goes on, Mr. Puri? These people live such different lives to us."

"He wasn't coming to see you, madam?"

"Me, Mr. Puri? What business would he have with me?" Mrs. Kasliwal's words were liquid indignation.

"Could be he was in need of assistance?"

"What kind of *assistance* exactly?"

"I'm told he was facing financial difficulties."

Mrs. Kasliwal rolled her eyes. "That is hardly news, Mr. Puri! Munnalal was always asking for salary advance. These types are in and out of trouble. So much drinking and gambling is going on."

"Did you ever give him anything extra?"

"Extra?" asked Mrs. Kasliwal, regarding him with mild contempt.

"Like a bonus, say?"

"I gave him his salary. That is all. *Buss!* Now I've answered enough of your questions, Mr. Puri. There's such a busy day ahead. Mr. Malhotra will be arriving at nine-thirty to go over the defense. And I'm hosting the monthly meeting of the Blind Society."

"No need to explain, madam," said Puri. "It's about time I pushed off. Till date, I'm without my breakfast."

Puri picked up Tubelight ten minutes later from behind the Sunrise Clinic.

He could hardly control his excitement.

"Boss, the security guard remembers a girl being brought in on August twenty-first night!" he said, clambering into the car. "Says she was covered in blood. But, Boss! She was very much alive!"

"He's certain of it?" asked the detective.

"One hundred—no, three hundred and fifty percent certain!"

"Why so certain?" Puri said skeptically.

"She was dropped off by a man matching Munnalal's description in a Sumo, and the very next night she left!"

"She left? How?"

"Taxi. Came and took her."

"She was with someone?"

"The guard's got confusion on this point," answered Tubelight. By this the operative meant that the guard had clammed up suddenly when asked.

"Could he tell you where the taxi went, at least?"

Tubelight grinned.

"No delay! Tell me!" insisted Puri.

"Train station."

"He's certain?"

"Overheard the taxi-wallah being told where to go."

"Very good!" exclaimed Puri. "Tip-top work!"

"Thanks, Boss," said Tubelight with a grin.

The detective instructed Handbrake to head directly to the station.

"Boss, you don't want to interview the clinic owner? He's Dr. Sunil Chandran."

"Naturally I would want to know why it was Mary was discharged and who all paid the bill," he said. "But I'll visit Dr. Chandran later. For now, let us stick on the trail while it remains hot."

On platform 2, where the Jat Express to Old Delhi was about to depart, hundreds of passengers with suitcases and bundles balanced on their heads were trying, all at once, to push through the narrow doorways of the already crowded second- and third-class carriages.

The weakest, including women with babies and the elderly and infirm, were ejected from the crush like chaff from a threshing machine, while the strongest and most determined battled it out, pushing, shoving and grabbing one another, their voices raised in a collective din.

Puri watched as an acrobatic young man clambered up the side of one carriage, scrambled along the roof and then attempted to swing himself inside over the heads of the competing passengers jammed into one of the doorways. But he was roughly pushed away and, like a rock fan at a concert, was passed backward aloft a sea of hands and dumped unceremoniously onto the platform. Unperturbed, he scrambled to his feet and clambered up the side of the train to try again.

The detective continued along the platform where the calls of chai- and nimboo paani-wallahs competed with train tannoy announcements preceded by their characteristic organ chords. A knot of migrant workers, evidently waiting for a long-delayed train, lay sprawled over sheets of newspaper on the hard concrete platform, sleeping soundly.

Near the first-class retiring room, he found the men he was looking for: three elderly station coolies who were sitting on their wooden baggage barrows taking a break from the grueling work of ferrying passengers' luggage on their heads.

Like the other coolies Puri had just interviewed at the main entrance to the station, they wore bright red tunics with their concave brass ID plates tied to their biceps. Their arms and legs were thin and sinewy.

Puri explained that he was looking for a missing girl called Mary who was said to have come to the station on the night of August 22. His description of the girl was cobbled together from the facts he'd gleaned about her during his investigation—together with a certain amount of deductive reasoning.

"She is a tribal Christian from Jharkhand in her early twenties. She would have been extremely weak and probably had bandages wrapped around her wrists. I believe that if she boarded a train, its destination was probably Ranchi."

The old men listened to the detective's description. One of them asked, "What was the date again?" Puri repeated it. No, he said after some discussion with his fellow coolies, they had not seen a girl who matched that description. "We would remember," he said.

The detective made his way to the last platform. There he found a young coolie who was carrying three heavy-looking bags on his head for a family traveling on the Aravali Express to Mumbai.

Puri walked alongside him as he made his way to one of the second-class A/C carriages.

"Yes, sir, I remember her well," said the coolie after he had dropped off the bags for the family and Puri had described

Mary to him. "She could hardly walk. She seemed sick. Yes, she had bandages around her wrists."

"Did she board a train?" asked the detective.

"A man put her on board the—" The coolie suddenly stopped talking. "Sir, I'm a poor man. Help me and I will help you," he said.

Puri took out his wallet and handed the man one hundred rupees. This was as much as the coolie made in a day, but his composed expression did not change as he tucked the note into his pocket.

"She boarded the Garib Niwas."

"You saw her get on?"

"Yes, sir, I helped her."

"Did you speak to her?"

"I asked her if she needed a doctor, but she did not answer me. She looked like she was in shock, just staring blankly, not even blinking."

"What happened to the man she was with?"

"He waited until the train departed. Then he left."

"Describe him."

Again the coolie pleaded poverty. Puri had to hand him another hundred rupees.

"Middle aged, dark suit, white shirt, expensive shoes— well polished."

Ever grateful for the observational powers of the common Indian man, the detective made a note of the coolie's name and went in search of the station manager's office.

Twenty minutes later, he was back at the car, where Tubelight and Handbrake had been waiting for him.

"There is one 'Mary Murmu' listed on the manifest for the Garib Niwas train to Ranchi on August twenty-second," he said. "Sounds like she was extremely weak."

"What's our next move, Boss?" asked Tubelight.

"You and Facecream keep a close eye on Bobby Kasliwal. He is up to his neck in this. I want him watched every moment of the day and night."

"Think he murdered Munnalal?"

"There's no doubt he was there on the scene."

"And you, Boss?"

"I'm going to Jharkhand tonight to locate Mary."

"Jharkhand. Could take forever. Where will you look?"

"The uranium mines of Jadugoda."

Twenty-two

The passenger manifest showed that whoever purchased Mary Murmu's train ticket on August 22 had opted for a seat in a non-air-conditioned three-tier carriage. The train from Jaipur to Ranchi had been a "local" and had stopped at every station along its 740-mile, 30-hour journey east across the subcontinent.

During his student days, Puri had always traveled in the cheapest trains and carriages out of financial necessity. He looked back on the experience with nostalgia. The hypnotic swaying of the train, the camaraderie between passengers, all of them poor, had been wonderful.

But he knew how unforgiving the conditions could be. And now, as he traveled in the comfort of a first-class carriage on a fast train (top speed 87 miles per hour) on the same route Mary had taken, he pictured her—weak, with nothing of her own to eat or drink, possibly fading in and out of consciousness—crammed into the corner of a bottom wooden bunk with the rough feet of the occupants on the bunk above dangling centimeters from her face.

Her carriage would have been heaving with laborers and rustics, who routinely clambered aboard slow-moving local trains between stations, occupying every inch of space. Mary would have been forced to share her bunk with up to six or seven other passengers. With no one to guard her place while she went to the toilet, she might well have found herself squeezed onto the floor.

When the train stopped during the day and the sun hammered down on the roof, it must have been like the inside of a tandoor oven. The circular metal fans bolted to the ceiling would have offered little respite. During the inordinate number of stops, there would have been no letup from the footfall of hawkers selling everything from biscuits and hot tea to safety pins and rat poison. Nor from the perpetual stench of "night soil," which, on all Indian trains, went straight down the toilet chutes onto the tracks.

Had someone taken pity on Mary and helped her? Perhaps a sympathetic mother who had given the poor girl some water and a little something to eat from her family's tiffin.

Had she had made it to Ranchi alive?

The odds were not good. And without Mary, or at least irrefutable evidence that she had not ended up dead and mutilated on the side of Jaipur's Ajmer Road, Puri was going to have an extremely hard time proving what had happened on the night of August 22. A train booking with her name on the roster would not be enough to prove Ajay Kasliwal's innocence.

The detective watched the striking Rajasthani landscape slip past his window. The sun was setting over an intricate patchwork of small fields—the dry, baked earth rutted with grooves made by ox-drawn plows in expectation of the monsoon rains.

His eyes followed the progress of a herd of black goats and a stick-wielding boy along a well-worn pathway that led to a clutch of simple homesteads. In front of one stood a big black water buffalo chewing slowly and deliberately. Nearby, on a charpoy, sat an old man with a brilliant white moustache and a bright red turban watching the train go by.

Puri reached Ranchi early the next morning. He had phoned ahead to arrange transportation and exited the station to find a driver who hailed from Jadugoda waiting for him.

Together they set off in a four-wheel-drive Toyota toward the mines.

· "Sir, it's not a good idea to make this journey at night," the driver told Puri once they had left behind the economically depressed city, which embodied little of the new India. "Nowadays the roads are extremely dangerous."

"Why's that?" asked Puri.

"Naxals," replied the driver.

Much of Jharkhand, along with great swaths of eastern and central India—the "Red Corridor"—were controlled by Naxals, short for Naxalites, or Maoist guerrillas. Their cause was ostensibly a just one: to fight against oppressive landlords and functionaries of the state, who had tricked or forced hundreds of thousands of people off their land. But like so many proxy rebel movements around the world, they had become the scourge of the people they claimed to represent. Naxal comrades levied taxes on villagers, robbed them of their crops and indoctrinated their children.

They also killed hundreds of people each year.

"Just last week they murdered a truck driver who refused to pay their road tax," explained the driver. "They burned him inside his cab. Last night they murdered an MLA in Ranchi. They put a mine under his car and BOOM!"

Puri had read about the murder in that morning's paper.

The MLA was the third to die in as many months. Little wonder the prime minister had recently called the Naxalites the single biggest internal security threat faced by India.

Puri asked the driver whether he thought the Maoist movement would continue to grow in popularity.

"Of course, sir," he said.

"Why?"

"Because now the poor can see what the rich have— expensive cars, expensive houses. So they feel cheated."

Yes, the genie has been let out of the bottle, Puri thought. God help us.

Despite all the potholes, which caused his head to jerk up and down and occasionally bounce off the window, Puri soon fell fast asleep.

He awoke when they were half an hour from Jadugoda town.

The landscape to his left was Martian: flat, rocky and arid. The only earthly features were the occasional thick, knotty trees—remnants of a great, primordial jungle, which had been cleared to grow monsoon-dependent rice. To the right rose hills with sharp escarpments. Here and there, the uphol-stery of patchy scrub was punctured by outcrops of rock and scarred by gullies made during heavy downpours.

The uranium mines lay deep beneath these hills. A barbed-wire fence encircled them. Large yellow Uranium Corporation of India signs warned trespassers to keep out.

Puri's vehicle was soon stuck behind a convoy of dump trucks. Each was carrying loads of ordinary-looking grey rock chips that, according to the driver, had been extracted from the mines and were being taken to the processing center a few miles away. There, the rock would be crushed, and after being put through a chemical process, the uranium extracted in the form of "Yellowcake."

"Sir, did you know our Yellowcake was used to make India's nuclear bomb?" said the driver, grinning with pride at his country's achievement and his native Jharkhand's contribution.

"Do you know anyone who works in the mines?" asked the detective.

"Sir, only tribal people do the manual labor underground," he replied.

There was a subtext to his answer: the driver was a caste Hindu and although he had grown up in the area, he did not mix with the tribals, or Adivasis, the indigenous aboriginals who traditionally dwelled in the jungle.

"I had a cousin who used to drive these trucks. He did the job for twelve years," said the driver cheerily. "But then he had to stop."

"What happened to him?" asked Puri.

"Sir, he got sick. The company doctors diagnosed him with TB and gave him some medicine. But he did not improve and then he died."

"What was his age?"

"Forty-two."

The driver fell silent for a moment and then, with a confused frown, said, "Sir, the antimining campaign-wallahs say the mines make people sick. They say people should not work there. But what else are people to do? There are no jobs. Driving a truck pays good money. If one or two people get sick, well . . ."

They were still stuck behind the dump trucks, unable to pass because of oncoming traffic.

A headwind had started blowing dust from uranium rocks

in their direction. Some of it settled on the windscreen. Although the windows were rolled up, Puri automatically buried his mouth and nose in the crook of his arm.

The driver laughed when he noticed the detective's reaction.

"Sir, don't worry, you can't get sick from a little dust! See?" He rolled down his window and took a deep breath. "There's nothing wrong with me at all!"

Jadugoda was virtually indistinguishable from tens of thousands of other little roadside settlements to be found across the length and breadth of India, thought Puri as they stopped at the main intersection to ask for directions.

A collection of rickety wooden stalls stood along the sides of the road that led in and out of the town. There were several paan-bidi stands stocked with fresh lime leaves and foil pouches of tobacco, which hung like party streamers. There was a vegetable stand, a fruit stand with heaps of watermelons, and a butcher, whose hunks of meat hung on hooks smothered by flies.

A fishmonger sat cross-legged on a plastic tarpaulin on the ground scaling a fresh river fish using a big knife that he held expertly between his toes. Next to him crouched an old woman selling meswak sticks for cleaning teeth.

The scene would not have been complete without a big neem tree by the intersection, which provided welcome shade for the local dogs and loafers who spent their days watching people and vehicles coming and going.

There was, however, one unusual feature about the place. In the middle of the intersection stood a statue of three Adivasis armed with bows and arrows—a memorial to local heroes who fought, albeit with primitive weapons, against the British.

In Chanakya's day, too, the tribals had offered fierce resistance to the Maurya Empire, staging raids on passing caravans from their jungle fastness. But since the formation of the Indian republic, these people had been exploited and disenfranchised, Puri reflected sadly. To their misfortune, their ancestral lands lay atop some of the largest mineral deposits in the world, and in the past fifty years, most of these had been requisitioned for pitiful compensation. Hundreds of thousands of Adivasis had been made homeless and nowadays, all across India, scratched a living digging ditches, carrying bricks and cleaning toilets.

As they sat at the very bottom of the social scale, there was a good deal of prejudice against them.

"The tribal people are not so friendly," complained the driver as they pulled away from the dusty intersection. "And they drink too much!"

A couple of minutes later they passed a small township built in the 1960s by the Uranium Corporation of India to house its full-time employees and their families, nearly all of whom hailed from elsewhere in India. Within its spruce perimeter there was a school, a hospital, blocks of flats and green playing fields.

Beyond the township, the driver took a left down a rocky lane and pulled up outside an ordinary, one-story concrete building. Had it not been for the cross above the entrance, Puri would never have guessed it was the local church.

The detective got out of the Land Cruiser and knocked on the metal doors. They were soon opened by a middle-aged man who could easily have passed for an Australian Aboriginal. He was dressed in a shirt, jeans and a baseball cap, and around his neck hung a small gold crucifix. His eyelids blinked in slow motion, giving the impression that he was half asleep, and his mouth broadened into a wide, childlike grin.

"Good afternoon," he said, welcomingly, as if it had been some time since he'd had any company. His pronunciation mimicked the way English is spoken on "Teach Yourself" audiocassettes.

"Good afternoon, just I'm looking for the priest," said Puri.

"I'm Father Peter," replied the old man. "It's a pleasure to meet you."

"Father, my name is Jonathan Abraham. I run a charity based in Delhi that offers assistance to Adivasi Christian families," lied the detective.

The business card he handed the priest named him as "Country Director" of the nongovernment organization that he often used as a cover: "South Asians in Need"—SAIN. The card listed two Delhi numbers—both of which, if dialed, would be answered by an extremely helpful lady by the name of Mrs. Kaur, who would offer to send out an information pack about the charity.

The priest studied the card and his eyelids blinked in slow motion again.

"Ooh!" he said like an excited child. "Are you from Delhi?"

"Yes, Father, my office is there."

Father Peter grinned again. He had a dazzling set of white, perfectly straight teeth, which might have belonged to an American high school student. "Then you are the answer to my prayers!" he said, inviting the detective inside.

Puri had reasoned that if he went around asking people in the local Christian Adivasi community about Mary's whereabouts, they would react with suspicion and he would be stonewalled. Furthermore, he didn't want Mary—assuming she was still alive—coming to know that an outsider was looking for her.

Ideally, he wanted to engineer a situation in which she would feel comfortable divulging the truth about what had happened to her in Jaipur. To do so, he would need to gain her trust.

Fortunately, the cover of a Christian was an easy one to pull off. Puri had attended a Delhi convent school as a young boy and the nuns had drummed the Lord's Prayer into him. The other sacraments of the Nazarene guru were also easily observed. (Pretending to be, say, a Muslim presented considerably more pitfalls. Mastering the Islamic prayers alone took hours and hours of practice.)

Christian priests, too, were easier to handle than the representatives of other faiths. They were generally nowhere near as greedy as Hindu pundits, who always had their hands out.

The only thing Father Peter really wanted was a new cross for his church. The existing one, which was made of wood, was being eaten by termites. "Now it is 'holy' in more ways than one," he joked as they drove back into town.

Over lunch—Puri took him to the dhaba on the main road, which was the only place to eat in Jadugoda—the detective promised to send him a new one from Delhi.

By the time they had finished their meal and sat cleaning out the bits of mutton gristle from the gaps in their teeth with toothpicks, he had learned that there were only forty families in the Jadugoda area who had converted to Christianity (far greater numbers were to be found around Ranchi). The rest still clung to their animist religion.

Of those forty families, seven or eight bore the tribal name Murmu.

Puri told Father Peter that he wanted to visit their homes

because the Government of India's Ministry of Development had identified the Murmus as the poorest and he wanted to assess their needs.

The priest accepted this explanation without question and offered to act as the detective's guide.

To reach the first house, they drove back to the main junction in the center of the town and turned left along the narrow road. It passed through the hills, which were cordoned with high fences. More yellow "No Trespassing" signs appeared and the driver explained that the uranium processing center was off behind the line of trees on their left.

"See the pipe coming out of the jungle? That carries the waste from the plant—a sludge of toxic chemicals and crushed rock," chimed in Father Peter.

Puri followed the path of the pipe with his eyes. It traveled under the road, crossed the narrow valley and climbed up the side of an enormous, 150-foot-high man-made dam that had been constructed across the mouth of the adjacent valley.

"The waste is dumped there, is it?" he asked.

"Behind the dam lies what they call the 'tailing pond,'" said Father Peter. "No one is allowed there. But when I was a boy, we used to go up the hill and throw stones into the mud." He grinned impishly at the memory of his childhood escapade. "It's very thick. Sometimes when it is very hot, the surface is hard and cows stray across it and get sucked down."

Their destination was a hamlet that lay in the shadow of the dam.

By now, it was early afternoon and the sun was at its hottest. The little sandy lanes that ran between the mud and straw compounds were empty save for a few chickens.

Father Peter knocked on the first door and an Adivasi man with coal black skin, wearing a sarong and a baseball cap, answered. He was obviously delighted to see the priest and after a good deal more grinning and pleasantries, the detective was invited inside.

A large well-swept courtyard lay at the center of the house. On one side, rows of cowpats were drying in the sun; on the other grew a banana tree, holding up a direct-to-home satellite receiver dish.

Their host arranged a couple of chairs in the shade provided by the overhanging thatch roof and soon his daughter served them glasses of cold water and a packet of cream-filled biscuits.

The daughter was too young to be Mary and Puri quickly established that she had no sisters. But he went through the motions of taking out his notebook and inquiring about the family's financial circumstances.

The couple had had two other children, both boys. The elder was working down in the mines, where he loaded rocks onto a conveyor belt all day without any protective gloves or breathing apparatus; the other son had been born physically and mentally handicapped and died at the age of seven.

"What problems did they face?" Puri asked them.

The father made a face as if he did not know where to begin. Usually, he said, his words translated for the detective by Father Peter, he worked alongside his son in the mines. But he had been feeling weak for the past few months and had not been able to work. Because of this the family's income had been halved. Like seven hundred million other Indians who were yet to see the benefits of the country's economic growth, they were surviving on less than two dollars a day. To make matters worse, the water in their well had been poisoned by the chemicals from the tailing pond.

"They can no longer drink it," explained Father Peter, almost jovially. "But they still use it for washing."

"Have you thought about moving? It is dangerous to be here, no?" Puri asked them.

"This is the only land we have left," said the father. "The jungle is mostly gone and we have nowhere else to go."

Puri made a show of writing down more details and, before heading off to meet the next family, gave the father a thousand rupees. He also tried to impress upon him that it was hazardous to use the water from the well. But the man shrugged, resigned to his lot.

It was not until the following afternoon, when the detective and Father Peter arrived at the eighth and final home on the list, that Puri's search came to an end.

The house, which was much smaller than the others they had visited, stood next to a sal tree. In its shade a teenage girl and a young woman squatted playing a checkerslike game called Bagha-Chall, or Tigers and Goats. The board was a grid drawn in the sand; for game pieces they were using twenty-four little pebbles. In shape and color, they were indistinguishable from the ones Puri had found on the windowsill of the servant quarters in Raj Kasliwal Bhavan.

"Hello, Mary, God bless you," said Father Peter in Santhal, the local language, greeting them both with a big, friendly smile.

"Hello, Father." Mary, who was wearing an unusually large number of bangles on her wrists, beamed.

She stood up, brushing away the hair from her eyes with her left hand, and a few of the bangles slid down her arm toward her elbow, revealing a scar on her wrist.

"Is your father at home?" asked Father Peter.

"He's inside, sleeping," she said.

"Well, go and wake him, child. This gentleman has come all the way from Delhi and would like to speak with him."

Mary shot Puri a suspicious look.

"What does he want?" she asked.

"He's here to help us."

"How?"

"Now, don't ask so many questions, my child. Run along and bring your father," said the priest.

Puri watched Mary walk over to the house. She was an attractive young woman, slim, with dark brown eyes and long black hair tied in a ponytail. Her features, dusky and distinctly Adivasi, were strikingly similar to those of the murder victim dumped on Jaipur's Ajmer Road. "That poor girl has suffered a lot," the priest told Puri when she was out of earshot.

"What happened to her?"

"I hate to think. She won't tell anyone, not even her mother. Like so many of our young women, she went to the city to find work. When she came back a few months later, she could hardly walk. It's taken her weeks to recover, God protect her."

"How did she get here?"

"The Lord was watching over her. She collapsed at Ranchi station, but a member of our community took her to a hospital."

Soon, Puri was sitting on a mat on the floor inside the house with Mary's father, Jacob, asking questions about the family's circumstances. Mary sat in the doorway listening to their conversation and sifting through a pot of lentils. All the while she watched Puri suspiciously.

Like most of the men Puri had interviewed in the past 24 hours, Jacob worked in the mines, which provided just enough money to feed the family. But he was getting old and complained that he had no son to help him. Last year, after the family's rice crop failed, he had sent his eldest daughter to the city to work. For a while, she sent money home.

"But she became sick and returned," said Jacob. "Now I'm afraid my health will give out and we will all starve."

Puri made a note of this and then explained to Jacob that he ran a charity willing to provide the family with assistance. He made a show of taking out a calculator and punching in some figures and then announced that because they had no sons, they were eligible for an immediate payment of four thousand rupees. This was more than Jacob made in a month, and the sight of so much cash left him speechless. He took the wad from Puri with tears in his eyes and said to Father Peter, "It is a miracle!"

Puri accepted the family's invitation to stay for dinner and, before the sun went down, managed to snap a surreptitious picture of Mary with his mobile phone.

After dark, by the light of a paraffin lantern, they sat eating a simple meal of fish, rice and daal. The food, which was prepared by Mary and her mother, was delicious. Throughout the meal, Puri complimented the cooking and ate seconds and thirds.

Afterward, as he, Jacob, Father Peter and the driver, who had joined them, shared the priest's pipe, he made his host an offer:

"I would very much like to give your daughter a job working in my house in Delhi," he said. "The salary would be four thousand rupees a month and she would stay in the servant quarters."

Mary looked horrified by this suggestion. "No, Father, I won't go!" she protested immediately.

Puri ignored her protest, adding, "Of course, I can understand why you would be concerned about her safety. You are welcome to bring her there yourself. I will provide the train tickets and we can all travel together. Perhaps Father Peter would like to come as well and we can find him a new cross for his church?"

The detective knew it was too good an offer for Jacob to turn down. It was the answer to all his prayers.

Sure enough, despite Mary's misgivings, her father soon agreed to Puri's terms. They would leave for Delhi the next day.

Twenty-three

Mummy's little Maruti Zen crept along the road in Mehrauli, southwest Delhi. The road was lined with imposing walls topped with shards of broken glass. Behind these lay "farmhouses," some of the largest and most expensive properties anywhere in the capital, all of them built on land illegally appropriated by the wealthy and well connected. Mummy had visited one a few years ago during Holi. It had been like a mini-Mughal palace—all marble archways and perfumed gardens.

"Twenty-two!" called Majnu, Mummy's driver, as they passed another set of ornate wrought-iron gates and he read from the Italian marble plaque, which had been engraved with the owner's name: "KAKAR."

Mummy was looking for number nineteen.

She had been reliably informed by Neelam Auntie, one of her former neighbors in Punjabi Bagh, that it belonged to Rinku Kohli, Puri's childhood friend. Apparently, he spent most of his time in Mehrauli these days, often returning to Punjabi Bagh and his wife, children and elderly mother in the early hours of the morning.

Everyone knew what Rinku got up to in his farmhouse. It

was an open secret. But his standing had not suffered in the community as a result. Punjabi Bagh's men admired him because he was rich, drove a Range Rover and liked to drink a lot of imported Scotch, watch cricket and tell dirty jokes. And the women were always ready to forgive a good Punjabi boy for his improprieties, just so long as he respected his elders, observed all the family rituals and raised strong, confident boys of his own.

"Must be making a packet," Neelam Auntie had commented admiringly.

Mummy, though, had always understood Rinku's weaknesses. The fact that he had turned out rotten like his father had come as no surprise to her—neither did the fact that he and Chubby had chosen such different paths. But Rinku had practically grown up in her house and she had always been kind to him.

Which was why Mummy felt confident asking for his help now. A serial adulterer and crook he might be, but nice, grey-haired Punjabi Bagh aunties still commanded his respect.

"There it is! Stop!" she shouted.

Majnu, who was sulking again because he had been working long hours helping shadow Red Boots, pulled up to the gate. A uniformed security guard approached his window.

"Tell Rinku Kohli he's got a visitor," Mummy called over the driver's shoulder.

"Madam, there's no one here by that name."

"Just tell him Baby Auntie is here. I've brought his favorite ras malais."

The guard hesitated.

"Listen, I know he's living here, na. So might as well get on with it!"

Reluctantly, the guard returned to his hut and picked up a

phone. Mummy could see him through the glass talking to someone. Another minute passed before he emerged again and opened the gates.

Majnu started the engine again and pulled inside.

The "farmhouse" was set on three acres of immaculate, emerald lawns trimmed with neat hedges and lush flower beds. The house defied elegance, however. A modern red-brick structure with oblong windows and yellow awnings, it looked like a House of Fun at a fairground. At the back, Mummy spied a swimming pool and two tanned goris in bikinis sunning themselves. A lean, attractive Indian man in shorts and sunglasses was standing nearby, talking on a mobile phone and smoking a cigar.

Majnu stopped in front of the house and, as Mummy got out clutching her Tupperware container, Rinku came bounding down the steps.

"Baby Auntie, what a surprise!" he said, bending down to touch her feet.

"Namaste beta. Just I was passing, na," she said, patting him on the shoulder. "No inconvenience caused, I hope?"

"Not-at-all! You're most welcome any time, Auntie-ji, *any* time. Come, we'll have some tea."

He was about to head back into the house and then thought better of it.

"Actually, let's go on the lawn. It'll be quieter there."

He led her to a spot where a garden table and chairs were arranged in the shade of a tree.

"Oi! Chai lao!" he called to a servant who had emerged from the front of the house.

Rinku and Mummy sat down and "did chitchat."

"Where is Chubby?" asked Rinku.

"Who knows where? So secretive he is."

When the tea arrived, Rinku served her himself and then tucked into one of the ras malais, making suitably appreciative noises.

"*Wah!*"

Mummy saw her chance.

"Beta, you heard some goonda did shooting at Chubby, na?" she said.

Rinku's face darkened. He took off the sunglasses he'd been wearing and placed them on the table.

"I heard, Auntie-ji. I'm sorry."

"So close it was. Just one inch or so and he'd have been through. Fortunately, his chili plants saved the day."

"Thank God," intoned Rinku.

"Problem is, beta, Chubby's not doing proper security. When I help, he gets most upset. You of all people are knowing how stubborn he can be, na."

"Only too well, Auntie-ji."

"You know and understand. That is why I've come," she continued. "But, beta, you're not to tell Chubby we've talked. Equally, I won't go telling him you're helping in this matter."

Rinku patted her fondly on the hand.

"Auntie-ji," he said. "Chubby has always been like a brother to me. And you've been like a mother. We are family. Just tell me what I can do."

Mummy proceeded to tell Rinku about how she had tracked down Red Boots, a corrupt police inspector called Inderjit Singh; and how he had met Surinder Jagga at the Drums of Heaven Restaurant, where, over spring rolls and whisky, they'd discussed a murder.

"Since then I've done checking. Turns out, this fatty-throated fellow has desire to build one office block on

241

Chubby's home. Already he's bought up some nearby plots. Recently one elderly neighbor, Mr. Sinha, sold out. Must be under pressure, but it has been hushed up."

"Did Jagga come to Chubby with an offer?" asked Rinku.

"Rumpi says Jagga visited some weeks back and offered Chubby a large sum for the land, but he turned him down flat. Jagga didn't threaten him, so naturally my detective son is unaware he did the shooting."

"Jagga and Singh must have decided the best course of action was to get rid of Chubby," said Rinku. "They probably thought someone else would get the blame and then Rumpi would take their offer and sell up."

"Jagga and Inspector Singh are bad sorts, that is for sure," added Mummy.

Rinku looked as if he couldn't make up his mind whether to congratulate Mummy on her brilliant detective work or scold her for taking so many risks.

"You've been keeping quite busy, isn't it, Auntie-ji." Rinku smiled, quietly impressed.

"Well, what to do, beta? Someone's got to look out for Chubby, after all."

"I know, Baby Auntie, we all worry about him. He doesn't look after himself, actually. But at your age you shouldn't be running around getting involved in this kind of thing. These people can be dangerous. Property brokers are the worst kind."

"Don't be silly, beta, I'm quite capable of looking after myself, na."

Rinku laughed. "I've never doubted that, Baby Auntie. But you've done more than enough. Leave this with me, OK? I'll take care of it."

"You know this Jagga fellow, is it?"

"I know people who know him," said Rinku, a little hesitantly. He paused. "Auntie-ji, I promise I'll sort it out. Trust me."

"Don't do rough stuff, beta, please."

"Of course not, Auntie-ji!"

"And not a word to Chubby."

"Not one word! Now I'll walk you to your car."

Flush was also busy while Puri was in Jharkhand. But he was finding keeping tabs on Mahinder Gupta deeply unsatisfying.

Never before had he trailed such a boring individual.

Mr. Gupta's routine was numbingly predictable.

On the day before Puri returned to Delhi with Mary, he woke at a quarter to six, spent ten minutes on his automatic toilet (which sluiced and dried his bottom and told him to "have a nice day"), changed out of his pajamas into his tracksuit, and made his way to the kitchen.

There he gulped down a protein shake.

At 6:30, Bunty, his one-thousand-rupee-per-hour personal trainer arrived and, for the next thirty minutes, put Gupta through his paces in his personal gym.

Afterward, the BPO executive had a shower and then changed into a smart business suit and tie.

At 7:30, he took the lift down to the underground car park to his BMW. Pavan, the car-saaf-wallah, had finished washing and waxing the blue paintwork to perfection, and for this he received payment of twenty rupees.

The car sparkled in the early morning sunshine as the driver pulled out of the gates and took the turning for the NOIDA expressway toll road. He did not have to fight too hard for space amid the frenetic traffic. Given the Beemer's Brahmanical status at the top of India's vehicular caste system (bicyclists being the dalits of the road), few cars dared to cut in front of it or venture too close lest they contaminate its uncorrupted, venerated bodywork.

Gupta, meanwhile, sat on the backseat with the automatic windows closed and the air-conditioning on, blissfully isolated from the diesel fumes and wretched hawkers. He kept half an eye on his in-car LCD TV, which was tuned to a morning business program, while reading his overnight emails from Hong Kong on his BlackBerry. He also put in calls to New York, Mumbai and Singapore.

At the main gate to Analytix Technologies, Gupta's employers, the guards stood to attention as the BMW left the dusty, bumpy feed road and glided over the pristine tarmac of the car park, pulling up at the entrance to the glass-paneled office block.

Briefcase in hand, Gupta took the elevator up to his office on the executive floor.

He stayed inside the building all day.

For lunch, he ate a dosa at his desk.

At precisely 8:15 in the evening, he left work, having already changed into his golf kit—green mock turtleneck, long Greg Norman plaid trousers and a Tiger Woods cap.

Gupta reached the Golden Greens Golf Course at 8:30 and teed off with a senior futures manager, Pramod Patel.

He scored an eagle on the fifth, a birdie on the eighth and finished seven under par.

Back in the clubhouse, he had a Diet Coke at the bar and, shortly after ten o'clock, returned home.

There he changed out of his golf clothes, took another shower and spent an hour talking on the phone, first with his parents and then his fiancée.

He fell asleep watching the second day of the Vallarta Golf Cup in Mexico.

"I bet all he dreams are about little white balls," Flush muttered to himself as he sat in his white van, which was parked near Celestial Tower, listening to his mark snoring.

A week of surveillance had thrown up nothing incriminating. Gupta's bank and phone records were clean. He had not visited any porn sites. He was not in touch with illegal bookies. He had not made any big unaccounted-for cash withdrawals.

When he wasn't working, playing golf or sitting on his automatic toilet, Gupta went to the Great Place Mall, where he liked to watch sappy Bollywood love stories in the super luxury Gold Class Lounge cinema and buy organic handmade lavender soap at Lush.

Flush was growing increasingly frustrated with his failure to dish up the dirt. Seeing middle-class Indians living such ostentatious lives while the vast majority of the population survived on next to nothing riled him. He wanted badly to put a dent in Mahinder Gupta's perfect life.

The only glimmer of hope was the unmarked bottle of yellow liquid Mrs. Duggal had discovered in the medicine cabinet.

But what could it be? Was he HIV positive, perhaps?

One thing was for sure: he was not taking recreational drugs. Gupta had not had contact with any of the hundreds of dealers now operating in Delhi.

"He's not even had pizza delivered, Boss," Flush had reported to Puri at the end of another fruitless day.

Twenty-four

After returning from Jharkhand and leaving Mary and her father with Rumpi, Puri drove to his office.

Sitting behind his desk and feeling especially pleased with himself, he sent Door Stop, the office boy, to fetch him a couple of mutton kathi rolls with extra chutney. These he devoured in a matter of minutes, ever vigilant about getting incriminating grease spots on his safari suit, and then got back to work.

His first call was to Tubelight, whom he informed about his success in Jharkhand—"A master stroke" was how he described his triumph. He also shared his plan, which did not involve breaking the good news to the Kasliwals just yet.

"I've something else in mind," he said. "What's Bobby been up to?"

"Doing timepass," said Tubelight. "He's hardly come out of his room. Facecream says he's depressed. Had a big argument with his mother."

"What about?"

"She couldn't tell, but there was a good deal of shouting. That apart, he's gone to the Central Jail to visit his Papa every day."

Next, Puri talked to Brigadier Kapoor to assure him that that the investigation was "very much ongoing." He promptly received a harangue on how he wasn't doing enough and should try harder.

Finally, Puri turned his attention to the small matter of the attempt on his life and put in a few more calls to some of the informers and contacts to find out if they'd heard anything useful.

One, a senior officer at the CBI whom the detective had helped on a couple of cases in the past, ruled out Puri's top suspect, Swami Nag. There had been a confirmed sighting of the fraudster at a Dubai racetrack on the very day of the shooting, so he had not been in Delhi as previously thought.

"Unless of course His Holiness can bilocate and be in two places at once," joked the officer.

No one else had any leads.

Exhausted from the overnight train journey from Ranchi, Puri tilted back in his comfortable executive chair, put his feet up on the desk and closed his eyes.

In seconds, he was fast asleep and dreaming.

He found himself standing before the legendary walls of Patliputra, the ancient capital of the Maurya Empire, with its 64 gates and 570 towers. Nearby, under an ancient peepul tree sat a sagely figure with a shaven head, ponytail and an earring in one ear. Across his forehead were drawn three parallel white lines denoting his detachment from the material world.

Puri recognized him as his guru, Chanakya, and went and knelt before him.

"Guru-ji," he said, touching his feet. "Such an honor it is. Please give me your blessings."

"Who are you?" asked Chanakya, busy writing his great treatise.

247

"I'm Vish Puri, founder and director of Most Private Investigators Ltd. and the best detective in India," he answered, a little hurt that the sage had never heard of him.

"How do you know you are the best?" asked Chanakya.

"Guru-ji, I am the winner of the Super Sleuth World Federation of Detectives award for 1999. Also, I was on the cover of *India Today* magazine. It's a distinction no other Indian detective has achieved to date."

"I see," said Chanakya with an enigmatic smile. "So why have you come to me for help? What can I, a simple man, do for you?"

"Guru-ji, someone tried to kill me and I need help in finding whoever it was," explained Puri.

Chanakya closed his eyes and gave the detective's request some thought. It seemed like an age before he opened them again and said, "Do not fear, Vish Puri. You will receive the help you need. But you must accept you don't have power over all things. All of us require a helping hand from time to time."

"Thank you, Guru-ji! Thank you! I'm most grateful to you. But please, tell me, how will I be helped?"

Before Chanakya could answer, Elizabeth Rani's voice broke in. She was calling him over the intercom. Puri woke with a start.

"Sir, I've the test back from the laboratory. Should I bring it?"

The detective looked at his watch; he'd been asleep for more than half an hour.

"Yes, by all means," he said drowsily, buzzing in his secretary.

The test Elizabeth Rani was referring to was the analysis of the mystery liquid Mrs. Duggal had retrieved from Mahinder Gupta's bathroom.

After looking over the results, and drinking a cup of chai, Puri called Flush on his mobile phone to tell him the news.

"It's testosterone," he said.

"Is that all, Boss?"

"You sound disappointed."

"It's very common for guys to take that stuff these days, Boss," Flush explained. "Everyone who goes to gyms is taking it. They all want Salman Khan muscles, so they're pumping themselves full of dope. It's readily available on the black market. Most chemists will sell it to you."

"I don't doubt Gupta wants big muscles," said Puri. "But from everything we've learned about this man and his habits, I have a feeling his motives are different."

"HIV, Boss? Maybe that's why so much of his hair is falling out."

"No, something else. Find out his doctor's name. Has he seen him lately?"

Puri had given Rumpi and the servants strict instructions to make Mary feel welcome and asked them to put away the Hindu idols for a few days (he had to keep up the pretense that he was Jonathan Abraham, after all). He'd also sent Sweetu to his cousin's house for a few days because he couldn't be trusted not to blurt out the wrong thing at the wrong time.

Mary's father only stayed at the house for a couple of hours and then headed back to the train station. His wife and younger daughter needed him at home, he explained to Rumpi.

A tearful Mary saw him off and then joined Monica and Malika in the kitchen, where she helped them prepare lunch.

When asked where she had worked before, she told them that this was her first job.

After lunch, Monica and Malika showed Mary the laundry room and taught her how to use the top-loading washing machine, which had to be filled with buckets of water because there was rarely any in the taps after eight o'clock in the morning.

Rumpi then took her shopping at a nearby market for new clothes. Mary picked out a few bright new kurtas, salwars and chunnis, some underwear and two pairs of chappals. Puri's wife also bought the new maidservant a hairbrush and various bathroom necessities.

The next stop was a small private health clinic run by Dr. (Mrs.) Chitrangada Suri, MD, who gave Mary an examination. The doctor found that she was suffering from dehydration, malnourishment, worms and lice, and immediately wrote out prescriptions for a couple of different medicines, vitamins, minerals and oral rehydration salts.

Talking in English so Mary would not understand, Dr. Suri also told Rumpi that the girl had tried cutting her wrists within the past few months and although the blood loss had probably been significant, she was young and seemed to have bounced back.

That evening, after Malika returned home to her family, Mary and Monica made the evening meal, did the washing up, took down the laundry from the roof, ate their dinner and then went for a walk in the neighborhood.

They passed many other servants working for other households out enjoying the cool evening. Monica stopped to chat and gossip and bought them both ice creams from a vendor with money that Rumpi had given them specifically for the purpose.

At 8:30, they sat down with Madam in the sitting room to watch *Kahani Ghar Ghar Ki*, one of India's most popular soaps. Set in the home of a respectable industrialist family, the serial nonetheless featured shocking twists and turns with ex-tramarital affairs, murders, conspiracies and kidnappings.

In the latest development, the main daughter-in-law had had a face-change operation and turned up as the wife of another man. But Monica said this was because the actress playing her had been fired after demanding a salary increase.

At nine o'clock, Rumpi said that Sahib was expected home and that it was time to sleep. A second mattress had been arranged on the floor in Monica's small room and lying on it was a new Bagha-Chall set. Mary's eyes lit up at the sight of the pitted wooden board and the bagful of pretty, polished stones, and she eagerly accepted Monica's challenge to a game.

Mary proved a demon player, easily beating her opponent.

"I'm village champion!" she said. "I could beat all the men if they would play me!"

The two of them then settled down for the night and Mary was soon fast asleep. But Monica lay awake for a while, wondering why her new roommate was so sad and why she wore her bangles to bed.

Around midnight, she awoke in a fright. Mary was sitting up, screaming.

Monica jumped up and turned on the light and then put her arms around her new roommate, telling her that it had only been a bad dream. Now awake, Mary fell back on her pillow and started crying.

"I lost him!" she sobbed. "I lost him!"

"Lost who?" asked Monica.

But she didn't answer and cried herself back to sleep.

Twenty-five

Flush called Puri the next morning to give him the name of Gupta's doctor.

"How did you find it so quickly?" he asked him.

"He went to see him before reaching office," answered the operative.

"What's the doctor's name?"

"Dr. Subhrojit Ghosh."

"Six-B Hauz Khas village," said Puri.

"You know him, Boss?"

"Indeed I know him," said the detective with a chuckle.

"Well, Boss, it's definitely Dr. Ghosh who prescribed Diet Coke testosterone. Afterward he went and bought more supplies."

"Good. Well done. Now pack up and get out of there."

"The operation is finished, Boss?"

"I'll be taking over," said Puri. "If Gupta is seeing Dr. Ghosh, there is only one meaning."

Puri drove to the leafy area of Hauz Khas in south Delhi, built amid the ruins of the ancient Delhi Sultanate.

Dr. Subhrojit Ghosh practiced in the basement of the same two-story house that his father had built and in which he had grown up.

It had been more than six months since Puri had been there, but he knew the place well. He and the doctor had met during one of his first cases. The erudite Dr. Ghosh had been recommended to him as an expert on a medical matter. In the years since then, Puri had turned to him on many occasions for advice and the two had spent many a pleasant evening sitting in the Gymkhana playing chess and talking politics.

Puri opened the gate and, instead of knocking on the front door, which led to where the family lived, he made his way down the side of the building to the clinic entrance.

After letting him in, Dr. Ghosh's assistant asked Puri to wait in reception. He sat down on the cane couch and picked up a copy of the Indian edition of *Hello!* The cover featured a leading Bollywood actress who had cropped up during one of Puri's more sensational matrimonial investigations a few years earlier—the Case of the Absconding Accountant. She had been an unknown then and in the process of bedding half the producers, directors and leading men in Mumbai.

The spread pictured her sitting on a white couch with her parents and her pet poodles. "Putting Family First" read the headline.

With a disdainful chortle, Puri tossed the magazine back onto the table just as the door to the doctor's office opened.

"Hello, old pal, this is a surprise!" said Dr. Ghosh with open arms. "Long time no hear, eh, Chubby? How long has it been?"

"Too long, actually," answered the detective, embracing his friend.

"Well, come in. You'll take some chai?"

"And some of those chocolate biscuits you keep hidden in your drawer."

Puri stepped into the office and sat down in one of the two chairs in front of Dr. Ghosh's desk.

"Extra sugar for my dear friend," Dr. Ghosh told his assistant before closing the door behind him and sitting down in the chair next to Puri.

"My God, it's good to see you, Chubby!" he said, giving him a friendly pat on the knee. "How are you?"

"World class," answered Puri. "You?"

"All fine. But you've been neglecting me for too long."

"I know, Shubho-dada." Shubho was short for Subhrojit; dada meant older brother in Ghosh's native Bengali. "But I'm nonstop these days. The city is going mental, I tell you. There's a crime wave like you wouldn't believe. Not a day goes by without some girl getting raped or a businessman getting kidnapped. You read about the shootings in CP?* Can you imagine? Goondas running around knocking off businessmen in daylight hours! Someone even took a pop at me just the other day."

"I heard. Rumpi called me. Said you're working too hard and your blood pressure's up. She asked me to have a word with you, Chubby. Frankly speaking, you *do* look tired."

"Oh, please, the woman is keeping me half starved. How am I meant to live on daal and rice?"

"You're off the chicken frankies, I take it?" said Dr. Ghosh, looking skeptical.

"Well, not entirely," admitted Puri with a roguish grin.

"Hmm, I thought as much. And when's the last time you had a holiday?"

"You're doing an examination, is it, Doctor?"

* Connaught Place, New Delhi.

"Tell me, Chubby. When was the last time you had even one day off?"

"I've no time for meter down, Shubho-dada," he said. "People look to me for help. Who else they can turn to? The cops? When the director general, Central Reserve Force, is getting his journalist lover stabbed and throttled to death? Do you know in NOIDA, where gangsters are nightly holding up commuters with country-made weapons, the constabulary's phones are cut off through nonpayment of bills? They're not even having petrol for their vehicles!"

"I know how bad it is, Chubby. Believe me. Only yesterday, Rajesh Uncle's house was broken into and they gagged and bound Sarita Auntie."

"By God," intoned Puri.

"Point is, it's not your responsibility. You're no caped crusader. This isn't Gotham City. It's Delhi. You can't clean it up single-handed."

"Someone's got to bloody well do something," said Puri, raising his voice. "Papa worked every day of his life to build a better India. I owe it to him to—"

"Your papa was a good man, we all know that," interrupted Dr. Ghosh. "No one with a shred of decency could ever doubt it. Never mind the whispers. Let them be damned! But it's not your responsibility to make amends for what happened. You've got to think of your own health and well-being. Let's face it, you're not getting any younger. Or slimmer! Think of Rumpi. She needs you, too."

The doctor's assistant brought in their tea on a tray and left it on the desk. Puri took his cup while Dr. Ghosh went behind his desk, opened the drawer and took out an already open packet of milk chocolate McVities digestives imported from the UK.

"I shouldn't give you these, but you'll only accuse me of

255

being tight," he said, handing Puri the packet. "There's only a few left anyway."

"I'm sure you're having more stashed away there some-where," chided the detective.

"Could be," said Dr. Ghosh with a wink.

They both bit into their biscuits and sipped their tea. By now the doctor was sitting behind his desk. On the wall hung his medical degree from the All India Institute of Medical Sciences and his certificate from Harvard.

"So, Chubby, I take it this is one of your professional visits. What is it this time? You need to consult me on some poison? Or you've got another crushed skull to show me?"

"Actually it's about one of your patients," said Puri.

"Oh?"

"Don't worry, Shubho-dada, I know all about your doctor confidentiality and all. No one's asking you to betray any secrets. Without naming names, I want to tell you what I know about a certain individual. If my theory is wrong, just say the word."

"Sounds fair enough, Chubby," said Dr. Ghosh.

"Your patient is male, thirty-one, a senior BPO-wallah. He's living in NOIDA in quite a fancy apartment. Has his own gym and talking toilet and all. Currently he is engaged and due to be married shortly. Quite the golfing fanatic, he is. He is worryingly obsessed with golf, in fact."

Dr. Ghosh leaned forward on his desk, picked up a Parker pen and started doodling on his blotting paper.

Puri switched to Hindi. "I've been studying his habits and they are extremely suggestive," he said. "At school he was a misfit, never had many friends and was prone to depression. Since then he has become extremely successful professionally, but he remains a private person in a way that very few Indians are. At the golf club, for example, he never uses the men's changing rooms, but comes home to shower. He never consumes alcohol, either, presumably because he needs to maintain control at all times."

Puri paused for a moment to finish his tea and reached for another biscuit, the last in the packet.

"You've been prescribing him testosterone," he continued. "I'm guessing he's been taking it since his mid-teens. Given your specialization, I would say that he has . . . well, let us call it a 'special problem' and it is something he has been keeping secret all his life."

Puri chose his next words carefully.

"The irony is that he has nothing to hide, and that is precisely the problem," he said.

The faintest of smiles played across Dr. Ghosh's lips.

"Chubby, might I ask why you need to know?" he asked.

"I've been retained by his fiancée's family. Now that I have discovered this man's secret, I'm concerned for her future. If she's not aware of the truth, then she is being deceived and I'm obligated to tell her."

The doctor nodded and, wetting the end of his finger, dipped it into the cluster of crumbs left in the packet and licked them off.

"It's certainly a *private* matter," he said. "All I can suggest is that you go and talk with the girl."

"Fine. In that case I'll arrange an interview," said the detective.

"Try to remember one thing, old pal," said Dr. Ghosh. "Love can move in mysterious ways."

The doctor stretched and looked at his watch.

"I've no more patients today. Shall we go to the Gym for a peg or two and a game of chess?"

"Think you can take me on, is it?" said Puri.

"As I recall, I won last time we played, Chubby."

"You had me at a disadvantage."

"How's that?"

"I was completely piss drunk."

Later that evening, Mary and Monica returned from their evening walk to find that Sahib had come home early.

Much to their frustration, he had parked himself in front of the TV and was watching the news; the prospect of being able to watch *Kahani Ghar Ghar Ki* now seemed remote. But Puri assured them he was only planning to watch the headlines and that afterward, the TV was all theirs.

Shyly, the two servant girls filed into the room and sat down on the floor at the foot of the couch, gazing up at the set in silence.

Five minutes later, the channel appeared to change (in fact Puri had pressed play on the VCR remote control) and a Hindi news report began about the Ajay Kasliwal case in Jaipur.

The pictures showed the High Court lawyer being led into court and Inspector Shekhawat telling the reporters that he could prove conclusively that the accused was guilty of killing his maidservant. The report, which was actually a number of reports Flush had edited together, cut to shots of the front of Raj Kasliwal Bhavan, then to a reporter saying that the maidservant, Mary, had been taken away in Kasliwal's Sumo and dumped on the Ajmer Road. There followed more scenes from outside the court taken on the first day of the trial, including a few shots of Mrs. Kasliwal. The report ended with a clip of Bobby addressing the cameras, insisting on his father's innocence.

Mary watched in wide-eyed disbelief, with her hand over

her mouth as if she was suppressing a scream. When Bobby appeared, she pointed at the TV and let out a startled cry. Then her head flopped forward onto her chest and she fainted.

Mary awoke to find herself lying on the blue leather couch with a cold hand towel on her forehead. Rumpi was sitting next to her; Mummy was nearby in an armchair doing some knitting.

"Are you all right, child?" asked Rumpi in a gentle, caring voice. "Try to rest; you've had a fright."

Mary stared up at her with dozy eyes and then took a sharp, frightened breath and sat bolt upright.

"Madam!" she exclaimed. "I saw him!"

"You saw who?" asked Mummy.

"Him!" she said, turning away from her and burying her face in one of the purple silk cushions.

Rumpi put a gentle hand on her shoulder, saying, "Please don't cry. Nothing is going to happen. Ask Mummy-ji, she will tell you."

"Yes, nothing bad will happen to you now," Puri's mother assured her, putting aside her knitting and joining Mary on the couch. "We will look after you. Now stop your crying and sit up and have some tea. It is freshly made. Come. Sit up now."

Mary did as she was told, rubbing her tear-stained face with the tissues that Mummy gave her.

"That's better, child," said Rumpi, handing her a cup of tea. "You are quite safe here. There's nothing to fear."

After Mary had drunk half her tea, Mummy asked her again what it was that had caused her to faint.

"If you tell us, then we can help you," said Rumpi.

"Madam, I cannot say," whispered Mary, looking frightened.

"Did it have something to do with what you were watching on television?" asked Mummy.

Mary bowed her head, staring down into her teacup. A few more tears fell into the brown milky liquid. Rumpi started stroking the back of the girl's head.

"Child, if you know anything about the case you saw on the TV, then you must tell us," she said. "It is very important. The man you saw, Shri Ajay Kasliwal, is accused of murdering a young maid who used to work in his house. She was called Mary—just like you. It is a serious charge. If he is convicted, Shri Kasliwal will spend the rest of his life in prison. There is even a possibility he will face the death penalty."

But Mary continued to stare down into her teacup.

"Dear me, child, this will not do," said Mummy, firmly. "Now you must finish your tea and tell us whether you worked for these people."

Dutifully, Mary drained the cup and Rumpi took it from her.

"Now, look at me, child," said Mummy.

Mary's brimming eyes met those of the older lady.

"Tell me. Did you work for this family?"

The maidservant's lower lip started to tremble. "Yes, I worked for them," she admitted, and burst into another fit of sobbing.

When it had passed, Mummy said, "If you are the same servant girl called Mary who worked for this family and you are alive, then Shri Kasliwal is innocent. You will have to go to Jaipur and help clear his name."

The suggestion engendered a terrified reaction. "No, madam, I cannot go!"

Rumpi took Mary's hand in her own.

"Would you want Shri Kasliwal to go to prison for a murder he didn't commit? He is innocent."

Mary hung her head again. "Madam, I cannot go," she repeated.

"You must," said Mummy. "It is your duty. You have no choice in the matter. The destiny of this man and his family is in your hands. But you will not have to face this alone. I will be with you."

Twenty-six

Before driving Mary and Mummy to Jaipur, Puri went to the Gymkhana Club to meet Brigadier Kapoor's granddaughter, Tisca.

Their meeting was set for eleven o'clock in the morning, but the detective arrived a few minutes early to peruse the noticeboard in reception. The lunch menu promised Toad in a Hole and Pinky Pudding. Three more names had been added to the list of membership applicants. And there was a new notification signed by Col. P. V. S. Gill (Ret.), pointing out that hard shoes were to be worn in the building at all times.

RUBBER SOULS CAUSE SQUEEKING AND ANNOYANCE, it stated.

Wearing his nonsqueaking shoes, which he'd changed into before entering the club, Puri made his way to the front lawn. There he ordered tea and cucumber sandwiches and sat down at the most secluded table he could find—a good twelve feet from a gaggle of aunties talking in loud voices about how much money they'd made on the stock market.

At the far end of the lawn, a mali was cutting the grass with a manual mower drawn by a buffalo.

"Uncle, I don't mean to be rude, but I don't have that

much of time," said Tisca Kapoor when she arrived, lowering herself into one of the cane chairs, which was barely wide enough to accommodate her wide girth. "Pappu Uncle asked me to meet you, but he wasn't at all clear about what it's about."

"Actually, my dear, I have come as a friend to discuss your proposed marriage," said Puri.

Tisca Kapoor rolled her eyes. "That's what I was afraid of," she said. "You've been asked by Brigadier dada-ji to talk some sense into me, no? Well you might as well save your breath, Uncle. Quite a number of aunties and uncles have tried before you. I love my grandpa very much and he's a national hero and all, but I've made my choice and I have my parents' blessing. That should be enough. *Buss.*"

"I'm asking for a few minutes of your time only," said the detective. "You are quite correct. Your grandfather asked me to look into this matter and, during my investigation, I've come across certain information. This information is of a most highly delicate nature, to say the least. I'm in no doubt—no doubt at all, actually—that if your grandfather came to know what I'm now knowing, the wedding would be most certainly getting over in a jiffy. That is why I have come to you first. So, please do me the courtesy of answering a few questions. I have your best interests at heart, actually."

"You're a private detective, is it—a kind of Indian Sherlock Holmes?" asked Tisca Kapoor.

"Sherlock Holmes was fictitious, but I am very much real," answered Puri. "Yes, I am a private detective. The best in India, actually, as many important personages will attest. They'll also tell you I am a man of great discretion."

He poured them both some tea.

"Now, tell me how came you to know Mr. Mahinder Gupta?"

Tisca Kapoor hesitated and then said with a sigh, "We studied together—him and me."

"At Delhi University, correct?"

"I see you've done your homework, Uncle."

"You were sweethearts, is it?"

"Just friends, actually."

"And then?"

"I stayed in Delhi; he went to Dubai. But we kept in touch. Last year he moved back to Delhi and we started spending time together. In August, we decided why not go the marriage way."

"You've not considered marrying before?"

"There've not been a lot of takers—not with my weight and all," she admitted.

"Why him all of a sudden?"

Tisca Kapoor smiled. "We've always got along, actually."

"So it's a love marriage, is it?"

"Certainly I love him, yes."

"And he loves you, my dear?"

Tisca Kapoor hesitated again. "I believe so," she answered. "Certainly he's very devoted and kind."

Puri drank half a cup of tea, stuffed a cucumber sandwich into his mouth and chewed.

"So I take it you won't be wanting a family," he said, his mouth half full.

"Why do you say that, Uncle?" she asked, sounding more cautious.

"You must be knowing about his problem."

"Problem? What problem? I don't know of any problem."

"It will do you little good to pretend, my dear," he said. "My investigation has been most thorough. I know *everything*. My only concern is you are not being deceived. If Mahinder Gupta has been one hundred percent honest, then

264

that is your business. Certainly, I would keep his secret safe from your grandfather."

She said nothing in response. Her expression betrayed both alarm and helplessness.

"It's my guess you've known what he is for many years. Perhaps he confided to you at university. Or you discovered it by chance," prompted Puri.

There was a long silence and then Tisca Kapoor said in a quiet voice, "It was at university. Everyone else teased me about my weight. None of the other boys gave me a second look. But Mahinder was always kind to me. We used to talk for hours and hours. About everything under the sun. I suppose I fell in love with him. One day I told him how I felt, but he ran from my room and after that he didn't talk to me for two weeks. Then, one day, he came to see me and told me that we could never be together. That was when he revealed his secret." She lowered her voice. "That was when he told me he was born a eunuch."

Tisca Kapoor's throat had gone dry and so Puri poured her a glass of water.

"You mustn't be embarrassed, my dear," he said. "In my profession I'm often called upon to put aside the detective and become the psychologist. There is little I have not heard."

Tisca Kapoor sipped the water gratefully and nodded.

"Understand, Uncle, this is something I've never told another living soul. Mahinder made me promise. He said his parents had hidden the truth from the world at his birth. Otherwise the hijras would have come and claimed him."

"They were right to do so," interjected Puri. "They would most certainly have taken him."

"That is why all through his childhood they kept it a secret. But also, had anyone at school ever found out, he would have been the laughingstock. That is why Mahinder has always been an extremely private person. He's kept himself to himself. But he's very sweet, I can assure you."

"So now all these years later you're getting married. Is it only for convenience sake?" asked Puri.

"I've always loved Mahinder," she said. "But, yes, partly it is for convenience. There's so much pressure to marry, Uncle. My mother has been after me for so long! Now at least she'll be off my back!"

"She'll be after you for grandchildren next," said Puri. "What will you do?"

"We'll adopt," she answered. "One girl and one boy."

"It's all decided, is it?" asked Puri

"We have it all planned out."

The detective nodded knowingly. "Well, it's as I suspected. Just I wanted to check you weren't being taken advantage of."

"So you won't tell anyone?"

"My dear, you can trust me on that score. Confidentiality is my watchword, actually," said Puri with not a little bravado.

Tisca Kapoor, soon to be Gupta, sighed with relief. "You're too kind, Uncle. I can't thank you enough."

The detective beamed with pride. "No need for thank you, my dear. I'm only doing my duty."

They walked back through reception and Puri saw her to her car. "What will you tell my grandfather?" Tisca Kapoor asked before driving away.

"I'll tell him you're betrothed to a good man," answered Puri, but it was not a conversation he was looking forward to.

Twenty-seven

Puri's Hindustan Ambassador reached the Jaipur courthouse at a quarter to five the following afternoon.

It was the first day of the Ajay Kasliwal "Maidservant Murder" trial and the proceedings had been under way for a couple of hours.

Outside the main entrance, the media had gathered in full force. Six uplink trucks were parked on the pavement, their satellite dishes emblazoned with the logos of the nation's English and Hindi 24-hour news channels. Eager, earnest reporters posed in front of cameras mounted on tripods, relaying live developments to tens of millions of potential viewers spread across the three million square kilometers that separated Kashmir from Kanyakumari. Photographers in sleeveless khaki jackets sat bent over their WiFi-enabled laptops transmitting the images they had captured an hour earlier of Kasliwal being led into court. Meanwhile a clutch of grizzled hacks milled around the chai stand, smoking laboriously, swapping disinformation and falling prey to their own self-deluding rumors.

Had any of them but known the identity of the shy, frightened young Jharkhandi woman who passed within a few feet of them, they would have surrounded her in much the same way Indian crows will ring and taunt a street cat if they spot it out in the open.

But the press-wallahs' scoop passed up the steps of the courthouse undetected.

Once inside, Puri led Mummy, who in turn was holding Mary by the hand, down the busy corridors until they reached the door of Court 6.

Already a crowd was waiting outside, all of them jostling for position and trying to cajole the peon on the door to let them in despite the sign that stated boldly, HOUSE FULL.

For once, Puri's powers of persuasion failed. The peon would not budge. "Naat possi-bal," he kept saying.

Mummy scolded her son for his failure.

"That's no way to go about things, Chubby," she said after he had been rebuffed for the third time. "How a son of mine ended up with cotton wool in his brain, I ask you? Evidently, a woman's touch is required, na. I will take care of it."

Puri bristled. He had had grave misgivings about bringing along Mummy. But he had been left with no choice. Mary needed a chaperon and Rumpi needed to be at home to oversee the preparations for Diwali.

"Mummy-ji, please. I told you, don't do interference. I will sort it out," Puri insisted.

"Chubby, when you'll accept you don't have power over everything, na? A helping hand is required from time to time."

Mummy's words echoed those spoken to Puri by Chanakya in the dream he'd had in his office; for once, he was dumbfounded.

"What did you say, Mummy-ji?" he asked her.

She tutted impatiently. "It's time to put away your pride, Chubby. I'm your mummy, after all. I've your best intentions at heart. Right now, a woman's touch is required. Now, you two go and sit. Jao!"

For once, Puri did as he was told and took a seat with Mary on a bench a few feet down the corridor.

With all the noise created by so many people coming and going from the various courtrooms, Puri was unable to make out what Mummy said to the peon on the door. But gradually the man's demeanor softened and then tears welled up in his eyes.

Finally he signaled to the detective that he could enter the court after all.

"What all you said to him?" asked Puri.

"No time for explanations, na," she answered. "Let us say mummies have their uses after all. Now go quickly. Might be he's changing his mind. So corrupt these people are. We'll wait right here."

Inside the courtroom, the gallery was packed with spectators, all of them sitting in silent, rapt attention to the cross-examination of Inspector Shekhawat by the defense counsel, Mr. K. P. Malhotra, who was living up to his reputation as a fearsome advocate.

"Inspector, you say you found bloodstains in the accused's Tata Sumo," he was saying. "But I put it to you that this blood could have come from anyone. Another passenger with a bleeding nose, perhaps."

"There is no doubt in my mind that the blood is the victim's," answered Shekhawat.

"Surely it is the responsibility of the police to offer proofs, is it not? Two and two should always equal four. Is that not correct, Inspector Shekhawat?"

"I can provide three witnesses who saw Ajay Kasliwal pull up in his Sumo and dump the servant girl's body on the Ajmer Road," he answered.

"We will come to that in a moment," said Malhotra. "But let us first consider these bloodstains. I put it to you . . ."

Malhotra lost his train of thought as he read the note Puri had managed to pass to him.

"Mr. Malhotra?" prompted the judge. "Are you with us?"

"My apologies, Your Honor," answered the lawyer, looking up from the note with a bewildered expression. "I have just been informed of what could well be an extremely dramatic breakthrough in my client's defense. Might I take a moment of the court's time to confer with one of my associates?"

"This is highly irregular, Mr. Malhotra, but I will grant you sixty seconds."

"Thank you, Your Honor."

Lawyer and detective exchanged a few quiet words and then Malhotra continued with the cross-examination, taking it in a new direction.

"Inspector Shekhawat, how can you be so sure that the Kasliwal family's maidservant Mary and the body found on the Ajmer Road are one and the same?" he asked.

"Two of her co-workers identified the victim from a photograph taken by the mortuary photographer. Three part-time employees at the house did the same."

"And if Mary was alive today—let us imagine she walked in here right now, for example—those same witnesses you mentioned would be able to identify her?"

Inspector Shekhawat replied confidently with an arrogant smirk. "Without doubt."

"I have no further questions for this witness," said Malhotra. "But I reserve the right to recall him."

Shekhawat was excused.

"Your Honor, I would like to call a new witness who, I feel confident, could save a great deal of the court's time," said Malhotra as the inspector resumed his seat in the gallery to watch the rest of the proceedings.

"It is teatime," grumbled the judge.

"Your Honor, if you will allow me five minutes, I believe we can clear up this whole matter."

The judge gave his consent.

"The defense calls Mary Murmu," announced Malhotra loudly.

"Who is Mary Murmu exactly?" asked the judge.

"Mary Murmu is the alleged victim, sir, the Kasliwal family's former maidservant," replied the lawyer nonchalantly.

Malhotra's answer elicited a collective gasp. Every head in the court turned to look at the main door.

In the dock, Ajay Kasliwal stood on his toes and craned his neck to see above the sea of heads.

The door opened again and Mary stepped through it, her head covered by her pallu and eyes cast down, with Mummy by her side. Together they walked slowly through the gallery until they reached the bench and the former maidservant was escorted to the witness stand.

"State your name for the record," she was told by Judge Madan in Hindi as Mummy took a seat nearby.

Mary mumbled a response.

"Speak up, girl, and show your face!" he ordered.

She stated her name again and pulled back her pallu.

"My name is Mary Murmu," she said clearly for all the court to hear.

"Liar!" screeched a woman's voice in the gallery.

Mrs. Kasliwal was standing, pointing an accusing finger at the witness.

"That's not her!" she screamed. And then she fainted and fell to the floor.

The courtroom descended into bedlam.

Twenty-eight

Facecream was crouched behind a shrub in the back garden of Raj Kasliwal Bhavan. It was nearly eight o'clock and pitch dark. She had been there for over an hour keeping watch at the rear of the house in accordance with Puri's orders—delivered by Tubelight when the Kasliwals were still in court.

"Boss will arrive around eight," he'd explained. "Munnalal's murderer is still at large. He might try to take out Boss. So be on your guard."

Facecream's position to the right of the servant quarters provided a commanding view of the garden and the interior of the sitting room. The curtains had not been drawn, which was unusual. But then, today was proving to be anything but routine.

At breakfast, Madam had been in an uncommonly pleasant and buoyant mood, talking confidently on the phone about how Mr. Malhotra was going to make short work of Shekhawat's case.

"It will soon be over," Facecream had overheard her tell someone.

But at around 6:30 in the evening, when her freed

husband had brought her back from the courts, Mrs. Kasliwal had been completely hysterical.

"Vish Puri will ruin us all!" she'd screamed. "Don't let him into the house!"

Shortly afterward, the family doctor had arrived and given Madam a sedative that had put her to sleep. His patient was not to be disturbed, he'd insisted. The arrest and trial had exhausted her.

In accordance with the doctor's instructions, Ajay Kasliwal had excused all the servants from their duties for the evening—apart from Jaya, who'd been told to make sure there was a ready supply of cold hand towels to cool Madam's forehead and ice for Sahib's whisky.

Facecream could see Jaya through the kitchen window now; she was taking something out of the fridge.

The other servants were all accounted for. Bablu had gone home. Kamat was in town watching a film. And the mali was stoned in his room, tendrils of sweet smoke drifting out of his open window.

Boss should be arriving any minute now, Facecream told herself.

If Munnalal's killer did make a play for him, he was likely to approach through the back way. But she was ready. Before taking up her position, she had checked her trip thread and it was still taut.

No one else had passed through the gap in the wall since Facecream had laid her trap and she was beginning to wonder if she would ever know the identity of the person who had tried her door that first night.

"Backside clear, over," she whispered into the minitransmitter Tubelight had smuggled into the grounds earlier along with the earpiece receiver.

"Frontside clear, also—over," responded Tubelight, who

was loitering on the main road in front of the entrance to Raj Kasliwal Bhavan.

Puri's Ambassador pulled into the driveway at 8:10. Tires crunched on gravel as the vehicle came to a halt.

"Boss has made penetration, over," reported Tubelight.

The detective stepped up to the front door and paused to take a deep breath.

Rarely had he found himself in such an unenviable position.

True, he had accomplished what he had been hired to do: against all the odds, he had managed to track down the missing servant and ensure that the spurious, half-baked charges against Ajay Kasliwal had been dropped. By any standard, it had been a brilliant piece of detective work—one that would rank in Puri's self-congratulating oratory in the years ahead.

But a great injustice had been done—not to mention a gruesome, premeditated murder—and Puri could not see it go unpunished no matter how devastating the truth might prove for his client.

The detective patted the outside pocket of his jacket, reassured by the feeling of his trusty .32 IOF pistol, and pulled the bell chain.

Footsteps clipped and echoed down the corridor inside the house. A lock was unlatched. The door opened and Ajay Kasliwal's face appeared in the gap.

"Puri-ji! Thank God you're here!" said the lawyer.

"How is she?" asked Puri.

"Sedated. The doctor's with her now. He says she's suffered some kind of mental breakdown. He's recommending she be kept here overnight and taken to his clinic in the morning for testing. She's been saying the craziest things, Puri-ji. Like you're out to ruin the family."

"I'm sorry it's come to this, sir," said the detective. "But I had to produce Mary in court. It was the only way."

"But I don't understand. Why did my wife insist it wasn't her?"

"I'll need to explain a few things," answered Puri. "But first things first. Something more urgent is there. Bobby has—"

"Yes, where is Bobby?" demanded Kasliwal, interjecting. "He was at the courthouse but disappeared. I couldn't find him anywhere and had to bring home his mother on my own. The media nearly ate us alive!"

"Sir, Bobby tried to—"

The detective's words were swallowed up by the sound of a vehicle tearing into the driveway and braking hard behind the Ambassador. It was a police Jeep. Inspector Shekhawat stepped out of it and opened one of the back doors. Bobby emerged into the light cast from the veranda.

"What's this?" exclaimed Kasliwal as the inspector led his handcuffed son to the door. "Bobby, are you all right? What's happened? Puri-ji, for God's sake, explain!"

"He was caught trying to enter Mary's room at the hotel where Mr. Puri and Mary are staying," butted in Shekhawat, officiously. "I was going to take him down to the station for questioning. But given Mr. Puri's cooperation in the past few hours, I agreed to do as the detective asked and bring him here first."

"Those handcuffs aren't necessary," said Puri. "He's not going to abscond."

The police-wallah appraised the prisoner like a fisherman trying to decide whether or not to put his young catch back into the river.

"I suppose you're right," he said, although he didn't sound convinced. "But I'm only willing to play along a little longer, Mr. Puri. I want to know what's been going on here. If I don't get some answers soon, then we'll do things my way."

Shekhawat unlocked the cuffs and Ajay Kasliwal ushered the party down the corridor.

Entering the sitting room, they found Mrs. Kasliwal lying deeply sedated on the couch, wrapped in a blanket. Her doctor, a man in his fifties with salt-and-pepper hair, was sitting at her side monitoring her pulse. At the sight of them, he made an irritated gesture.

"What's this, Ajay-ji?" he hissed, standing up. "I said no visitors. She's not to be disturbed."

Walking around the couch, he addressed Puri and Shekhawat directly.

"You must leave immediately! She's extremely sick. Ajay-ji, I don't know who these gentlemen are . . ."

"I'm Inspector Rajendra Singh Shekhawat," said the inspector, flashing his badge. "And this is Vish Puri, a private detective. Who are you exactly?"

"I'm Dr. Chandran, Mrs. Kasliwal's personal physician," he answered haughtily.

"Dr. Sunil Chandran, is it?" asked Puri.

"Yes, that's right."

"I understand you are Madam Kasliwal's rakhi-brother. Is that so?"

"Yes, we grew up together. We're like brother and sister. Now, what's all this about?"

"There's been a murder and we're here to find out who did it," Shekhawat answered.

"Well, now's not the time. She's had a mental breakdown. I've seen it before. The stress causes a kind of brain fever. You'll have to come back another time."

"I'm afraid it won't wait," said Puri. "Why don't you pour

yourself a drink, Doctor-sahib, and sit down? I'm glad to see you, actually. You've saved us time in coming here."

"But I'm finished here for the time being."

"You're *finished*, that is for sure, Doctor-ji," said Puri sternly. "Now sit down."

"I'll do nothing of the sort!" shouted the doctor. "Ajay-ji, I'm leaving. Take Savitri's temperature every hour and let me know of any change. You'll be able to reach me on my mobile."

Dr. Chandran gathered up his stethoscope and bag and made for the door. But he found his exit blocked by Shekhawat who had one hand on the revolver peeking out of his shoulder holster.

"Do as Mr. Puri says, Doctor-sahib," said the inspector, his muscular jaw rigid with determination.

Puri positioned himself by the fireplace. Bobby knelt next to his mother, a mixture of anger and anxiety clouding his young face. His father stood expectantly, looking at the detective for answers. The doctor was sitting involuntarily in one of the armchairs with his arms crossed in defiance. The inspector guarded the door.

"The case has been a complicated one and required all my skills as a detective, but fortunately I was up to the task," began Puri.

Shekhawat rolled his eyes and looked at his watch.

"Mr. Puri, please, I don't have all night," he interrupted impatiently. "Who killed Munnalal?"

The detective bristled at the younger man's impertinence. If there was one thing he couldn't stand, it was having people butt in while he was trying to conclude a case. This was his moment and he would not be rushed.

"During my many years of service and duty I have learned

not to share information about ongoing cases with my clients," he went on. "Often it is important they remain in the dark. This gives the impression that I am sitting idle. In reality, nothing could be further from the truth. Vish Puri does not do meter down. Thus, on the very day Munnalal met his fate, I went to his residence."

Puri paused to clear his throat and then continued.

"An extremely unpleasant and most slippery fellow he was all round. There and then, I confronted him with certain evidence. Namely, I told him I knew it was he who carried Mary's body from her room and placed it in the back of Kasliwal-ji's Sumo on August twenty-first night."

"Mr. Puri, please," said Bobby, suddenly snapping out of his reverie. "What's this about Mary's body?"

"Allow me to explain. The maidservant Jaya saw Munnalal carrying Mary from her room to your father's vehicle and placing her inside. At the time, she assumed he had murdered her. Terrified, she told no one."

"But what happened to Mary?" asked Bobby.

"This same question I put to Munnalal. He did not deny taking her away. But he denied totally murdering the girl. He said she attempted suicide only. Afterward he drove her to the Sunrise Clinic."

At the mention of the clinic's name, Bobby and his father both turned and stared hard at Dr. Chandran. "That's your place, Doctor-sahib," said the elder Kasliwal.

"I'm well aware of that," replied the doctor. "But I don't remember any girl. Clearly, this Munnalal was lying. The detective himself called him a 'slippery fellow.' "

"Munnalal was a first-class Charlie, that is for sure," said Puri. "But for once, he was not lying. Your night security guard remembers Mary most clearly, Doctor-sahib. He says after her admittance, you returned to the clinic. Must have been around midnight. Thus it seems you cared for her yourself."

"I've no idea what you're talking about," said the doctor dismissively.

"Then why is it, the following night, you took Mary by taxi to the train station?" he said. "Knowing full well she was too weak to make the journey and might easily die along the way, you bought her a ticket on a local train to Ranchi. A coolie identified you at the scene."

By now Bobby was glaring at Dr. Chandran contemptuously. "Uncle is . . . is this true?" he asked him.

"Not one word of it, beta. Don't listen to him. He's trying to blacken the family name, divide and conquer like the British."

"He's doing nothing of the sort," snapped Kasliwal. "But what I don't understand is how a maidservant tried killing herself in my own home and I knew nothing about it?"

"Sir, you are never around. Your work keeps you at the office, and at night you are out a good deal. You're a very *sociable* individual, we can say. Running of the house, with servants and all, is Madam's responsibility. Thus the facts were kept secret from you.

"But to continue," added Puri, urgently, before anyone else could get a word in, "after dropping Mary at Sunrise Clinic, Munnalal returned here to Raj Kasliwal Bhavan. In the wee hours, Mary's blood was washed away and her possessions taken. The kitchen knife she used Munnalal threw over the back wall from where it was recovered and is now in my possession. Only things left behind were two wall posters and a few stones."

Puri modestly revealed his foresight in having Mary's stones analyzed and how they had led him to Jadugoda. But his client could not have been less interested.

"What about Munnalal? Why was he murdered?" Kasliwal asked.

"Just I was coming to that, sir. You see, he was an instrument only. Some other person did direction of his actions. When he found Mary bleeding to death in her room, he called that person to ask what to do. Thus he was ordered to rush the girl to the hospital. But along the way Munnalal got thinking. For him, Mary's suicide attempt was a golden egg. Such a man knows many secrets. He stores gossip for rainy days. Thus he understood why Mary tried the suicide and why it had to be hushed up. Next day, he demanded compensation to the tune of many lakhs."

"But that can only mean . . ." said Kasliwal.

Bobby finished his sentence in a flat monotone. "Ma. It had to be Ma."

There was a long silence. Every pair of eyes in the room save Mrs. Kasliwal's were now riveted on the detective.

"The boy is correct: it was your wife, sir," said Puri. "She told Munnalal to take Mary to the Sunrise Clinic and asked her rakhi-brother, Dr. Chandran, to patch her up and send her on her way."

"Puri-ji, I've been married to this woman for twenty-nine years and I can't believe she'd do that." Turning to Dr. Chandran, he implored him, "Doctor-sahib, tell me this isn't true!"

"I tell you, Ajay-ji, every word is a filthy lie." The doctor sneered. "We should call Mr. Malhotra and ask him to come here immediat—"

"Dr. Chandran, your mobile phone records show you made four calls to Mrs. Kasliwal on the night Munnalal was murdered," interrupted Puri. "One was twenty-five minutes after he was killed."

"We've always talked a lot. She was having trouble sleeping and—"

"Oh, shut up!" broke in Ajay Kasliwal. "I want to hear the rest. Carry on, Puri-ji; tell us what happened."

The detective went on to explain that, minutes after his meeting with Munnalal, the former driver had called Mrs. Kasliwal. He'd asked for more money to buy Puri's silence. She in turn had asked him to come to the house after dark. That evening, he'd set off by auto. Following behind on his motorcycle was Bobby, who wanted to ask Munnalal if he knew of Mary's whereabouts.

"Bobby followed him all the way into the empty property behind the house only moments after Munnalal was murdered," said Puri. "Stumbling upon the body in the dark, he got blood on him and ran from the scene." Shocked and totally confused, Bobby passed the time since mostly in his room. Must be he was asking himself many unanswered questions about what all happened to Mary and why someone killed Munnalal. Also he was scared he'd get accused of doing the murder. But he was never Vish Puri's suspect."

"Well if it wasn't Bobby who murdered Munnalal, who was it?" demanded Shekhawat.

"From the wound, I could make out it was a professional. He surprised Munnalal from behind. One hand drove the knife into the neck, the other was placed over the mouth— hence there was so much of betel juice on Munnalal's lips and chin. Must be you came to the same conclusion, Inspector?"

"Yes, of course," lied Shekhawat, shifting uneasily. "It was obvious. But you assured me earlier today you knew the identity of the killer!"

"Most certainly I know, Inspector," said Puri. "He is one hit man called Babua."

Bobby piped up, "But, Uncle, are you saying Ma . . . she had . . . she had Munnalal . . . *murdered* . . ."

"It is hard to believe she could not have known. But there's no conclusive evidence connecting her to Babua. Dr. Chandran took out the contract. He made a number of calls to the killer in the hours before the murder."

"How do you know that?" asked Shekhawat.

Puri hesitated before answering. "We all have our ways and means, Inspector."

"But for God's sake, why?" broke in Kasliwal. He was gripping the back of the couch where his wife lay. "Why, Puri-ji? None of this makes any sense!"

"Unfortunately, it makes perfect sense, sir," answered the detective calmly. "An Indian mother will do almost anything to protect her son and his reputation."

There was another long silence. And then Bobby broke into deep, shameful sobs.

"Papa, I . . . I should have told you," he said. "But I . . . I didn't know what had happened. I . . . I never meant . . . for *any* of this . . ."

"*What* happened, Bobby? I want to hear it from you. Tell me once and for all," said Kasliwal, now standing over his son.

"Papa, I . . ."

"Out with it!"

The boy swallowed hard.

"It was this summer, before . . . before I went to London. Most days I . . . I was here alone in the house studying . . . and Mary . . . well, you see, Papa, sometimes we'd, um, talk. She was . . . so . . . so *nice*, Papa. And *smart*. We used to sit together . . . in my room. I . . . I was teaching her to read and write and we used to play Bagha-Chall. She always used to beat me."

283

Bobby's lower lip was trembling. "Well, one day . . . you see . . . I loved her, Papa . . ."

Ajay Kasliwal held up a hand to silence his son.

"I understand," he said. He turned and addressed the detective. "I take it my wife found out, Puri-ji."

"About a month after Bobby left for London, Mary discovered she was pregnant," said Puri.

"Pregnant?" exclaimed Bobby.

"Desperate, she went to Madam. But the idea of a servant—a dirty tribal being with her son disgusted her. She abused Mary verbally, threatened her and ordered her to leave the house immediately."

". . . And so that poor girl took a knife from the kitchen, went to her room and cut her wrists," murmured Ajay Kasliwal.

Facecream watched the evening's events unfold through the French windows of the sitting room.

First Boss appeared with Inspector Shekhawat and Bobby. Then Boss gave one of those long-winded soliloquies he so enjoyed. And finally, Ajay Kasliwal broke down in tears and attacked the doctor, punching him in the face.

Bobby, Shekhawat and Boss tried to restrain him and in the confusion, the latter was knocked over.

Now, Facecream watched as the inspector clapped a pair of handcuffs on the doctor and led him away.

Puri came and stood silhouetted by the French windows nursing his bruised cheek, while Bobby sat with his distraught father.

Facecream decided to stay put. Munnalal's murderer was still at large, after all.

Another five minutes passed. Jaya appeared again in the

kitchen, standing at the sink, her face framed in the window. Suddenly, in the quiet night, Facecream heard the sound of the bell tinkle inside her room.

Someone had come through the gap in the wall.

A twig snapped underfoot. And then a man of average height appeared around the corner of the servant quarters carrying something long and narrow in one hand. He stopped, looked furtively from left to right, and then set off across the garden, sticking to the shadows on the left side of the lawn.

Facecream sprang forward and raced after him, her bare feet moving nimbly and silently over the grass.

She covered the distance that separated the two of them in just a few seconds and tackled the man from behind. He went down flat on his face and, in a flash, she pinned him to the ground, pulling back one of his arms.

The intruder let out a cry of agony and begged to be let go. His pleas brought Jaya running from the kitchen.

"Seema, what are you doing?" she cried. "Have you gone mad? Let him go!"

"No, Jaya, stand back!" insisted Facecream. "This man is dangerous! He killed Munnalal!"

"Dangerous? That's Dubey! He's a rickshaw-wallah! He's my . . . friend."

"You're sure?"

"Of course I'm sure! He wants to marry me."

Facecream released Dubey and the poor, shaken man stood up. He was still clutching a red rose that he'd brought for Jaya, but it had been badly crushed.

"I'm so sorry. I thought you were . . ." said Facecream.

But the rickshaw-wallah had taken to his heels with Jaya hurrying after him.

• • •

Ten minutes later, Puri stood with Shekhawat next to his Jeep in the driveway. On the backseat, in handcuffs, sat Dr. Chandran. He was glaring with venomous eyes at his captors through the window.

"You think he'll give her up?" asked the inspector.

"I doubt it," said Puri. "To do so would be to admit his guilt. He'll claim he's been framed, try to buy off or intimidate the witnesses. His trial will go on for years. It takes time to put away a man with his kind of connections."

"And her? She goes unpunished?"

"Oh no, Inspector. It is all over for her. She might have escaped prison, but no human being ever escapes punishment. One way or another, justice is always served. All of us must answer to the God eventually."

Puri rubbed his stomach and grimaced.

"Personally I'm now answering for the kachoris I ate at lunch," he added with a smile.

Shekhawat remained stony faced and aloof. His pride was too badly wounded. And he was not about to admit his mistakes—not here and now, and certainly not in his official report.

"Well, I'll be going," he said. "There's the killer Babua to track down and I've got a good idea where to find him."

"Oh, there's no need, Inspector," said Puri airily. "Didn't I tell you, I've got him locked in the trunk of my Ambassador?"

For once, Shekhawat was visibly dumbstruck.

"There?" he asked, pointing to the car, his eyebrows knitted together.

"That's right, Inspector. One advantage with Ambassadors is they have large secure trunks."

"But . . . ?"

"I picked him up this afternoon after tracing his mobile phone. Let me show you."

They walked over to the car and Handbrake opened the back. Inside lay a burly man, bound and gagged, his eyes defiant and angry.

"Allow me to present one Om Prakash, alias Babua," said Puri triumphantly. "A right bloody goonda if ever there was one."

Twenty-nine

At the end of every big case, Puri dictated all the details of his investigation to his personal secretary Elizabeth Rani, who could do speed typing.

He did so for two reasons.

Firstly, it was not uncommon for trials to drag on for years, sometimes decades. So it was imperative to keep a detailed record of events, which the detective could refer to when he was called upon to give evidence.

And secondly, Puri was planning to leave all his files to the National Archive because he was certain future generations of detectives would want to study his methods and achievements.

The detective also liked to entertain the idea that someday a writer would come along who would want to pen his biography. He had thought of the perfect title: CONFIDENTIALITY IS MY WATCHWORD. And what a spectacular Bollywood film it would make. Puri's favorite actor, Anupam Kher, would play the lead, and Rekha would be perfect for the part of Rumpi. Her screen persona would be that of a good, homely woman who also happened to be a talented and alluring exotic dancer.

"Sir, one thing I don't understand," said Elizabeth Rani after Puri had finished relating the twists and turns in the Case of the Missing Servant. "Who was the dead girl found on the Ajmer Road?"

Puri's secretary always asked such elementary questions. But he didn't mind spelling it out for her. Not everyone could have a mind as sharp as his, he reasoned.

"She's just one of dozens upon dozens of personages who go missing across India every year," he explained. "No doubt we'll never know her name. So many girls are leaving the villages and traveling to cities these days. And so many are never returning. Just they're turning up dead on railway tracks, in canals, and getting raped and dumped from vehicles. With their near and dear so far away, no one is there to identify the bodies. I tell you, frankly speaking Madam Rani, it is an epidemic of growing proportions."

Elizabeth Rani moved her head from side to side mournfully.

"Such a sad state of affairs, sir," she said. "Thank the God there are gentlemen such as yourself to protect us."

"Most kind of you, Madam Rani!" Puri beamed.

The two of them were sitting in the detective's office: he behind his desk; she in front of it with a laptop computer. Elizabeth Rani saved the document in which she had typed his dictation and closed the screen.

"Sir, one other thing," she said as she stood from her chair to leave.

"Yes, Madam Rani," said Puri, who had been expecting more questions.

"You said Mary got pregnant, sir. But what happened to the baby?"

"Sadly, she lost it on the train to Ranchi."

"That poor girl," commiserated Elizabeth Rani. "How she has suffered. Is there any hope for her and Bobby?"

"Sadly, there is no Bollywood ending. Mary refused to see him. Most likely, it is for the best. Too much hurt is there, actually. The poor girl has suffered greatly. This morning we brought her to Delhi, Rumpi and I. We've made arrangements for her to start work with Vikas Chauhan's family. Ajay Kasliwal has also promised to pay for her dowry so she might one day go the marriage way. He's being most generous and appreciative, I must say."

"And Bobby, sir?"

The detective rubbed the end of his moustache between his fingers in a contemplative fashion before answering.

"Seems like he and his mother will never speak again, Madam Rani," said Puri sadly. "He's sworn he'll not so much as be in the same room with the woman."

His secretary sucked in her breath and said, "Hai, hai."

"Mrs. Kasliwal's actions were certainly deplorable. Which one of us could forgive her in our hearts? But Bobby's actions, although innocent, were hardly decent. Such a well brought up and educated young man should have known better, actually. There is a right and proper place for physical relations and it is between husband and wife only. When young people go straying outside those boundaries, there can only be hurt and misfortune."

"Quite right, sir," said Elizabeth Rani.

Puri tucked a pen he'd been using into the outside pocket of his safari suit next to two others.

"India is modernizing, Madam Rani, but we must keep our family values, isn't it? Without them, where would we be?"

"I hate to think, sir," she said.

"Well, Madam Rani, that will do for now. Place the file

290

in the 'conclusively solved' cabinet. Another successful outcome for Most Private Investigators, no?"

"Right away, sir."

Elizabeth Rani returned to her desk, closing the door to his office behind her.

Puri leaned back in his chair and looked up at the portraits of Chanakya and his father on the wall, both of them wreathed in garlands of fresh marigolds. Putting the palms of his hands and fingers together, he respectfully acknowledged them both with a namaste.

With Diwali, the festival of lights, the biggest holiday in the Hindu calendar, due to begin the next day, Puri gave his staff the afternoon off and asked Handbrake to drive him to the airport to pick up his youngest daughter, Radhika.

He could hardly contain his excitement as he waited outside the arrivals hall. It had been three months since he'd seen his chowti baby, the longest they'd ever been separated. He'd missed her sorely.

As the other passengers emerged from the building, pushing trolleys piled high with baggage, and taxi-wallahs vied for their custom, the detective stood up on his toes, trying to peer over the heads of the crowd gathered around the exit.

When he finally spotted Radhika, her young, eager face searching for his among the banks of strangers, he felt a lump form in his throat and cried out his nickname for her: "Bulbul! Bulbul!"

"Hi, Papa!"

Grinning from ear to ear, she skipped forward, flung her arms around him and gave him a kiss and a big hug.

"By God, let me look at you," he said, holding her by the shoulders and giving her a fond, appraising look. "So thin you've become, huh! They're not feeding you at that college or what? Come! Mama's making all your favorites and she can't wait to see you. Mummy-ji's at home, also. Both your sisters are arriving tomorrow."

He took hold of her trolley and they headed into the car park to find Handbrake and the Ambassador.

"So, all OK?" he asked.

And from that moment until they reached the house, Radhika regaled him with everything that had happened to her in the past few months.

"Papa, you know we've been learning . . ."

"Papa, you'll never guess what my roommate Shikha said . . ."

"Papa, something amazing happened . . ."

"Papa, did you know that . . ."

Puri sat basking in her youthful enthusiasm and innocence, succumbing to her infectious laughter. Occasionally, he reacted to her anecdotes by saying things like, "Is it?" and "Don't tell me!" and "Wonderful!" But for the most part, he just sat and listened.

By the time they pulled up in front of the gates and Handbrake honked the horn, he felt that the weight he'd been carrying on his shoulders—the weight he'd become so used to—had vanished.

Like millions of other Hindu, Sikh and Jain households across India, every inch of Puri's house had been cleaned ahead of Diwali. In the kitchen, all the cupboards had been emptied and the shelves wiped down. The marble floors had been scrubbed and scrubbed again. Dusters had swished away cobwebs. Special lemon and vinegar soap had left all the taps, sinks and mirrors gleaming. And all the wood in the house had been lovingly polished.

The exterior wall that surrounded the compound had been whitewashed and a cracked tile on the porch replaced.

Rumpi had also been busy making preparations for entertaining all the family members and friends who were expected to visit them over the next few days.

Gift boxes of dried fruit, almonds, cashews and burfi had been packed and wrapped, and then stacked in one corner of the kitchen. Monica and Malika had been preparing huge pots of chhole and carrot halva, and deep frying batches of onion and paneer pakoras. And Sweetu had been sent to the market to buy bagfuls of "perfect ice," savoury matthis and oil for the diyas.

Puri's remit (he knew it only too well but Rumpi reminded him more than once) was to buy all the liquor, firecrackers and puja offerings—in the form of coconuts, bananas and incense—that would be made to Lakshmi, the goddess of wealth.

It was also his responsibility to pick up new decks of playing cards and some poker chips. No Punjabi Diwali could be complete without a bit of friendly gambling. And if this holiday was anything like last year's, they were in for at least one all-night session of teen patta.

After dropping Radhika at home, Puri went to the nearest market. He found it packed with people rushing around buying last-minute items. The shops were decked with colored lights and tinsel decorations. Devotional music blared from the temples. Every few seconds, bottle rockets whizzed and exploded overhead.

He returned after dark to find Rinku's Range Rover—license plate 1CY—parked in the driveway.

Before entering the house, Puri gave Handbrake his Diwali bonus and enough money to get an auto to Old Delhi railway station. By mid-morning the following day, he would be home with his wife and baby daughter in their village in the hills of Himachal.

"Thank you, sir," said the driver, beaming with happiness. "But, sir, one thing you promised me. The first rule of detection. What is it?"

Puri smiled. "Ah yes, the first rule," replied the detective. "It is quite simple, actually. Always make sure you have a good aloo parantha for breakfast. Thinking requires a full stomach. Now you'd better be off."

Puri saw Handbrake to the gate and made his way inside the house.

"So we've got out first visitor, is it?" he shouted as he stepped into the hallway.

He found Rumpi, Mummy and Radhika sitting with Rinku having tea and sharing platefuls of pakoras.

"Happy Diwali, Chubby!" Rinku said, greeting Puri with a hug and the usual matey slap on the back.

"You too, you bugger. Let me fix you something stronger."

"No, no, I've got to be off," said Rinku. "The traffic to Punjabi Bagh will be murder."

"Just one peg! Come on!" insisted Puri.

"OK, just one," replied Rinku who never needed much convincing when alcohol was on offer. "But you're going to get me into trouble."

"Then we'll be even!"

The detective poured both Rinku and himself generous glasses of Scotch, and soon they were telling Sardaar-ji jokes and splitting their sides with laughter.

Forty minutes and several more pegs later, Rinku stood to leave.

"Baby Auntie, have you seen my car?" he asked Mummy, his eyes twinkling.

"No, I must see what everyone is talking about," she answered, gamely. "Just I'll fetch my shawl. Such cold weather we're having, na?"

Rinku said good-bye to the rest of the family at the door and he and Mummy stepped outside.

"I've taken care of Chubby's little problem," he said in a hushed voice as they walked over to his Range Rover. "Those two gentlemen won't be troubling him again."

"I heard Inspector Inderjit Singh is suspended pending an inquiry into illegal activities," said Mummy.

"And it seems his friend has dropped plans for building a new office block," added Rinku.

"Just they're saying the market is doing slowdown, so it is best, na," said Mummy.

Rinku stooped down to touch her feet and wished her a happy Diwali.

"You too," she said. "And, thank you, beta. I'm very much appreciative."

She waved him off and returned to the house.

"What were you two talking about, Mummy-ji?" asked Puri, who had been watching them closely from the doorway. "It can't be such a long chat about a car?"

"Just I've been discussing one investment proposition."

"With Rinku?" The detective laughed. "What's he trying to sell you? The President's Palace?"

"Don't do sarcasm, Chubby. Rinku has given me one hot tip. Just some land is coming up and we're in discussion."

"You watch your back, Mummy-ji. He's a slippery fellow," said the detective, closing the door behind them.

"Oh, Chubby, when will you learn, na? Just I can take care of myself. Now, come. Let's play cards. Tonight I'm feeling very much lucky!"

Glossary

AACHAR | a pickle. Most commonly made of carrot, lime, garlic, cauliflower, chili or unripe mango cooked in mustard oil and spices.

"ACCHA" | Hindi for "OK," "good" or "got it."

ADIVASI | literally "original inhabitants." These Indian tribals comprise a substantial indigenous minority of the population of India.

AGRAWAL | a community in India, traditionally traders.

ALOO PARANTHA | flat Indian wheat bread stuffed with a potato and spice mixture, pan-fried and served with yogurt and pickle. Often eaten for breakfast.

ANGREZ | Hindi for "English" or "British." Also means "Englishman" or "Britisher." Angrez noun, Angrezi adjective.

ASHRAMAS | the four phases of a Hindu's life.

AUTO | short for autorickshaw, a three-wheeled taxi that runs on a two-stroke engine.

AYAH	a domestic servant role that combines the functions of maid and nanny.
"AY BHAI"	Hindi for "hey, brother."
BAGHA-CHALL	a strategic, two-player board game that originates in Nepal. The game is asymmetric in that one player controls four tigers and the other player controls up to twenty goats. The tigers "hunt" the goats while the goats attempt to block the tigers" movements.
"BHAANCHHOD"	Punjabi expletive meaning "sister fucker."
BABA	father.
BABU	a bureaucrat or other government official.
"BADIYA"	Urdu word for "wonderful," "great."
BAKSHISH	a term used to describe tipping, charitable giving and bribery.
BAHU	daughter-in-law.
BALTI	a bucket.
BANIA	a trader or merchant belonging to the Indian business class.
BARSAATI	from *barsaat*, meaning rain. A barsaati is a room at the top of the house used for storage or servant's quarters that bears the brunt of the falling rain. Today, barsaatis in posh Delhi neighborhoods rent for hundreds of dollars per month.
BASTIS	colonies of makeshift houses for the poor.
BATCHMATES	students who attended the same school, college, or military or administrative academy.

BETA	"son," or "child," used in endearment.
BHAI	brother.
BHANG	a drink popular in many parts of India made by mixing cannabis with a concoction of almonds, spices, milk and sugar.
BHAVAN	home or building.
BHINDI	okra.
BIDI	Indian cigarette made of strong tobacco hand-rolled in a leaf from the ebony tree.
BINDI	from the Sanskrit *bindu*, "a drop, small particle, dot." Traditionally a dot of red color applied in the center of the forehead close to the eyebrows worn by married Hindu women, or by any girl or woman as a decoration, often colored to match the clothes they are wearing.
BUCKS	as in America, but used to mean rupees instead of dollars.
BURFI OR BARFI	a sweet made from condensed milk and cooked with sugar until it solidifies. Burfi is often flavored with cashews, mango, pistachio and spices and is sometimes served coated with a thin layer of edible silver leaf.
"BUSS"	Hindi for "stop" or "enough."
CAR-SAAF-WALLAH	*Wallah* is a generic term in Hindi meaning "the one" or "he who does." Car-saaf-wallah is typical Hinglish, a mixture of Hindi and English, in this case meaning "he who washes the car."

"CHALLO"	Hindi for "let's go."
CHAI	tea.
CHANNA	spicy masala chickpeas, also known as *chhole*.
CHANNA BHATURA	Indian fried bread, very oily, chewy (and delicious!), served with curried chickpeas.
CHAPPATIS	see roti.
CHARAS	handmade hashish, very potent.
CHARPAI	literally "four feet." A charpai is a woven string cot used throughout northern India and Pakistan.
CHAPPALS	Indian sandals usually made of leather or rubber.
CHAT	a savory, spicy, tangy street food common to northern and western India. Chat comprises crispy fried papris or savory biscuits, topped with yogurt, spices, sliced onions, mango powder, and tamarind and green chili chutneys.
CHAVAL	rice.
CHHATRIS	literally "umbrella" or "canopy," a dome-shaped pavilion commonly used as an element of Indian architecture.
CHHOLE	see channa.
CHIKAN KURTA	Kurta is a long shirt worn by men and women in Pakistan and northern India. Chikan refers to a unique embroidery style from Lucknow, believed to have been introduced by the emperor Jehangir's wife, Nur Jehan. Traditionally,

it uses white thread on white muslin cloth.

CHOWKIDAR	watchman.
CHOWTI BABY	in Hindi, *chowti* means "little."
CHUDDIES	Punjabi for underpants.
CHUNNI	long scarf worn with drawstring trousers and a knee-length kameez or kurta.
CHURIDAAR PAJAMA	a style of leg-hugging drawstring pajamas with folds that fall around the ankles like a stack of churis, or bracelets.
CRORE	a unit in the Indian numbering system equal to 10 million.
CROREPATI	an extremely rich person, a multimillionaire.
COUSIN-SISTER	a colloquialism emphasizing that in India a first cousin is like a sibling.
DAAL	spiced lentils.
DABBA	a lunchbox, usually round and made of stainless steel with several compartments.
DACOIT	a member of an Indian or Burmese armed robber band.
DALITS	untouchables, low caste; means "suppressed" or "crushed."
DANDASANA POSITION	in yoga the simplest form of the sitting position.
DHABA	roadside eatery, popular with truck drivers in northern India, which serves spicy Punjabi food.

DHARMA	a Sanskrit term that refers to a person's righteous duty or any virtuous path.
DHOBI	person who washes clothes.
DISHDASHA	an ankle-length garment similar to a robe worn in the Arab world, most commonly in the Gulf states.
DIYAS	a lamp usually made of clay with a cotton wick dipped in vegetable oil.
DOSA	a South Indian crêpe made from rice and lentils.
DOUBLE-ROLE	one actor often playing two opposing roles (good brother/bad brother) in Indian films.
DOUBLE ROTI	sliced white bread.
DUPATTA	in women's dress, a scarf usually worn over the head and shoulders, made of cotton, georgette, silk, chiffon, etc.
GHEE	clarified butter.
GOBI	cauliflower.
GOONDAS	thugs or miscreants.
GORA/GORI	a light-skinned person; the term is often used in reference to Westerners.
"HAAN-JI"	Hindi for "yes, sir/madam."
"HAI!"	an exclamation indicating surprise or shock.
HAKIM	a Muslim physician.
HALDI	turmeric, deep orange-yellow spice made from the rhizomes of the turmeric plant.
HALVA	a dessert made from wheat flour,

semolina, lentils or grated carrots mixed with sugar and ghee and topped with almonds. Often served in Hindu and Sikh temples as blessed food for worshippers to eat following prayers.

HIJRA   a member of "the third sex," neither man nor woman. Most are physically male or intersex (formerly known as hermaphrodites). Some are female. Hijras usually refer to themselves as female and dress as women. Although they are usually referred to in English as "eunuchs," relatively few have any genital modifications. A third gender has existed in the subcontinent from the earliest records, and was clearly acknowledged in Vedic culture, throughout the history of Hinduism, as well as in the royal courts of Islamic rulers.

HINDUSTAN AMBASSADOR   until recently India's national car. The design, which has changed little since production started in 1957, is similar to the British Morris Oxford.

INCHARGE   noun meaning "boss."

JAINS   a small but influential and generally wealthy religious minority with at least 10 million followers.

"JALDI KARO"   Hindi for "hurry up."

JALEBI   pretzel-shaped, bright orange sweet made of fried batter soaked in sugar syrup.

JAO!   "Go!"

JEERA   cumin seeds.

-JI   honorific attached to the end of nouns.

303

"JI"	"yes."
KACHORIS	a snack eaten in north India and Pakistan. The Rajasthani variety is a round flattened ball made of fine flour filled with a baked stuffing of yellow daal, beans, gram flour, red chili powder and other spices.
KADI CHAWAL	Kadi is made from gram flour fried in butter and mixed with buttermilk or yogurt to produce a spicy, sour curry. Served with chawal, rice.
KATHI ROLL	a type of street food similar to a sandwichlike wrap, usually stuffed with chicken tikka or lamb, onion and green chutney.
KHANA	Hindi for food.
KHICHRI	a cupful of rice cooked with yellow lentils and spiced with cumin, salt and coriander. Generally eaten when one is sick or in need of comfort food.
KHUKURI	a carved Nepalese knife used as a tool and weapon.
KIRPAN	a ceremonial sword or dagger that all baptized Sikhs are supposed to wear.
KITTY PARTY	women in India organize kitty parties to socialize, but also as an interest-free way of loaning one another money. The kitty is a collective fund. The carefully chosen guests bring their next installment of cash to each party. One name is drawn from a hat, with that woman receiving twelve installments all at once to use as she pleases.

KOH-I-NOOR	the "Mountain of Light," a 105-karat (21.6 g) diamond that belonged to various Mughal and Persian rulers and is now part of the British crown jewels.
KOHL	a mixture of soot and other ingredients used predominantly by Middle Eastern, north African, sub-Saharan African and South Asian women (and to a lesser extent men) to darken the eyelids and as mascara for the eyelashes.
KOORAY WALLAH	one who collects the rubbish. See car-saaf-wallah.
KUNDAN	a style of jewelry dating back to Mughal times in which precious and semi-precious stones are set in pure gold, often with colored enamel at the back, so that each piece of jewelry has two equally beautiful surfaces.
KURTA PAJAMA	long shirt and drawstring trousers.
KSHATRIYA	the military and ruling order of the traditional Vedic-Hindu social system as outlined by the Vedas; the warrior caste.
LADOOS	a sweet that is often prepared to celebrate festivals or household events such as weddings. Essentially, ladoos are flour balls cooked in sugar syrup.
LAKH	a unit in the Indian numbering system equal to 100,000.
LAL MIRCH	ground red cayenne pepper.
"LAO"	Hindi for "bring."
LASSI	drink made from buttermilk; can be plain, sweet or salty, or made with fruit such as banana or mango.

Glossary

LATHI	length of bamboo or cane carried by police or schoolmasters.
LOAD SHEDDING	a phrase referring to the period when Indian power companies cut off the electricity to different neighborhoods when they cannot meet demand.
LUNGI	a garment that covers the lower half of the body and is tied around the waist.
"MAADERCHOD"	literally "motherfucker" in Punjabi.
MAALISH	oil massage.
MALI	gardener.
MANDE THUNIS	a turban worn by the Coorg men of southern Karnataka.
MANGAL SUTRA	a symbol of Hindu marriage, consisting of a gold ornament strung from a yellow thread, a string of black beads or a gold chain. It is comparable to a Western wedding ring and is worn by a married woman until her husband's death.
MANGLIK	astrological term referring to a person born under the negative influence of Mars. It is believed that a non-Manglik marrying a Manglik will die. Two Mangliks marrying each other cancel out the negative effects. Mangliks can also perform a ceremony in which they "marry" a tree or a golden idol to transfer their bad luck.
MASALA CHAI	spiced tea.
MATTHIS	fried savory biscuits, often served with tea.

MEMSAHIB	formerly a term of respect for white European women in colonial India, but now used for well-to-do Indian women.
MESWAK	a natural toothbrush made from the twigs of the *Salvadora persica* tree, also known as the Arak or Peelu tree.
MOONG DAAL	a split bean that has a green husk and is yellow inside.
NAAMAALUM	like a John or Jane Doe, a corpse or hospital patient whose identity is unknown.
NAMASHKAR/ NAMASTE	traditional Hindu greeting said with hands pressed together.
NIMBOO PAANI	lemonade, usually with salt.
"OOLU KE PATHAY"	Punjabi curse literally translates as "son of an owl."
PAAN	betel leaf, stuffed with betel nut, lime and other condiments and used as a stimulant.
PAAGAL	Hindi for crazy.
PAKORA	a deep-fried snack. They can be made from pretty much anything dipped in a gram flour batter.
PALLU	the loose end of a sari.
PANEER	unaged cheese made by curdling heated milk with lemon juice.
PARANTHA	a flatbread made with whole-wheat flour, pan fried in oil or clarified butter and ususally stuffed with vegetables like potatoes and cauliflower.
PEG	a unit of measurement for alcoholic spirits. Peg measures can hold anywhere from 1 to 2 fluid ounces (30–60 ml).

PRESS-WALLAH   a journalist.

PUJA   prayer.

"PUKKA"   Hindi word meaning "solid, well made." Also means "definitely."

PURANAS   a group of Hindu, Jain or Buddhist religious texts.

RAJMA   red kidney beans cooked with onion, garlic, ginger, tomatoes and spices. A much-loved Punjabi dish eaten with chawal, rice.

RAKHI-BROTHER   the Hindu festival of Raksha Bandhan celebrates the bonds between brothers and sisters. The sister ties a rakhi, or holy thread, on her brother's wrist in exchange for a vow of protection. Any male can be adopted as a brother by tying the thread.

RAS MALAI   dumplings from cottage or ricotta cheese soaked in sweetened, thickened milk delicately flavored with cardamom.

RAVAN   the demon king of the Hindu epic the Ramayana, who kidnaps the wife of Lord Ram.

ROTI OR CHAPATTI   Indian wheat flatbread cooked on a hot griddle.

"SAALA MAADERCHOD"   "bastard mother fucker."

"SAALE"   "bastard."

"SAB CHANGA"   Punjabi for "all well."

SADHU   a holy man who has renounced the material world to devote himself to spiritual practice.

SAHIB	an Urdu honorific now used across South Asia as a term of respect, equivalent to the English "sir."
SALWAR	baggy trousers worn by men and women common to Afghanistan, Pakistan and northern India.
SAMOSA	a triangular fried savory snack stuffed with potatoes, peas and spices.
SANYASI	a Hindu who has renounced the material world.
SARDAAR	a male follower of the Sikh religion.
SARDAAR-JI JOKES	Sikhs are traditionally the butt of jokes in northern India.
SARI	India's national dress for women. Usually six yards of material wrapped and pleated over a blouse and petticoat.
SHRI	a Sanskrit title of veneration. An honorific, whose equivalent is "Mr." in English.
SINDOOR	a red powder used by married Hindu women and some Sikh women. During the marriage ceremony, the groom applies some to the parting of the bride's hair to show that she is now a married woman. Subsequently, sindoor is applied by the wife as part of her dressing routine.
SONF	plain or sugared fennel seeds eaten to aid digestion and to freshen the mouth after a meal.
SUBZI	a vegetable.

309

SUBZI-WALLAH	vegetable seller.
TACHEE	Indian English for suitcase, derived from "attaché case."
TAVA	a large, flat or slightly concave disc-shaped griddle made from cast iron, steel or aluminum used to prepare several kinds of flat breads.
TEEN PATTA	an Indian card game, also known as Flush. Usually played at Diwali, the Indian new year, it is a betting game in which the player with the best hand (three aces or three consecutive cards of the same suit) wins the pot.
TIFFIN	steel lunchbox usually with three round, stackable compartments.
TIMEPASS	Hindi/English word meaning any pointless activity to pass the time.
TULLI	Punjabi slang for "drunk."
TONGA	a horse-pulled cart.
"YAAR"	equivalent to "pal," "mate" or "dude."
ZARI	a type of thread made of fine gold or silver wire woven into silk to create intricate patterns; Mughal in origin.

NOTE

The rupee exchange rate at the time of writing is
£1 = 84 Rps
$1 = 48 Rps